Then, Now and in between

EDDIE WHITHAM

Order this book online at www.trafford.com
or email orders@trafford.com

Most Trafford titles are also available at major online book retailers.

Note for Librarians: A cataloguing record for this book is available from Library
and Archives Canada at www.collectionscanada.ca/amicus/index-e.html

Printed in Victoria, BC, Canada.

ISBN: 978-1-4251-8967-9

*Our mission is to efficiently provide the world's finest, most comprehensive
book publishing service, enabling every author to experience success.
To find out how to publish your book, your way, and have it available
worldwide, visit us online at www.trafford.com/10510*

Trafford rev. 8/10/2009

 www.trafford.com

North America & international
toll-free: 1 888 232 4444 (USA & Canada)
phone: 250 383 6864 ♦ fax: 812 355 4082

**FOR
SAMARA
&
JESSICA**

INTRODUCTION

ON THAT DAY when I stood before the headmaster's desk, quivering with the expectation of another seven 'cuts' with his heavy leather strap, I was surprised at the calmness that the Head was showing - given that he had seen me in his office several times previously on the same charge, truancy. When he asked me to take a seat I was relieved. Then, reaching toward his huge library of books straddling many shelves adjacent his desk, he selected about five.

He said that he realised I was bored. I was to take these books home, read them and return them when I had finished. They were of course the classics - *Kidnapped*, *Treasure Island*, two Biggles books, and the fifth was a collection of English poems. That was the catalyst for me to commence reading decent literature instead of comics.

My mother was another influence. She read in many languages, was a keen short story reader and a cryptic crossword exponent. She would buy the *Argosy* magazine, read the stories, complete the crossword and leave it in my room. We often discussed the stories and I developed the feel for cryptic and twisty stories.

I later discovered Poe, Twain, Alfred Hitchcock's collections, and the rest of the exponents of excellent writing. Second hand bookshops are a delight to indulge in. To find a well-worn article means a lot of readers enjoy what I enjoy most of all, a good human story.

My collection before you, the reader, may reflect some of my personal life and experiences. There are chapters about others as well. These I have gleaned as Barbara and I travelled extensively in our own Australia, as well as through more than sixty other countries.

Everybody is a dreamer, so all of us have tales to share with other human beings, thus keeping the age-old art of story telling alive.

THE DECISION

Ushenko held his Kalashnikov close to his side, just in case he might be discovered, as he viewed the landscape ahead of him. From the ridge where he was lying, he could see the four buildings surrounded by massive aprons of concrete. He was more interested in the largest one of the quartet. It had a huge double-hung doorway, which housed a smaller door, for personnel to use when the massive doors were closed.

The shed was constructed of metal. There were few windows in the gigantic structure and these were high up in the walls close to the guttering. That was all he could see from where he was viewing. A skylight, protruding from one side of the roof, would be useless this time of the year, while the murky grey clouds held out the sun.

The winds of change had swept across the former Soviet empire in the past few years, leaving the Generals with nothing to do but to fiddle whilst the Union shrivelled up, and became a shell of its old self. It was that time when the leadership, watching the disintegration of their pride and joy the USSR, decided to inflict punishment on those who dared to step out of the fold.

This mood was turned into belligerent hostility when the Ukraine annexed the Black Sea ports. Consequently, the great fleet of nuclear shipping and allied industries fell into their hands. Nuisance strikes, such as stopping the flow of essential commodities like gas and petroleum from time to time, served notice on the recalcitrant neighbours that the old boss was still the one to deal with.

He positioned himself about fifteen hundred metres from the nearest shed. The woods behind him, held his concealed snow bike, which he used to convey the sled of deadly weapons. The mid-Autumn weather could turn from cold to freezing at the wink of an eye. Although the weather forecast he was issued with indicated a mild night, he had prepared for most of the scenarios that the night might throw at him. Along the track, four kilometres away were two of his back up team, Sergeant Ivanoff and Private Gregor, along with the snow bike. A plane, sitting on a military runway at a not too distant airfield, was ready for immediate deployment, armed with the appropriate missiles.

Major Uri Ushenko swept the scene before him with his night glasses. His gaze was transfixed on a building, the smallest one on the extreme left. There was no visible sign of vehicles or any movement about the place, nor a light to show that humans were in attendance. The apron of concrete, which surrounded each storehouse, was bathed in moonlight, which tended to reflect an uncanny gloom around the area. He watched the second shed for a while, but it also showed no light or life. The lazy Ukrainians are either very stupid or have laid a trap, he mused to himself.

He glanced at his watch. It was now two-thirty a.m. He had two hours to complete the mission or to abort it. That was plenty of time. He was twenty kilometres from the border and could return there in an hour providing nothing went awry. His attention turned to the third building, the second largest. There seemed to be nobody in attendance at this one either. The windows were shuttered for the impending winter but not a slither of light appeared from the place. He rolled over as the snow began to fall lightly. He cleaned the glasses then concentrated on the large construction on the right side of his viewing line.

Ushenko favoured this one for the demolition. It would make the biggest bang, cause the largest amount of collateral damage and make his superiors ecstatic. They of course would be in absolute denial in the halls of international politics as per usual.

He reached into his overcoat pocket and retrieved a portion of his rations without relish, a stale piece of biscuit and a small block of cheese. These he munched on, as he reflected his position with the Russian Army. He, like the majority of his compatriots had not been paid for months.

His wife Alena was due to deliver them an heir within the next few weeks. If it were not for their immediate families' assistance, they could never make ends meet. Uri buttoned up his coat then went back to perusing the enormous building. As he concentrated his eyes on the construction, he saw for the first time, a slight flicker of light advancing from a crack in the doorway of the fourth building.

Life at last, he thought to himself. He wondered who or how many people were in the shed. He kept vigil for a few more minutes, trying to decide whether to go and check, or just sit and watch for a little while longer.

Curiosity was getting the better of him, but he lay motionless nevertheless in a prone position, watching intently at the door, and the small flicker of light. It seemed to him to be that of a fire, opposed to the glow that a lantern would make in such conditions. He first thought was that it was coming from an oxy-acetylene welder, but he dismissed that, owing to the lateness of the hour. The moon was burying itself behind the small mass of cloud. As darkness became more pronounced, Uri considered whether he should take a careful look at the source of the light.

The lack of a glimmer from the heavens would give him sufficient cover to cross the white landscape, and allow him to find out what was transpiring behind the huge doorway. Then he changed his mind. He would watch a while longer then decide on his next move. So the soldier laid alert and wide-awake, intent on completing his task. After a short time, he changed his position by sitting upon the frigid ground, and rubbing his legs to stimulate the blood circulation. As the clock moved to three a.m., the twinkling light gave him an eerie feeling. Perhaps there were fathers or expectant fathers in there. Then he thought of the futility of the matter of war. Peace would make him redundant, but he would be home, work or no job. The flickering light inside the big building cast eerie spectres across the walls and the ceiling. The glow of a tiny fire was all that the young woman had, to keep herself and her child from the extreme cold, in the steel room. The building inside was of greater capacity than most of the great cathedrals of Europe.

There was the incessant sound of water dripping as condensed moisture fell from the lofty, unlined, frigid ceiling. The woman, dressed in peasant clothing was lying on an ancient couch, trying to catch some sleep. The infant was asleep in a cot nearby, close to the flickering embers of the fire. The woman stirred herself, looked at her watch, then with great reluctance, moved to the fire, and placing two pieces of wood on it, fiddled a while with the fiery embers and left it to take its course. She checked the child. Satisfied that the babe was warm, she left it and returned to the couch.

Nita, the mother and Samara the baby were waiting for Gregorian to return from his clandestine trip to the border. His booty of Sable pelts would fetch enough money to see them out of The Ukraine, to the safety of America. Gregorian was a Russian and Nita a Ukrainian. Neither wanted a future in their poverty-stricken homelands. Her husband had worked a clever trade with a merchant in Kharkov, one of the country's large cities. The merchant had rented the buildings from the impoverished Ukraine government, and stored massive quantities of goods, which the merchant could off load through his vast outlets of dodgy representatives. Self-seeking officials were as corrupt as Judas was, with every man woman and youngster on the make in this part of Eastern Europe.

Ushenko noted the time. He had forty-five minutes to complete his mission. He must decide which of the buildings he would waste, then, after honing the laser, call the plane and the pilot would do the rest. He would link up with his team, then, quickly disappear from this land. He was pleased that the moon had divested itself from the shroud of cloud and beamed down on the landscape before him. His mind wandered to his wife, who had no idea where he was based, or what type of operations he had to carry out. It was better this way.

Nita had roused herself and prepared the samovar. She would make tea the instant she heard the footsteps of her husband approaching the building. The baby had not stirred. She sat, staring absent-mindedly into the fire, soaking in any warmth she could, taking comfort in the red and golden embers assembled in the portable grate. Her husband had played a smart deal, collecting half his money in local currency and the rest in American dollars.

He was able to send his uncle in Kiev, the dollars to purchase the tickets, and to organize the travel arrangements. She expected him at any time now, and when he arrived, he would load the sable furs onto the truck and make ready to go to Kharkov.

The usual practice was to put the animal skins onto the tray of the truck, then cover them with the hay. The shed, in which the woman was waiting, was filled mostly with hay, boxes and huge crates of assorted goods. Nita had absolutely no knowledge of their contents, nor did she wish to know. Her main aim was to flee with her small family to the west, as quickly as possible.

When Gregorian reached the merchant's warehouse, he would park the vehicle in the building then take another truck which would be prepared, stacked high with goods. The stock would be stored in the defunct military depot for the time being. This was the way the dice rolled for the young couple. Over the past few years they had saved and skimped, in order to release themselves from the grip of the old ideology and the recent mindset of this new world, consisting of a species of old Communists, Stalinists, and others whose use-by date was long overdue.

Tonight was to be their last evening in the shed. They had enough money to satisfy their early travel aspirations. The final cache of illegal sables would be delivered. Gregorian with his young and beautiful wife, child in arms, could escape the misery of the post Soviet era forever.

The Russian soldier had made his decision as to the target he would set the laser beam on. He commenced to call the aircraft to arrange the offensive. He looked towards the woods, to ascertain how much time would be required to exit with extreme haste.

Whilst he was contemplating this matter, he failed to notice the moving shadow which was approaching the number four building. Gregorian slipped in unnoticed by the soldier. He was ignorant of the Russian's presence. Gregorian loaded the sable pelts onto the truck then joined his loving wife, just as major Ushenko called the pilot and announced his decision.

LONREGAN'S
PIGSTY

West of Bendigo, not far from Moliagul, was the place where Pat Lonregan bought his ill-fated farm lot. Not that any thing was wrong with the five hundred acres he owned. The problem lay with Lonregan himself. He deserved all that he got, because he was just a lazy Irish sod. Pat arrived in Victoria, and through an uncle purchased Shamrock Park. He named the place himself, though he had never seen or smelt a shamrock in his entire life. He was just like most of the pseudo Irishmen of his ilk and era. They were descendants, living off untruthful or dubious memories of their fathers and grandfathers, peddling blarney that folks had come to expect from that type of loud and graceless breed.

The land was a surprise to him and his wife Mary and the three children. The block he had acquired was long and not very broad. It was level for the first couple of hundred acres but rose and fell towards the rear. This area of the place Lonregan dismissed as useless. The back end of the property had a small gully running through it, which swelled to rivulets during the wet periods. For eight months or more they had dust up to their ankles and for the rest of the year if it rained, and that resulted in mud up to their knees.

Not withstanding, all of the farmers and graziers made the most of the land. Some fared well, others toughed it out, then found their niche in the community, and organized places to sell the produce and animals that they so painstakingly nurtured. When the wind blew, red and yellowish powder settled on everything. The lady of the house resigned herself to the fact that if Lonregan couldn't make a go of it in the bush, she would, despite him.

Lonregan flopped. Every thing he tried failed. He did not have a clue when it came to cropping or animal husbandry. To demonstrate his ineptitude, his pigs died but his wife's chickens flourished. His corn, wheat and maize withered whilst his spouse's vegetable garden blossomed and produced in abundance. He built a large pigsty down the back, far away from the house. The three sows and the boar didn't make it through the first summer. The man had ten thumbs whilst his wife green fingers.

Lonregan blamed every living mortal for his woes, while his ever-suffering wife held her tongue. He was arrogant in his poverty, never seeing himself for what he was. He cleaned out the pigsty, then surprising Mary, joined the local council's road repair gang. There he stayed for many years, talking more and working less.

One day when he returned home from his work, his good lady informed him of her new enterprise. She had this day rented the pigsty. The person who rented it would pay two shillings a week. Lonregan's jaw dropped; that was half of his weekly salary and his wife just collects it. Then he asked her who the lucky person was. When she told him he nearly fell out of his chair.

Wing Lee, a Chinese gardener from over the other side of the range called on Mrs Lonregan that morning, asking if she knew of any accommodation in the area. After a while he noticed the pigsty, and inquired as to the possibility of renting it. She told him that it wasn't much of a place to live, but he insisted that he would make it habitable, so what could she say. Then he offered the two shillings and the deal was struck. Wing Lee quickly set about to establish a garden, put a floor in the hut and procured a bed and a table. Mary noted that all the possessions he had were an old overcoat, the clothes he stood up in, a wok, a skillet and two pieces of rolled up canvas.

The oriental gent, much to Lonregan's surprise, painted the hovel bright red and put gravel on the floor, as though he was there for the long haul. The children loved Wing Lee, who kept to himself most of the time. However he had a little time when pottering around the garden, to stop and talk with them. They were curious about the strange vegetables he was growing. Lonregan wasn't a bit interested in the Chinaman or the garden, just the money his wife received from him, whisky money. Try as he may she didn't let him get his hands on a penny. It was earmarked for things around the house.

Wing Lee hovered around the place for about three years. One of his strange habits was, when the rains came, he would disappear for a few days. He went away wearing his old coat, carrying his two pieces of canvas, the wok and the skillet. He would return without a word to any one. The Lonregans were curious as to this trait but were timid about approaching Wing Lee about it. They dismissed it with the theory that it may be some oriental peculiarity. Wing Lee came and went as he pleased, still paying Mary his rent as well as supplying her with some of his unusual produce.

Mary Lonregan, much to her husband's astonishment, purchased a treadle sewing machine and an ice-box with the rent proceeds. She was moving the house along whilst he was standing stock-still. Lonregan held on to his job despite his lack of effort and his inherited Irish temper. The long-suffering spouse prospered and kept adding comforts to the home and kept her counsel.

One bright and sunny morning Wing Lee called on Mrs Lonregan and informed her that he was leaving the property. She was surprised but gracious, wishing him well. Then he told her that he was opening a café in town, a Chinese Café. He said it would be next to the Victoria Hotel. He invited her and the family to dine there without charge for making him so welcome and so comfortable. This news hit Lonregan like a sledge-hammer as he was counting on the rent to take the pressure off his drinking cash, now he would have to front up with his pay packet.

Lonregan arrived in town on Monday morning to report for work. Then he saw it. Nestled right next to the Victoria Pub, was a bright red building, two storeys high with a sign, in black letters, proclaimed the building, "PEKING CHINESE CAFÉ". Lonregan bemused to say the least, trudged off to his work place. Wing Lee was no pseudo china man, he was the real thing, born and bred in Peking and he spoke the language clear and precise.

Lonregan fronted the dinner table at home that night in a not too congenial mood. Then when his meal was put in front of him, he took one mouthful, let out a scream and ran out of the house to the water tank. That was his first encounter with madras curry, which his wife bought from Boa Singh the Indian peddler the day before. Foreigners were getting him down. When he had calmed down and returned to the house, his good woman told him that she had rented the paddock and the pigsty again. Who this time he thought? Wing Lee's brother had just arrived from China to assist in the café and needed it, three shillings this time.

Chi Lee had the same habit as his brother, disappearing from time to time after the rains came. Then he left, and Wan Ho, another relative took his place, worked in the café tended the garden and went walkabout after every shower of rain. Chi Lee opened a café near Bendigo and Wan Ho joined him. Then Wing Lee upped the ante to four shillings, reclaimed the pigsty for its original purpose and filled the yard with swine.

Mary began to toss over in her mind the way in which the Chinese were exploiting the farm; not that she was troubled, but that her womanish instinct told her that they were profiting at her families expense, although they paid fair compensation for the land and the shed. So she, without a word to anyone waited for the rain. The café had prospered and Wing Lee had relatives cooking with the local girls employed to wait on the tables. Wing Lee still left when it rained, allowing the trusted kin to attend the day to day running of the establishment.

On the tenth of May the heavens opened up across the whole region. The storms bucketed down in torrents. When the rain ceased Mary decided to go into town. Her husband was at work and the kids at school, so she left a note and departed. Standing across from the café Mary waited patiently. Sure enough Wing Lee scurried from his premises and hastened down the street, towards the end of town her farm was situated. Mary followed at a distance. It wasn't difficult, the man shuffled along the gravel thoroughfare and out of the small town.

The road had a junction a couple of miles further along. The gravel course on which they were travelling went a further five miles, connecting with the Bendigo road. The right branch forked toward Lonregans farm, and beyond to several other properties, which were scattered throughout the scrub. Lonregans road, as it was known was more or less a dirt track. It had been hastily constructed. Trees had been cleared, then a primitive grader pulled by horses was engaged to level the surface and allow the flow of traffic, which consisted of horse drawn carts and carriages of various sorts. It was not a pleasant ride, because after it rained, the thorough-fare was reduced to a quagmire and nigh impassable. When the long dry spells occurred, the vehicles were like bone crunchers, bouncing along the way.

Mary Lonregan kept tracking Wing Lee, keeping to the verges and out of his view. If anyone had been observing this unusual sight they may have thought that Mary was losing her marbles. She had the determination to see out what she had set in her mind to do. The lady was a pocket dynamo and was never deterred by her size. The way she commanded respect from her husband was the only evidence one would require, to give her the respect she deserved. She was a no nonsense woman who devoted her energy to her family and those she had befriended in the district.

Wing Lee turned off the gravel road and headed into the scrub. Mary let him disappear, and then followed at a safe pace. She knew where she was heading, so time was not of the essence in this case. It was simply confirmation of her conclusions - reached by a little amount of deduction - something that her husband was incapable of doing.

As she moved through the bush on what seemed at a glance, a well-worn footpath, she wondered what her reaction would be when the chase came to its finality. She was nothing like her husband who felt the only way to resolve anything was to roll up ones sleeves and sort it out. He was sorted out more times than not.

The Chinaman quietly ascended to the summit of a slight ridge, then descended the incline to the gully below. He was now at the extreme rear of Lonregan's acreage which was a quarter of a mile ahead. It was four hundred yards from the pigsty where he sojourned for three or so years. He faded from Mary's sight, and as she attained the base of the ridge she heard an inaudible cacophony of voices, Chinese utterances, Oriental dialects and lots of laughter as well.

She edged her way to the brim of the hillock and ventured a peep over the top. Wing Lee, Chi Lee and Wan Ho were standing by the creek chatting ten to the dozen to each other. In the water, not far distant were half a dozen men, panning the residue from the soil washed down from Lonregans farm. The woman watched in amazement as Wing Lee collected the small sacks from the two men, placed them in the large pockets in the old overcoat and handed some money in return.

Mary Sheila Rose Lonregan slipped away from the hillside, and quickened her pace as she headed for home on foot. The distance did not perturb her as she walked three miles or more into town and carried her purchases home by foot every few days. Her whole being was seething with rage. Not just for what she had seen, but the indignation it bore her, because of her husband's lack of insight, which allowed her to be hoodwinked by the oriental men. The pieces came together clearly now - Wing Lee's canvas roll, the wok, the skillet, the absences after the rains, and the choice of the pigsty.

Her land had more or less been milked by the immigrants, whilst her spouse had never ventured past the outhouse to check on the low end of his land, her land.

She made up her mind to make things right. After she saw her children off to school, the next morning, she saddled her horse and headed toward Bendigo. She left a note, which advised her family, that she would be late home. She went to the town feeling in great spirits, resolving to teach her husband and the Chinese a lesson.

That day Mary Lonregan staked sole claim to the entire region surrounding her family property.

ORANGE
CARTWHEELS

The small town of Milo Springs was abuzz with excitement. Tonight, after years of planning and hard work by a large percentage of the populace, the Centenary Ball and Mardi gras was truly about to come to fruition. The accommodation was booked out for more than a hundred kilometres radius of the town, and anybody who claimed to be associated to this tranquil haven, either was invited, or would just turn up to be a part of the celebrations.

Ten decades of rural prosperity, five scores of unstoppable progress, was the hallmark to the fame of Milo Springs. Seven thousand people lived in the town, which lay beneath the shelter of the Lazy Mountain range. The town was serviced by the friendly and abundant waters of the Mellow River, which wound its way from the hills to the broad plains west of the town. The river flowed with an unending source of domestic and irrigation water, which coupled with a temperate climate, gave the locals the best of both worlds.

The first glimmer of dawn crept over the mountains. A few dozen early risers were wending their way through the streets of town - some to the swimming pool for the customary dip, others, going to the first shift of their respective businesses. Little did these souls, along with the rest of the town, have an inkling of what the day would bring. The inhabitants were totally unaware of the frightful tragedy that was to come upon them all as the next twenty-four hours unfolded. No one noticed the glow of the sun as it climbed higher, lifting itself off the skyline. Not a single person showed concern at the eerie colouring that the sun seemed to have picked up, as it rose into the heavens.

That is, nobody except Alby Jones, a cereal farmer out on Deadman's Plain, some seventy kilometres from Milo Springs. Alby commented to his wife over breakfast. "I'll be danged Mildred; the sky's got a funny shade of orange in it today." And that was that. Mildred acknowledged his statement then went on devouring her meal. Alby trudged to the field, occasionally looking to the sky and uttering, "Well I'll be danged." He made no report of this. By lunchtime, the sky had a greater tinge of orange and the temperature was on the rise. By noon, the thermometer had reached thirty-one degrees Celsius, about six above the average for the town for this time of the year.

Rod Wills and his wife Emma, were commencing an attempt to conquer the sheer face of Arthur's Peak, five kilometres north of the town. They set their base camp at the lookout, just above the first small hill. This gave them a view of the proceedings in town as they climbed. The temperature was much warmer than they had anticipated. The pair prepared to make a start.

The townsfolk were very industrious, putting the final touches to the Town Hall, where the grandest event of the century was to happen this evening. Dignitaries where arriving and were being tucked into their accommodation. Catering firms attended to the finer details, whilst the small business enterprises were cashing up their tills, ready to cope with the demand on their wares, which would be unprecedented in the town's history.

As the morning progressed, the streets were bustling with last minute shoppers, as the people raced for the items which would most likely disappear from the shelves before the day was out .The throng were starting to feel the heat as the gauge was still moving upwards. They all were so involved in the matters at hand that scant regard was paid to the sky, even though most commented on the warmth of the day.

Out in the field Alby Jones was mopping his brow, then reaching for his water flask, more often than he would most days, except in the very middle of summer. But this was not summer it was halfway through autumn. Alby perceived a further brightness in the orange colouring of the heavens and had a good mind to go back to the house, to ring the radio station and see if something was happening with the weather. He didn't; he just kept mopping his brow and working at his chores in the paddock.

Rod and Emma were moving slowly up the face of the hill, so focused at keeping a safe footing that they were not looking to the sky at that time. They did feel the warmth, as the temperature started to rise, but with a deadline to meet, but were not concerned about this.

At four-thirty, the heat was becoming unbearable. It had reached thirty-five. Now the townsfolk were putting on a serious face. What was happening to the temperature? Nobody had the foggiest idea of what was about to happen. The town's womenfolk were in a panic. All were prepared for a cool evening and had arranged outfits to suit. What would they do now? At five, the mercury registered thirty-seven. The dusky sky had an aura of foreboding, in its colouring. The twilight was setting in. The people were not in festive mood. The weather had caught them off guard. The phones to the radio stations and the weather instrumentality ran red hot. They wanted answers, and scalps.

Out on the farm, Alby was a very frightened man. His mature crops had withered in two hours of heat, so he thought; that was until he took closer scrutiny. It wasn't the heat of the sun that had damaged his crops; the plants had turned orange. The stalks of the plants were bent over so that the top of them hit the soil. They were as dry as a bone, as if something had sucked the very life from them. He had watered them heavily for the past three days so he and his wife could attend the celebrations.

At seven o'clock that evening, one hour before the ball, the temperature fell dramatically. People who had already prepared for the ball, abandoned their regalia, and put on the original attire. There was mayhem in the majority of households as families tried to cope with the weird conditions imposed upon them. Why? No one could hazard a guess. The weather gurus about town were inundated with inquiries. But still no answer! At seven-thirty the mercury had fallen to seven, more than a quarter of the four pm reading. The night sky reflected a strange orange glow.

Rod and Emma had reached the point of no return on the mountain, and decided to stay on the ledge until daybreak. Rod cleared a small patch to settle down. Thank God for lightweight sleeping bags and ration packs. Their backup team would meet them at the summit at ten in the morning. The couple could watch the goings on in town from their lofty vantage point. Rod had his night glasses, so they could monitor events as they happened. There came a sudden chill in the air. Emma shuddered and reached into her bag for a wind jacket.

The town clock struck eight as a great cheer went around the main square, for the gong was sounded to commence the festivities. His Worship the Mayor opened the show with the usual waffle and the Grande Ball began. The other townsfolk were wandering around the streets, testing the wares at the myriad of stalls, set up for the weeklong fair. All the common show exhibits, along with the latest in gimmickry were on display. All were set for what they believed would be a great seven-day bash.

Alby made it home to get himself ready for the evening. His wife had retrieved his ancient dinner suit from the dry cleaners yesterday and she purchased a new outfit for the ball. He had lost his desire to go out in the wake of the devastation to his crops. He knew in his inwardly that his wife would be very disappointed if they missed out, as she was one of the driving forces behind the festival. In fact, Primrose Jones, mother of five, grandmother of nine, was the president of three of the largest women's clubs in the district. She was a very well respected person in the area. So Alby said nothing to her about the crops, or the strange sky, deciding to keep his counsel, until the next day.

The town's activities were in full swing by eight-thirty. Every one was having a ball. Rod, taking his glasses, leaned on the edge of the hill and gazed down to the town. Through the still night, he could see the movement of the crowds in the streets, although it was not possible from the distance to make out any individual thing. He was pleased just to feel a part of the show. He handed the glasses to Emma who watched for a while making comments on various lights and landmarks that she could identify.

Suddenly she exclaimed "What are the orange lights moving toward the town from the west?" She handed the instrument to Rod, who lined them up with assistance of Emma's pointing. "Yeah, that's weird; I don't have any idea. Maybe it's some kind of procession. They look like cigarettes glowing in the night." He stared for a few minutes and as his eyes adjusted and focused, he saw an alarming thing. As the orange glows moved closer to town, the surrounding fences glowed. A large tree also lit up, in a queer sort of way, as the strange vehicles rolled on past it.

He tried to count the number of moving objects. He guessed that there were at least thirty. They seemed to be rolling towards town at a slow pace. He noted the glow in the sky. He gave Emma the glasses. She did not speak for sometime. When she did, she said in a soft tone, as though she was talking to herself. "Cartwheels, they're like cartwheels on fire." He wrested the glasses from her, then, after watching the scene below for a short period, agreed with her. He was apprehensive, but from where they were situated, could not do a thing about it.

The Grand Ball was sailing along smoothly. Business was brisk at the bar, as the patrons swallowed the free alcohol, liberally supplied by the organizing committee. The dancing and the music were marvellous; the people were making the most of it and enjoying themselves. They were so focused on the event that they paid scant regard to the screams, which were coming from the street, outside the hall. That was, until the main door burst open. Dozens of people, with fear etched on their faces and terror in their eyes stumbled into the great room, waving their arms, and gesticulating to the crowd. They were yelling incoherently and some were lying prostrate on the floor, as in some kind of epileptic fit. The mayor moved swiftly to the stage to try and restore order as the din was reaching a crescendo.

Meanwhile, at the tavern known to the locals as Riley's Brawling Bar, the party was in full swing. The swilling and foul language, filtered through the open door, out into the beer garden, where a throng of drunken men and women where carousing the night away. Riley himself was attending to the needs of a few boozers, when his attention was drawn to an orange glow, coming from the end of the street. He stepped out to investigate the extra-ordinary colouring of the night sky. He froze in his tracks, when he saw what was rolling down his street. A huge orange cartwheel, completely lit up, It was about three metres high and as wide as a car. However, it was not the size of the object that held him in awe. There was no one in control of it. Then there were two more of the things turning the corner.

The Mayor lost control of proceedings, as pandemonium was reigned. More people were spilling into the hall from the streets, pushing and screaming. Some just swooned and dropped to the floor, frothing at the mouth and convulsing. A middle-aged man struggled to the stage and grabbed the mayor. "Aliens! Lots of them! Cartwheels - burning, murdering!" With this, he fell dead to the floor at the mayor's feet. The town leader bent down to touch the body, but recoiled in horror and stood up abruptly, when he saw the man's face. The man's face had turned a shade of orange. Others gathered close by were startled as well. Panic ensued, as some headed for the front door to see what the trouble was about. Others charged to the back exits, like proverbial rats deserting a sinking ship. The young couple, who had settled on the mountain, were watching the evening revelry in the town, with incredulity. Rod had kept a vigil for the past two hours, surveying and contemplating what was transpiring below. Emma was becoming increasingly agitated as the night wore on. They were an unwilling audience to a frightening event. The cartwheels were all over the town, rolling around the busy streets like overgrown cotton reels. Wherever they went, Rod observed that fires commenced beside each of the illuminated vehicles when they passed by an object. He figured out that some sinister force was usurping the town. However, he was really unaware of the chaos and uproar that was going on in the main area of town. The cartwheels were now in every part of it.

Riley stood very still outside his pub, staring at the scene unfolding before his very eyes. He was trying to comprehend the situation, attempting to take stock. Perhaps, he would try to attack. But he couldn't raise his legs. He stared at the orange contraption rumbling toward him. He noticed a person standing in front of him. The man had his back to Riley. Riley finally found his legs and staggered forward. He drew level with the other then turned to see who it was. It turned out to be one of his clients, Barry O'Toole. Mr O'Toole stood stock still, as a dead person. Riley touched him on the shoulder and greeted him. As he pressed his hand on the man's shoulder, the whole body crashed to the ground. It hit the pavement, and to Riley's absolute horror, fell to pieces into a mound of tangerine dust.

The publican bolted toward the park, looking back to see where the cartwheel was situated. It was moving after him, he thought. It was, yes, following him. He ran like a man possessed. His feet crunched on the gravel as he pounded forward. His breathing sounded like drumbeats in his ears as he tried to keep ahead of his pursuer. Crackling sounds came from his ill-fitting boots, which were for use indoors only. His coat rustled in the night air, but he dare not look back. Even the small change in his pocket jangled as he blundered onwards. The less noise he tried to make the more pronounced his presence was. Rushing on gasping, wheezing, stepping in and out of potholes, he stumbled on, his whimpering adding to the uncontrollable clamour that he was making.

Riley tripped on an uneven section off pathway and fell heavily on his face. He hurt himself quite badly, but struggled to his feet. It was too late. He fell to his knees. The lumbering wheel was nearly upon him. He stared at the contraption in sheer horror. The wheel ceased its momentum, emitting tangerine rays directly at him. He died instantly, without uttering a single word, turning into a terra cotta stone like substance. The monstrous, driver-less contrivance gyrated past the remains of the former innkeeper to its next mission.

Back at the Town Hall, all hell had broken loose. The under-staffed police presence was inadequate to tackle the potent force that was assuaging the community. Four policemen, who tried in vain to halt one of the vigorous wheels, were over powered in an instant and were reduced to ash. The fire brigade attempted to hose the wheels as they confronted two in High Street, but fell victim of the eerie rays of the machine. There was no indication as to where the macabre devices originated. The folk were in hysterics and out of control. Many rushed hither and thither, with no plan in mind. Some had headed over the two bridges, to the safety of the hills. The rest just ran to their houses or places of work to bury themselves under whatever they could find, clinging to the slight chance of a reprieve from the horrors of the night. The phones were out of action, both fixed and cellular. Communication was in disarray.

The late flight was due thirty minutes before midnight. How to stop it from coming in to land was the one of a myriad of problems that beset the remnants of the town's bureaucracy. Some people ran to the river to elude the giant robotic circles. They jumped in, only to be boiled alive in the now steaming waters. Shrieking, wailing, and bellowing came from every quarter of the once, docile country town.

Alby and Primrose had made it to their vehicle. They took a back street, to avoid the turmoil, only to be cut off by one of the giant cylinders. Then Alby had an idea. He would ram the spooky beast with his 'indestructible' automobile. He and Primrose were transformed to stone, as they sat in the car, even before his foot could hit the pedals. The car turned a brilliant hue, similar to the plant pots in poor Primrose's garden. The rig reeled onwards, advancing, with the slightest of sound. The only noise that was audible to onlookers, who were becoming scarcer by the moment, was the effect the machine made on the road. Frightened out of their wits, and half demented, folk, with countenances that resembled haunted, bewildered souls, running from the devil, Satan himself, sought refuge anywhere possible.

Elevated in a prominent position on the hill, Rod and Emma were doing it hard. They could not move from their spot until daylight, but could hear the mayhem which floated up in the air from the town. Emma was distraught and near to dementia with the knowledge that her parents, siblings and most of her friends lived in the town. Rod, holding to the premise that things might not be as desperate as they were perceived from their vantage point, was trying to keep his wife in one piece, so that they could commence the final climb with safety as the dawn appeared. The thing he was ignorant of, was that the whole town would be under the control of the sinister cartwheels by the rising of the sun.

Milo Springs was now partially reduced to stone. The relentless onslaught of the alien wheels was turning the place into brick-coloured dust and rock. Half of the population was now, what one could only describe as 'rock solid' as the cylinders cycled on and on. They seemed to roll around with no visible controller, or leader; there was no apparent motor or device in the wheels, except for the rays that advanced, from the robotic machines.

The stone statues, standing or lying around the town, formally citizens, now firmly cemented, made the town resemble a gigantic graveyard. The outside world was not aware of the carnage and devastation reeked by these unearthly and mysterious creations. There would not be a soul left alive in the place by sunrise, to even ponder a question as to where these uncanny things came from.

The orange circles kept up the pace, as the night moved into the wee small hours. An hour later a plane carrying forty or so passengers en route to Milo Springs attempted to abort the landing. The pilot was in the process of bringing the plane around, when a draught of air sucked the vehicle into a spin. It crashed, then a huge ball of flame engulfed it. The pilot could not call for assistance owing to the total collapse of the control system.

Several carloads of travellers proceeding to Milo Springs came to an abrupt end, as gigantic pumpkin coloured circles reduced them to dust.

The monstrous machines continued the precise and calculated destruction into the hours before dawn. As the final homes succumbed to the rays, and were turned into dry heaps of paprika-like powder, and the last mortal was extinguished, the cartwheels began to withdraw from the town, returning the way they had come early that evening. Rolling, each in its own good time, and headed in the direction of Alby Jones former home, they tumbled along the road, their lights slowly dimmed until only a faint gleam could be discerned.

Rod kept vigil as his wife slept uneasily. He noted the departure of the wheels and felt a relief that they were spared. If they hadn't made the climb, he and Emma would be gone as well. The tinted fingers of dawn revealed themselves, signalling the time to finish the event. Only one hundred metres climb to reach the top, where the back-up party was camped. The ascent proved much easier than they both had anticipated when they had commenced yesterday. With the last twenty metres left to accomplish, Rod could smell the meat cooking at the top camp. He pushed on to the top, his wife being only four metres below him. This meant that ten minutes would see them through.

Rod's hand touched the last ledge, and he pulled himself to the top looked around for the source of the cooking smells, then called to his companions. There came no answer. He suddenly guessed what had become of his friends. Three massive, menacing cartwheels loomed ominously in front of him.

The one nearest to him began to radiate a warm orange beam in his direction.

BONE OF
CONTENTION

It was Friday afternoon; the abattoir usually closed early. Brutus, the largest dog in the neighbourhood was waiting at the gate of his house for his treats. It was three o'clock. On these afternoons, his master would regularly arrive home early. He often brought a large bone. Brutus was a prolific burier of bones. He had quite a collection scattered around the paddock, interred in all sorts of places, wherever he could scratch the surface to conceal his treasure.

Lately, his favourite digging spot was the vegetable patch, a section of which had been abandoned by his master for some time – ever since Bob Melville disappeared about four months ago. Brutus was able to bury the bones deep or shallow without human complaint. From time to time, he would dig up some of his favourite ones, then move them to other parts of the grounds or leave them at the back door of the house for his master to toss to him when he was in the mood.

There was only ever one bone he did not appreciate. It was a very large one his master left on the step without actually calling him to fetch it. This bone had an odour which his canine instincts told him was not to be played with, so he took it to a spot near the old sycamore tree down in the back paddock and buried it as deep as he could in the soft soil. The bone was evil, so the large dog thought in his doggy way, but it was gone now. Somehow, he noticed that his master had lost interest in him as well as the vegetables and he was feeling very lonely.

His master was late. A strange car pulled up in the driveway. Four men alighted from the vehicle and walked towards the gate, the same gate where Brutus was waiting. The large dog began to snarl at the men who were all dressed in blue uniforms. One of the men opened the gate

21

and bent unafraid to pat the pet on his head. "He likes dogs" one of the others remarked as they gingerly sidled past the huge animal, walking in different directions around the place. After a short while, looking here and peeking there, one of them said. "It seems no one's home but the place is pretty orderly. Let's go." And as they left, the dog watched them as they faded from view. "He's a very big dog" one of the men thought. "His master's none too small either".

Ted Prosser was at his place of employment at that very minute, sterilizing his boning knives. He had quite a collection of meat workers' knives, which had been accumulated from many different sources. Some were from retired workers; others had been handed down from his late father, who had been the leading boner at this slaughterhouse, and a few new ones. However, he liked the old knives the best. Ted's father was the longest serving boner who had worked at this slaughterhouse.

He was a huge man with a round ruddy face, with receding hair. He had very large hands, big feet, and a surly countenance. He was a thoroughly boring person devoid of softness, and he grunted instead of speaking clearly, unless he required something. Even then, he was short with words.

He did his work in the factory satisfactorily according to his peers, and no complaints could be levelled at his skills in his trade. He clocked on and off with precision each working day. He held no opinions that he wished to share audibly and kept to himself, which is quite a chore when one is a part of a team of eighty or so. Several years earlier, Ted was offered the leading foreman position, but he turned it down with no explanation. It was a common view that he had resented the management for even suggesting the job in the first place. The position was given to Bob Melville, who from all accounts did a fair and reasonable fist of it. Ted thawed a little under Melville's leadership. Ted was a great boner. Bob knew how to handle him and did so with tact and sensibility.

Bob disappeared on Easter Monday, about four months ago. Inspector Lyall Watkins took charge of the situation. He had to determine the classification of the missing man. By that he was to establish whether the missing man absconded, met with foul play, suffered an illness which caused him to wander off, maybe even had committed suicide, or used any other manner of making him fade from everyone's sight. Watkins swiftly set his team to work. The local rescue apparatus swung into full gear behind the police, searching high and low for the missing man. But he had vanished without a trace.

Easter Monday, being a major holiday, did assist to clear up the whereabouts of many people whom the police had reason to feel may assist them in certain lines of inquiry.

The inspector also was able to glean a lot of information about those who were assisting him with the task. However, the job proved a monumental disaster. After interviewing countless people, sifting through hundreds of statements and leads in just about every point of the compass, he was totally stumped.

Watkins had exhausted every single lead. Still he could not find Bob Melville, alive or dead. The wife of the vanished mortal, and the Press, wanted answers and were continually pressuring him. They nearly sent the senior policeman crazy, looking for finality and answers. Watkins reduced his staff to the best four men he felt he had with him and sent the rest home. Four months passed. It was nearly five, when Watkins decided the only way to get ahead with the case was frontal assault. This could make or break him, make him a rooster or feather duster. He sat with his colleagues, who respected their superior, but they were all aware of the pot-holed road ahead in this investigation.

"Here are my plans boys." He spoke determinedly. "I have a gut feeling and I believe you also have a similar hunch. I believe Bob Melville is dead, and I feel that the answers lie with that insolent fellow Ted Prosser, or at least some of the knowledge of this affair. We have been over the district with a fine-tooth comb and examined every skerrick of information, listened to every wise man and 'loon', heard every scenario till we were blue in the face. The three things we need to find are a body, a motive or a weapon.

We haven't got a single clue. Find one, and then we will certainly gather up the others in time. We are going to attack Prosser first thing tomorrow. We've been there before and we have interviewed him along with several others a couple of times.

So let us look at all the facts and take stock of our position."

"This is how I see it. Melville goes to his workplace on the Monday, being a holiday. He, as foreman needs to know his staff situation for the coming short working week. This is not unusual for a person to do this. Then he has a chat to the security guy for a short while, leaves apparently in good spirits, and that's the end of him. His car was still in the reserved parking lot with his briefcase and the rosters intact. The vehicle was locked. It appears to me he was drawn from the place by somebody, either voluntarily or by force.

"Melville's family can shed no light on the matter. His financial situation appeared sound - no strange developments there, or any other irregularities to surface as yet. He had no axes to grind. In fact, he led a clean, orderly and happy life.

"Now, Prosser is a point to ponder! Let us take a minute to reacquaint ourselves with him. Well, he is a bachelor, follows his father's footsteps to work at the abattoir, works to schedule, is dull, has no humour, few people skills, lives alone in his old family home along with a dog as big as himself.

"This man does have the weakest alibi on the short list in my mind of the most likely.

Now this fastidious loner turns up to work the day after the holiday with a dirty utility truck. Not like him to do that. The canvas cover is missing from the back of his vehicle, stolen he says, on Saturday night whilst he is boozing at the local. But he does not tell a soul about the cover. The first time we heard about it was after a few of his co-workers told us, and when you, Brentnall, as the interviewing officer, tackled him at the station, he agreed with their story.

"The next point to question is his movements on that Monday. He was seen at Harry's Takeaway shop, collecting food for his fishing trip that afternoon. He says he was at Miller's lagoon. Then he left at six o'clock that evening, after listening to the football. He said he was fishing all of the time.

"Nobody saw him coming or going in any direction. I have no hard evidence and will not pursue him again if nothing is found in relationship to this case, once we have checked his home and undertaken a thorough search of the surrounds. So we must make the most of it, but also remember this is not a witch- hunt and if we come away without a result in our favour, so be it."

"Any questions?"

"Sir," Brentnall interjected. "I was wondering about the cover from his vehicle.

The general public may think that it is just a discarded motor vehicle cover. You see, my point is that nobody but this group, and some of his work mates, and possibly Prosser, himself, know anything about its disappearance.

If we can find just a small piece of evidence that he has a notion as to Melville's disappearance then, perhaps we could advertise the missing canvas utility cover without prejudice." "Yes, I get your drift, so we will be mindful of that at the appropriate time." "How do we check Prosser's house without attracting the attention of the media, Sir?" chipped in one of the constables." "That is easy. Two of us, Brentnall our dog fancier and me, will dress down and drop in on Prosser before he goes on shift very early in the morning, with his consent of course. You two will dress as official members of the force and make nuisances of yourselves at The Daily. Inquire as to a reported case similar to this several years ago, which you, of course had heard rumours of during your lines of inquiry."

"Waste about an hour to keep the heat off us, then leave, no doubt empty-handed. Then proceed at a great pace out of town heading in the opposite direction as far from us as you can. My brother is coming tonight with a vehicle, which will give us some privacy for a few hours. The neighbours should not take much notice of him. He's a painter, so that should hide our presence for a little while. Also he will drop into Prosser's favourite watering hole and drop a few hints and help rumours, nothing concrete, just local gossip."

He turned to the uniformed men. "Go off now and do your job. Tomorrow, we will meet here unless something satisfying transpires due to our efforts." The two left, leaving the senior policeman and his eager subordinate to plan the logistics for their foray into the unknown.

The dawn proved to be overcast, cool with little breeze. The inspector had called Ted Prosser at six-thirty a.m. which, seemed to annoy the big man no end. He grumbled, but when Watkins explained the reason for the early time, which he said was to not affect the man's work routine, nor to draw attention to him unduly, he considered this and then agreed to allow them to come and check out his house.

The young policemen approached the editor's desk after a hurried appointment had been arranged. "We would like to ask for your assistance to check articles appearing in your papers several years ago concerning a similar disappearance to the one we are interested in at this time", one of the constables convincingly explained.

"Fine" replied the editor, sniffing a fill-in to help a lean week, nothing like rehashing some old scandal. "Our records are not computerised completely as yet, but I'll give you an assistant who will show you the records. However you may need an hour or two to peruse the amount of information. Let me know how you get on. I have only been here a short while so one of the locals may be able to assist you."

Feeling jubilant, the two followed the young helper to the Records room. "You should have been an actor" one policeman said to his mate with a grin. Then they slowly went to work at their appointed task. They had two hours to fill in as the diversion.

Watkins spent half an hour with his brother, conferring about the previous evening at the hotel. Then he returned to Constable Brentnall, who was preparing his kit for the assault on Ted Prosser's ten acres. Watkins drove his government owned vehicle to the appointed rendezvous and picked up his brother's painter's truck, a vehicle of several-years vintage and showing its age. The senior police officer drove the van whilst the constable placed batteries in a dicta-phone, which would be concealed in his coat pocket during the visit. Then he un-wrapped a small parcel of meat, which he had one of his friends cleverly doctor. This would also be hidden in his coat and held for emergencies only.

The under-cover agent, discretely nestled in the trees beyond the entrance of Prosser's property, dialled the number that would get in touch with Inspector Watkins. The message was brief - "Very agitated." The senior policeman was pleased and moved the vehicle quickly to their destination. When they arrived, Prosser was at the gate with Brutus, who appeared to be as sullen as his master was.

"Get on with it then", the owner said in a surly manner. Watkins stepped down from the painter's van, closely followed by his assistant, who was wearing a large overcoat. The early morning was proving to be quite cool. The dog, seeing the young constable became excited and stretched up to lick him as he came through the gate, but the big man restrained the animal and came between Brutus and the policeman. Watkins explained that this was their last call as they were winding up the case.

This made the slaughterman considerably more at ease, as he followed the men in the manner of his dog who was hanging about searching for affection. Watkins commenced to search the house, room by room. The house was spacious, clean, neatly kept and filled with simple furnishings he suspected were the parents' hand-me–downs. He moved slowly and deliberately around the interior of the dwelling with Prosser ever at his elbow watching with an indignant look on his face. He was forced to ask Prosser with tact to give him space. The fellow grumbled and complied, withdrawing to keep an eye on Brentnall outside.

Lyall Watkins was not faring as well as he had hoped. There were too few places in the house to stash even as much as a case of beer let alone a body or something that could give him a break in the case. Maybe he was barking up the wrong tree, he mused. They spent a long two hours and knew they were outstaying their welcome when a strange thing happened.

The dog, which was fossicking around the yard, commenced to dig up the vegetable patch. Prosser took to him with a stick causing Brentnall to try and restrain him, calling to Watkins, who came to his assistance with great haste. Watkins warned Prosser to stay put on the veranda whilst they concluded their work, which he did with great reluctance.

The younger policeman reported to his senior that the other two had completed their assignment and were heading out of town. He instructed Brentnall to call it quits just as the dog started bounding down the back of the yard to the sycamore tree.

They had reached the gate as the dog raced toward them with a very large bone between his teeth. He dropped it at Brentnall's feet. It was partially covered with soil.

The policeman instinctively bent down and picked it up and was about to throw it to the dog when he stopped and stared at the bone.

"Boss, look at this. The bone has been sliced across and glued back together."

"You're right son. Give it to me". He held the bone aloft, and then shook it. It rattled.

"That's funny, how can a bone rattle in it? It takes more than one bone to make that happen". He swung the bone against the gatepost, smashing the joined end off. He then tipped the bone on its end. Something shiny fell out of it landing at his feet. It was a long thin boning knife. He looked in the direction of the despairing face of Prosser.

"Well, somewhere at last." he smiled, as the great dog bounded away, glad finally to be rid of that 'evil' bone.

WHAT'S MINE IS YOURS

Mrs Alice Farmer gazed across the spacious lawns of her large house block. She was standing by her living room window, admiring the roses which were her pride and joy. Precisely at six-thirty every morning, Alice arose from her bed, pulled the drapes back from the windows and spent a few minutes contemplating her achievements as a gardener. It was a habit born from years of loneliness. Since her husband passed on to greater pastures, Alice's only lot in life was to build a bigger and a better garden displaying more radiant arrays of blooms than any other of her contemporaries in the district.

She, at this time, was totally unaware that today's sojourn in the garden would bring her enormous heartache and despair. While she was at the window, she cast a glance toward the neatly manicured parkland directly across the road. Oh how she and her late husband fought the local council to force them to terminate the proposed housing development, those many years ago. She stepped away from the window, moved her attention from the outside to peruse the many stylish cabinets that adorned the room. They all had lead-light glass doors, perfectly manufactured by master craftsmen and kept in immaculate condition. Each showed the workmanship of a bygone era.

The several cabinets were filled to capacity, displaying trophies, medallions, plaques and other memorabilia. The contents of her cupboards generally reflected the dedication and prowess of Alice Farmer's prize garden, except for two which housed a mass of china and silverware. So dominant was she in the horticultural scene throughout the district, that many aspiring 'green fingers' chose not to enter any of the local competitions. Alice was also president of three garden clubs. This gave her an envied power base and that did not go down well with many of the townsfolk. However, she was dedicated and always available.

Alice's husband had detested gardening, suffering her bullying unto the grave. The poor mortal could hardly sit down for a moment after a hard day's work. Just as he opened his paper or lifted the lid of his favourite draught, the voice of Alice would boom into the house from some remote corner of the yard, be it front or back, demanding that he, with the shovel and barrow, report to her post haste. Life wasn't rosy for Jim Farmer. Even when he passed on, she buried his remains, after the visit to the crematorium, with the flowers near the back fence. Now he's kicking up daisies. That was his lot in life and death, to be in involved somehow in her confounded garden.

Today a pallet of seedlings was expected to arrive. A good hour or two in the garden would do her just fine. Then the phone rang. It was her close friend and confidant Julie Muller, calling to invite her to morning tea. She accepted and decided to plant in the cool of the evening. Now, that's a good day, eating and planting. The morning melded into late afternoon and the well-nourished Alice arrived home, ready to set to work and place the seedlings into their appointed spots in the orderly landscape of her expansive garden. She had two hours to achieve this before the sunlight gave away to the shadows and dusk, but she was an expert and was a very fit seventy-four year old.

Alice worked diligently for an hour or so in the solitude of the yard. Suddenly an unfamiliar sound assailed her ears, then an unsavoury odour her nostrils. She looked up and there it was straight in front of her. A large truck, with a covered back, something like a furniture removalist used, had pulled up by the park and was disgorging a couple of beings. The beings turned out to be a woman and a small child. Alice peered at them for a while to see if she could recognise them. No, they were strangers as far as she could ascertain. She continued with her planting and panting as the effort was straining her a little. Not that any one would have noticed by the manner in which she carried out her work so efficiently. She was just about finished at the same time as the sun was retiring behind the hill, when she noticed the lady with the child cross the road in her direction. The woman was neatly attired, as was the tot. Alice stood up and in her usual courteous manner, used for everyone except her late husband, and greeted them.

The younger woman, who called herself Rita, complimented Alice on her extraordinary array of well-kept flowers and shrubs. Rita explained that she couldn't keep a garden as she and her husband resided in a unit in the city and there was just no space for plants at all. Alice asked her why she was waiting in the park. The lady replied that her husband was a furniture carrier and delivering a load in the area. Alice then inquired as to when she expected him to pick her up. The night was setting in swiftly. It was not good for a young nipper to be out late. Her new acquaintance said that she was all right, that the trip broke the monotony of sitting around the house as a single parent whilst her man was on the road. Alice sympathised with her, although her late husband would never have been allowed to travel without her as back seat driver.

The older woman offered to get something to eat. The younger said she would be grateful for some hot water for the child's bottle. "You know; here in the country we have a motto of 'what's mine is yours' she beamed. Alice did not know what was in store for her as she uttered those words. Alice Farmer was so glad to oblige, opening the front gate and leading the two visitors to the house. They followed her, walking up the four steps on to the porch and then into the house. Alice had left the front door ajar as she worked in case the phone rang. As they entered the spacious living room, the young woman remarked with great surprise at the number of glass cabinets that were placed around the walls. Alice stopped and with great pride explained her passion - that of gardening, and she proudly showed the trophies of her exploits. Then she guided the other to her chiffonier laden with her finest silver ware. She had accumulated this collection over many years, through inheritance and just picking up sundries at auction sales and the like. She digressed from her diversion, moved toward the kitchen to heat the water for the infant. Mother and child followed her.

Alice placed the kettle on the stove saying loudly to her self that it would not take long for the water to heat. She then offered the girl something to eat. The woman accepted, and then asked to use the phone to find out how long her husband would be delayed. Alice talked to the tot like a long lost friend whilst the woman occupied herself with the phone. Alice did not listen explicitly to the woman's conversation but it sounded to her a very cordial conversation. "About an hour" the girl said, and that was that. Alice said that it was quite a while since young feet pattered around the house. Her children lived far away. They had little ones of their own and seldom visited.

She became so preoccupied with arranging the food for the two, and conversing, that the time slid by. As they entered the kitchen earlier, the younger lady suggested to Alice that the door of the living room be closed. This would assist to keep the youngster from moving around the house willy-nilly. Alice agreed, promptly closing the door. Time passed as the two chattered, chewed and attended to the child who had settled on the floor; he seemed to amuse himself with out much ado. Alice had warmed to her unexpected guests and fussed around them. During the kettle-boiling period a little earlier, Rita peered out of the window and suggested that she would like to view the back garden before they left. Alice thought that would a splendid idea as it was a sight to behold, and besides it needed to be watered tonight anyway. She had sufficient lighting due to the layout of the latest blooms.

They chattered a little longer, until the woman felt that she should go out and wait for her husband. He'd indicated that he would be finished by seven. It was nearly that now, Alice observed. Goodness gracious have we been talking that long?. How time flies when you are enjoying yourself! They left by the back door, circumnavigating the plots, eyeing the extensive quantity of flowers and shrubbery, which the owner had toiled over so lovingly for years. Rita thanked the elderly woman for her hospitality, said farewell, and then went around to the front of the house by way of the side path. Alice waved goodbye. She resumed the role of mistress of the garden and commenced to dampen the plants in the cool of the evening. The mother and child disappeared from Mrs Farmer's life forever as they left her view.

Alice Farmer, aged seventy-four, after watering her beloved garden plots and picking off some dead pieces of plant, switched off the tap and slowly ascended the steps to the front door once again that evening. She paused at the front door to look back and admire her plants. And reflect on her visitors! They were just what the doctor ordered. Young company was a scarce commodity for old folk to indulge these days .She caught her breath while noting it was a clear moonlit night. Then stepping to the door, she opened it. Alice Farmer, horticulturalist extraordinaire, switched on the lights of her orderly living room. Her eyes swept around the huge room. She clutched her chest, let out a muffled cry and fell heavily to the floor. What she had seen was what she couldn't see. The large rectangular room was laid bare. Not one cabinet, one chiffonier, a single trophy or a Persian carpet was left.

Every single piece was gone.

The Queen of Smugglers

Maja's grandmother lumbered along the bumpy cobble-stoned street whistling an ancient Italian tune. The melody and words had been adopted and adapted into a Slovenian folksong centuries before. The elderly woman warbled along with it most afternoons as she waddled home from her devious pursuits, pushing the four wheeled pram, as she had for most of her senior years. The tune had another purpose as well as keeping her cheery. Her customers knew that if they heard it, then she had procured their goods and they would be in the street ready as she passed by.

She paused for a moment outside a dingy building, collected a parcel wrapped in brown paper from the pram, pushed the ugly grey door open and threw the parcel onto the first step, let the door slam, then proceeded along the street.

Anyone who observed the elderly woman as she meandered along her path through suburbia could have thought of her as the local postal delivery woman. However Ludmilla Dragonju plied her shady trade day in, day out without hindrance or question. She plodded through the streets of Kranj early each day, collecting meagre orders from its inhabitants, and then would set out to fulfil those obligations.

As she approached her home, a second floor two bedroom unit one could hardly call an apartment, her breath came in short spasms and she began to wheeze. She sat down on the dilapidated seat provided by the Party for the convenience of its faithful members, opened her coat from which she extracted a shabby purse, removed a lozenge from it, sat and sucked at the sweet, while contemplating the world around her, a very small world indeed.

A passing acquaintance stopped and bid her good day, inquired of her health, then placed an order for a special perfume which was only available in Italy. However the same chattel appeared in the suburban markets under the label "eau de toilet." Ludmilla advised her client that it was a tough assignment and that she would need a deposit before she attempted to search for foreign perfumes - and of course there was the matter of danger money.

The Party's watchers were about in numbers these days. Any hint of inequality would bring a heavy hammer down on those who sought to be different from the masses. Ludmilla would be out of business and she was not going to let that happen. There was the winter to contend with, and her arthritis would not allow her joints free movement in the cold misery of an eastern European winter.

She farewelled the prospective client with the wave of her hand and a stifled smile and reached for her bags. Her breathing returned to normal which really wasn't that much an improvement at all, she stood up and left to find her front door. Some front door - paint-less and hanging by a hinge. It had holes kicked in it by street urchins and occasionally by a rare dissatisfied customer. The paint which was left, that ugly paint of the regime's plan for sameness, had fled the iron and wood, and the handle was no longer a part of the door.

She pushed at the door with her foot, then backed against it so as to drag the nondescript pram into the building and then onto the first landing. Ludmilla braced herself to attempt the stairway, dragging the pram with its contents, ever so slowly up to the first floor, and finally gasping and wheezing she made it to her level. Her apartment door was ajar, and music, young people's music, trickled through it. She leaned on the door to push it further, and pulled the goods wagon and her dishevelled self into the room. Immediately she left the pram to turn the gas stove on and fill the kettle. She breathed heavily as she prepared her cup of tea in an old chipped cup.

The cup of tea now in hand, she commenced to empty the pram. Small brown parcels one by one left their hideaway and were neatly tucked away in a refrigerator. There were three 'fridges' along the wall, two working and the third, which had seen better days, now defunct. It served as storage for non perishables. The room was crowded but the living space was not a priority for this woman. She was a merchant and the queen of Slovenian smugglers at that.

The 'dry' fridge was the first to gain her attention. Among its contents was a bottle of Italian perfume. 'Hanna can sweat over that,' she mused to herself. Never produce items too quickly or the sods will expect a discount, the longer the wait the better the profits. After all of the goods were safely stowed away she locked the dry fridge. It had a robust chain her elder son had procured from a shipping yard, bolted to its frame.

Once her cup of tea was finished, she walked to the door of the bedroom. She rapped on the plywood panel and muttered to the room's occupant that the moon would be around soon if the lazy lay about didn't attempt to move herself, to check if the sun had appeared. A few moments later a young girl's head appeared, eyes blinking, hair uncombed, but smiling nevertheless. "What goodies did you find today, gran?" The grandmother smiled and as she spoke, an array of stained teeth appeared, not one parallel with the other. "Pickled herrings and a ducks egg dear," the old lady replied.

The girl's head disappeared behind the door. The grandmother called to her and said, "Why are you bothering with a sailor? You know that sailors just drift from place to place and girl to girl. They are usually up to no good, they're just drifters with the tide. If you could find a nice electrician that would be better, then he could look after my refrigerators as well." Her grandmother was an expert at seeing to her own needs first. Maja had heard every angle. If her grandmother had a vehicle, then a mechanic would be first priority for her granddaughter's affections.

However the young woman had a mind of her own, and was about to head in a different direction in ideology from the elder. How to tell the old lady was the next issue, but that could wait for now. Maja was saving a little of her cash, which was left over from the textile factory, and had promised her boy friend Janko she would travel with him as soon as her funds were sufficient. That goal was still a long way off.

The girl dressed, then after kissing her 'gran' on the cheek, left the building and entered the somber colourless world that interlocked the communists together with the weather in that part of Europe, namely dull sky, grey houses, blank minds. The old lady started to attend to her chores and dreamed of how to fill the list of orders that her clients requested this morning. Her first task was to water down the Italian perfume. This was easily achieved. She always collected all the empties from her customers, telling them that there would be a refund of five tolars on each clean bottle. The clients, who had lined up daily for goods at most stores, were easily sucked in. Ludmilla handed them a discount after she jacked up the price first. Each day she dressed the same in her simple shabby attire. Completely enveloped in a dark brown long coat complemented with a green scarf dangling on each side of her, she meandered throughout Kranj, passing as a harmless old timer. In fact this small woman was the finest smuggler in the country. She knew where to find every illicit commodity, cultivated each of dozens of 'fences' in the district, and if things were hard to procure, she would ride the train to Ljubljana and find her goods there.

Ludmilla carried a string bag out and about. The bag contained two old shoe cartons, innocent enough to the cursory glance, but the sole method to convey the smuggled wares in. She had to pass the best of the Party's scrutineers, who usually lurked on every street and corner. The boxes hid a multitude of sins for decades. She had never been stopped and searched so far.

Since the authorities took her husband Maricek to a labour camp for 'crimes against the State', namely swearing at a Party Official during a contrived public meeting, Ludmilla Dragonju took a silent belligerent stand against officialdom, namely running her small but lucrative operation. At eighty four not out, she was going to survive the Party and prosper. Her grand daughter was her sole joy and Maja would benefit as a result and hopefully, get away from this decaying country.

Of course the granddaughter had her own plans which she wisely had not discussed with her elder relative. However she would, when the time was right for them both. Maja, being young and aware, smelt the winds of change moving in her land, whilst the incumbent leadership were in denial that the people would make the final decision sooner than later.

'Milla, one morning, trussed herself in the usual manner and as the freezing drizzle was imminent, so her bones told her, she shovelled the pram down the rickety stairway to head out into the front street. She hesitated at the doorway, pushed it slightly ajar and peered out into the gloom. Quickly she pulled her head in, closed the door as well as it let her, and scurried out the back way. She had observed a high ranking official taking notes and questioning people who were heading off to their respective jobs or schools for the day. 'Milla despised these officials and kept her distance. The good fortune she had was that she had three escape routes, the front, the back of the building and a fire escape which led to a basement, then to an outside exit seldom used.

This day she had an appointment with Mort Levin, a cobbler who was a friend of long- standing. He and his wife Ruth kept her in shoe boxes and shared in certain 'spoils' that she procured in the course of her trading. Mr Levin's shop was known around Kranj as 'the hole in the wall' and that is just what it was a little door squeezed between two ancient buildings. It was a room stocked with footwear and had a tiny space where Mort repaired shoes and assorted leatherwear.

He and his wife seemed to have been there a long time, except for a few years before and during the war, when they fortunately made it to America. They returned when the liberation was completed only to find a new and idealistic regime in power. The Levins were the ones who assisted Maja to spend a year in Italy by pulling strings and greasing palms.

Maja was supposed to be schooling at that time, but nineteen year olds have different priorities and she was no exception. She had tasted the good life and was determined to have some more as soon as she could get out of her present situation. She kept her counsel, not telling her grandmother, whom she knew would be greatly upset at the thought of losing her.

Milla spent an hour with Ruth and Mort then left. Ruth gave Milla a small portion of halva for Maja that her daughter had brought back from Israel a week or so ago. The 'empty' shoebox she collected was full of contraband, perfumes, eau de toilets and fragrances, all sourced by the Levins, her partners in crime. She exited the shoe shop and shuffled for home. Hobbling up the stairs, pulling her dilapidated pram behind her into the kitchen, then after shutting the door, she quickly unloaded the ill gotten gains into the 'dry' refrigerator.

Milla made her tea and just as she was about to sit down there was a robust rap on her front door. Opening the door cautiously she beheld the countenance of the Party official she had eluded that morning. She had no option but to let him in to the room. She invited him in. Mr Jansa said he was from the Ministry of something or other. She didn't quite hear it and didn't care either as they were all nuisances at the best of time. He explained that he was calling on the elderly in the neighbourhood to ascertain their wellbeing. However she smelt a rat. She offered him a tea, and like all the leeches in the Party he said "Yes, and do you have something to eat as I have been too busy to…" She replied that she could not supply any food. She lied when she said that it was hard enough to survive on the meager money she received. He settled for the tea. She watched him eye up the refrigerators. She knew his thoughts. Three refrigerators; nobody has three refrigerators. Even his cousin in Australia, who is wealthy, only has one refrigerator.

"How did you get these?" pointing to the white goods.

"Oh, them! Well, that one." pointing to the dry fridge. "Its defunct. I store my kitchen linen in that." For good measure she opened its door and sure enough, tea towels and tablecloths were arranged neatly on the shelves. Now, if the lazy sod had gotten off his chair and took a closer look - but he didn't. "These haven't much in them as I can't afford to fill them. One day when my granddaughter brings home a strong man he could take them out of here but nobody can be bothered, so I keep them until that happens."

Then with guile she posed him a question "Could you lift that one down the long steps for me."

"Me! Oh no! I've got a bad back. You will just have to wait till some young men do it for you." Then he stood up and prepared himself to leave adjusting his coat and scarf. She had bluffed him and she knew he wouldn't come back. These types escape from any kind of physical work. Offer them some and they'll run for cover. He left speedily and she smiled. She shut the door, went to the dry fridge and lifting the tea-towels out of the way, pulled out the perfume bottles. "Tomorrow I need four."

A FRIGHTENING
SHADE OF GREEN

What was to have been a great day for the Holden family was to become a nightmare. Joan and Greg Holden had planned their vacation at the quiet coastal retreat of Dolphin Cove.

Greg, as a self-employed furniture builder and his wife–cum–secretary rarely had an opportunity to take a break during the working year, so they sneaked the odd weekend, a short time at Easter, and a few extra days between Christmas and New Year.

Life rolled on as they raised their three children, schooled them, and married them off at an early age.

At 47 and 49, Greg and Joan found themselves together and eager to get out and about, a restlessness that often manifests itself in couples who suddenly realise they have an empty nest. So the trip was arranged. Joan was excited. "Maybe we'll see a few whales this year", she told Greg with great anticipation. Greg was pleased that his wife of 27 years was a great companion. Although they differed in their political views, they had, at an early time in their relationship, agreed to disagree on this matter and both were content with this. Joan was a supporter of greenish matters, and Greg a conservative at heart.

The day was bright and cool with a cloudless blue heaven which was a perfect way to commence their journey. Dolphin Cove was a three-hour drive from their part of suburbia, a nice and non-threatening journey with abundant greenery, fields of lushness and verges - wooded and undulating toward the sea. It was whale season and expectations were high. The last whale sighting by the Holden's was when they took their young brood to South Africa fifteen years previously. That time they saw, on their way to the Cape of Good Hope, a pod of eight or ten in a small bay. This was the highlight of their overseas experience.

Greg, in his meticulous fashion, checked the travel gear as he packed the suitcases in the boot of the car and hung Joan's clothes in the back seat area; noting that their own pillows which they always took, served as packing. His favourite travel sweets were already in the glove box, as was the phone and drink bottles. All was ready, and believe it or not, Joan was for once on time – flushed with excitement, and with work far from her mind, was standing by the car when Greg finally checked the security arrangements and locked the front door.

He noticed as he stepped toward the car, that her favourite potted plants had not been watered. "Jeez," he thought, "She's certainly in a holiday mood today." But he decided not to mention the plants.

❧

They left the city behind them and within half an hour, they were passing through small villages on the outskirts, moving closer each minute toward the coast.

His favourite bakery was an hour away along the road. They often stopped there on weekends when they could get away for a couple of days.

The morning was pleasant for driving - the time one gets to reflect on things and drift into a space between the pressures of life and the peace of nothingness. It's a wonder vehicles ever make their intended destinations as people unwind and become inattentive to things around them. They plunge into a time of anticipation, of doing whatever interests them - at their leisure, not pushed by the demands of commercial constraint.

The Bakery lived up to expectations. The cappuccinos were tops and custard slices fresh and delicious. Joan commented to Greg as they strolled along the small town's main street that it would be a pleasant place to retire to, but that was years away. Silently, Greg's thoughts were on the same level.

They passed through a few small hamlets, some perched on the undulating hills and some nestled below in lush verdant valleys. Just before noon, as they were approaching a seaside town, Greg glanced to his left and noticed a large crowd of people on the beach below. Suddenly Joan's body lurched forward, her head drooped, and her only restraint being the seatbelt; she seemed to have fainted.

Bringing the car to a stand still in seconds, Greg found an area by the side of the road with barely enough space to park. In a kind of panic leaning over to attend to Joan, he found no response. Leaping out of the driver's seat to the passenger side, he lifted Joan's head back while simultaneously feeling her hands and staring into her face. He became extremely alarmed.

A stroke! A heart attack! Or something even worse!

He opened a back door, pushing goods from the seat. He released the seatbelt from Joan's body and placing one arm behind her back and one under her legs, he gently raised her and lifted her from the front of the car. He moved carefully with his fragile armful and placed her on the back seat with the gentleness of a mother with a newborn infant. His face was damp with tears; his heart thumping with fear, he trembled as he checked her breathing. It was slow and she had a weak pulse.

He made her as comfortable as could be and then looked around him. The only people he could see were those gathered at the beach. He left Joan in the car and sprinted down the hill to the sand dunes below. His tears were blurring his vision. Desperation lifted his resolve and he ran as he had never run before. Crossing the dunes onto the sloping sand, down towards the water he raced. Sand filled his shoes making running a little harder but he was near them now. Out of breath, he reached the crowd, about twenty or thirty people. They were congregated around a small whale which was beached, the waves stopping just short of the whale's tail.

Girls and young men were tossing water on to the creature. Others were rubbing it down; some were talking to it. It was a blur to Greg. He spoke to the first person he encountered, "My wife's sick. I need a phone and some help", he blurted out.The practically naked surfie blonde, standing near yelled, "We can't help you mate, the tides coming in and we must have the whale ready to float him out."

Someone yelled, "Phone's up there at the Life Savers Club".

He turned and set off in the direction where the 'someone' had pointed.

He reached the surf clubhouse just as a veteran surfie was pulling down the roller shutters.

"Can I use your phone sir, Greg yelled, "My wife's ill, she's had a heart attack, I think"

"Cant help you mate, I'm closed and I've got to help with the whale. There's a phone box up the hill about three hundred metres, see." The phone box took coins; he didn't have coins. He saw a young girl with a cell phone. She had just completed a call. She refused him, saying that she needed to get more people to the beach to assist the whale.

Almost exhausted, he ran back to the car, checked his wife. She was unconscious but breathing. He drove like a demon, through the small town toward the next town where there was a hospital. He was totally oblivious of everything around him; just looking for the blue board with the big 'H'.

Arriving at the emergency area Greg drove right to the door. An emergency team had Joan Holden in the appropriate ward in a few minutes. Greg just stood dazed and completely drained.

As one could expect, the hospital staff were full of empathy, love and compassion. Everything that could be done was done. Greg appreciated this.

Joan Holden died at precisely twenty-nine minutes past two that afternoon, just as that exuberant group of young greenies freed the whale and enabled it to swim free and healthy back into the ocean.

THE LAST DAY

Albert Johnson adjusted his tunic which was standard Government Issue, doffed his well-worn cap, said a few parting words to his wife, then stepped out of the house in which he had lived for the past thirty years.

His mind was travelling in many directions at once. The morning air was bracing, as it always was at this time of the year in Ellenville. It was precisely seven-thirty. It had been precisely seven-thirty every working day morning for the past three decades that the Station Master left his home and proceeded via the newsagent, to walk his domain. His employment was static and boring - hence the newspaper, which assisted him to move through the morning slightly faster than twiddling his thumbs.

Today would be his last day at the station. After forty-eight years of faithful service to the system, thirty as Station Master, his time had come. A man of habit, regular as clockwork, a human married to the iron and steel steam and diesel giants that fetched and carried, would be tonight divorced from them forever at a civic reception in the village hall at precisely eight o'clock.

Albert Johnson entered the newsagency, collected the station's papers, then arranged that the home delivery of his and his wife's merchandise would cease from today; the walk each day to collect them would do him the world of good. Leaving the paper shop, he checked his government-issue fob watch and noted that it was seven-fifty. Spot on time. He walked briskly toward the station nodding and smiling to passers-by that greeted him, in the same manner as he always did, born of habit over the years.

Mrs Johnson was standing in front of her wardrobe. Tonight would be the climax of her husband's decades spent in this small town as a public servant. No more of the ritual, up at six-thirty, breakfast at seven, lunch at twelve and dinner at six. She would be able to put her feet up, sleep in and casually enjoy each day as it came. She stopped her dreaming, realising that her husband was a creature of habit, a person who would be difficult to wean off his accustomed ways, instilled by a lifetime of devotion to the job. Anyhow, she would at least try.

She turned her attention to her dresses, selecting the one she felt suitable for tonight's formal occasion. Yes, the green with the peter pan collar, the one she wore to her niece's wedding last June. She wondered if it still fitted, but it was a bit late to worry now. Five minutes later, she was satisfied that the dress made her appear a little slimmer.

Albert opened the railway station's doors as the clock struck eight, just as he had done thousands of times before. His assistant Laycock, considerably younger, but an experienced trackman, would be installed on Monday as the new chief. Albert Johnson would pass the baton to his junior with a handshake and a well wishing smile and speech at the staff's afternoon tea party, which had been arranged for that purpose.

The Superintendent of Railways would arrive on the nine-thirty with a few others who were also guests of the town for this evening. Of course, the gold watch would accompany the superintendent. Why they gave you a gold watch at the end of your working life was a mystery to Albert Johnson. He mused about this as he toured the
Station to do his checks. - especially in those areas that the part time employees were in charge of. The cleaning of the station was attended to after hours by a young couple, whose laxness of attitude toward their duties was a concern, which would not be his after four-thirty today. He kicked the toilet doors open, remembering for the moment the time a few years ago when he had to remove the town vagrant out of the place practically every morning. He pottered past the parcels office, stuck his head inside the room and spoke to Rundle, who dropped his newspaper and stood up to acknowledge his boss. He checked the time.

The nine-thirty would be here in twenty minutes and with it the superintendent and his entourage, and of course, one other thing, the gold watch. He walked on the passenger platform in a pensive mood; a small disquiet hovered over his person regarding how he would fare in the ranks of the retired. He expected to receive his well-earned lifetime pension certificate on which he and Dora would be able to live, as they say in fairy stories, happily ever after.

The Johnsons would move from the railway house at the end of the year to make way for the Laycock family, whose brood of four would fill every nook and cranny in the house. Albert had purchased a small but adequate dwelling at the far end of the village, near the golf course and with a pleasant aspect.

The train had arrived and gone after disgorging a carriage of visitors amongst others. It was on time as usual. This pleased Albert as he wished to go out on a winning note.

He was so pleased that his flowerbeds which adorned the railway precinct were in full array, an eyeful of radiant splendour for his guests. The day passed quickly. After the formalities and speeches, he managed to extricate himself from the stories, anecdotes, and general remembrances of years past to spend a short time with his lady.

Railway business was usually the men's domain, or it was until these last few years, when women were recruited for the light jobs around the station. His wife as usual had the matters for the evening in hand. She was concerned more for her husband than herself. She would handle the next part of their life with ease. But would he? Satisfied, he returned to the ongoing celebrations at the railway station. There were no trains that afternoon, so, until closing, things were very loose indeed.

At seven-thirty sharp, the Johnsons paraded to the town hall, walking along with a few neighbours and the local doctor, a good friend, and Master of Ceremonies for the events of the evening. Albert proudly wore his gold watch, which he had received that afternoon from the 'Super'. Dora wore the dress she had selected that morning. The evening went without a hitch, thanks to the good doctor who carried out his duties so ably and the caterers did themselves proud.

The now 'former Station Master', as he would be known henceforth, arrived home at eleven-thirty with his good wife, weary, but thankful for the send off his peers and the people around him afforded them. Before he retired to the bedroom, he collected the newspaper, which for the first time he could remember he was unable to read at work. He sat up in bed and perused the paper whilst his wife removed her make-up before coming to bed. She looked at her husband of many years declaring that he deserved breakfast in bed tomorrow, as he would be sixty-five. He was born at ten a.m. according to his mother's advice. He told her that would be a great idea. Finishing his paper then placing his watch on top of the pension papers, he tucked in for a good night's sleep.

Mrs Johnson rose early, being careful not to disturb her sleeping husband and prepared his breakfast, bringing it into the bedroom on the wooden tray that he bought her for a wedding anniversary a few years before. After noting that he actually read the paper in bed the previous night, her heart was hoping for other habits to fall by the wayside as well. She placed the tray down on the bedside table. She leaned over to rouse him. It became apparent to her immediately that she would not be able to wake him. At sixty-four years, three hundred and sixty-four days and twenty-two hours, Albert Johnson had joined his Maker.

She trembled then in a sort of trance, picked up the gold watch and the certificate of lifetime pension and then held it to her breast for a few minutes.

Suddenly she uttered a cry "I'll have to have the papers delivered again."

THE NEW TEAM COLOURS

Henry Betts watched with anguish from his shop window, as the last of the football-mad community left for the game on Saturday's special buses. He had seen it all so many times before. The laden buses had hardly moved out of sight when Henry clenched his fists, banged them on the shop counter, then in an exasperated manner, yelled after it, "You mongrels, spend all your money in Sandy Springs! Let us all go broke. See if I care." He had hardly finished his usual tirade when his wife interrupted him. "Don't be so angry dear. If we had a football club of our own in the competition, then people would come to Borderville once a fortnight and spend their money here, too."

Henry Betts, the towns only butcher an ardent football follower of the State Football League all his life, stared at his wife with utter amazement. "Why didn't I think of that?" he thought suddenly. "You're dead right woman! Why haven't we done something about it all these years? We've been letting their money drift away to other towns and we've been putting up with empty shops every second Saturday morning. It's all right when the games are close by - we can close at noon and get to them. But when they are played at the other end of the comp then we sit at home doing bugger all".

The butcher sank into the shop chair wrung his be-whiskered chin. He fell into deep thought as though the surrounds about him ceased to exist. After a short while in deep contemplation, he sprang from the seat, flung off his apron, then lifting a piece of butcher's paper from the counter, seized a black pen, and commenced writing down a list of able bodied young men who resided in and around the town. Meantime his spouse leaned on the counter without uttering a word and watching bemusedly as her husband, who rarely picked up a pen,

48

scribbled furiously away. He grunted names out loudly and before he knew it, had a list passing fifty young men he believed, would play the game for the town team. Then without a breather he began to list all of the people he thought could be enticed to become committee or support personnel.

His wife glanced at the list then tapped him on the shoulder. "Hate to interrupt your eagerness, Henry, but there are women in this town that could fill just about any leadership roll you need, not just wash football gear and cook food, and maybe some could play just as good". The butcher shuddered; suddenly a good idea had impediments. "I just thought that, if we got the boys together first, we could ascertain the level of support for your splendid idea, then we could put the whole project before the townsfolk to have their say" he cunningly replied. That seemed to satisfy her and the subject of women and the football team was buried for the time being.

Not that our Mr. Betts was against the ladies movement. He gauged the matter in a different light. He was of the selfish opinion, that, with many pilot meetings to be held around town and with the three pubs to be involved, no doubt, which meant quite a considerable amount of drinking to be done, he didn't need females to circumvent these new opportunities. In between customers, he finished the first lists of potential players and officials, including some potential female administrators for good measure.

He felt elated when his wife left for home early, for his plans for the football team were moving briskly, in what he considered a positive direction. Henry was bubbling with youthful enthusiasm yet he was no chicken. He needed to sound out his ideas with the right people. The right people, according to the meat-man, were usually congregated at the local pubs on a Saturday afternoon. For the first time in his role as owner of the butchery, which spanned more than thirty years, he abandoned the shop, without even completing the usual daily clean up, which was against the health regulations. Noting that the noon hour was nigh, he put the 'closed 'sign on the front door of the shop. After locking the premises he strode across the dusty street to the safe haven of the Imperial Hotel. He was a man on a mission.

The 'home and away' game was well away from Borderville, so there were plenty of patrons in the main bar, and a few of the 'well heeled' clientele hovered about in the club lounge. Henry wasted little time in greeting the lounge dwellers, who were also the ones whose pockets would be tested if the scheme was to get afloat. When he had the attention of the bulk of those assembled, Henry Betts laid out his butcher's paper, outlined his wife's idea which he knew would be forever remembered as Henry's baby. He watched their reaction with bated breath. The listeners became animated for the next half hour; the din was one of earnest approval. The message was picked up in the club lounge as patrons moved freely about.

When Henry entered the Club lounge, the throng fell silent. Even when someone turned off the wireless, which had broadcast the horse races since Adam was a boy, nobody said a word. The butcher had them and he was going for broke. "Now what we need is to test the water to find out who will jump on board with my way of thinking, then move on and see if we could get into the comp next year". The lawyer Carmody chipped in "We will need a lot of cash, probably have to run raffles and a few ventures. Many of them are dodgy as far as the law is concerned." He broke off when someone replied that it was his job to dig the right information up to keep the project on the straight and narrow.

The solicitor grinned, said he liked the idea, and subject to this and that, he was on side. So it went on. The conversation bounced from one positive to a negative back and forth until it was four-thirty when Henry, very much under the weather, called it an afternoon at the Imperial Hotel. He excused himself, and slid out through the back door just in case his honour, the local constable, was lurking around looking for wayward citizens, which was his favourite pastime these days. Off to the Railway Hotel next! He had hardly moved ten paces when he bumped into 'Uncle Boxer' the local undertaker, who was heading for his Saturday afternoon nourishment and a few illicit bets at the 'Impy'.

The Mortician, bailed up, listened to the butcher with patience for a short few minutes. Then with sudden irritation, after realizing that his drinking time was being eroded, he turned to move on, leaving the butcher with the understanding that he would be of assistance when required. What he would do, he didn't really know at this particular time. Inwardly he thought, "Maybe I'll be able to bury some unfortunate who gets felled on the field or a supporter who passes on after watching the locals lose all their games for a season or two." Any way he would help.

The enthusiastic butcher bustled on, talking and drinking until he ran out of pubs and listeners, then staggered out into the street and found his way home. What he was completely unaware of was that his ever-loving wife Loris had been bending the ears of her peers with great success, but using her idea to enlist support from her gender using a different angle from that of her husband. She had a list of posers for her man. He would need to supply answers from both supporters and sceptics.

To shorten the narrative, the public meeting called by the Shire President came and went and the proposal to form the club was more or less unanimous. Those who verbally opposed the idea were discouraged from attending the meeting by the ones who were in for the long haul. A Steering Committee comprising of ten was elected and then requested to report back in a month with a comprehensive overview of how to proceed. The ten were, of course, men. However the women pointed out at the public meeting that the Borderville Football Club Committee would be commissioned after the steering committee reported back and there would be female representation.

Henry Betts could not have dreamed of the strange turn of events that would take place from this point on. Firstly, his business picked up no end and there seemed to be more male customers than female. Men who never darkened his door in the past seemed to materialize with orders larger than their spouses ever purchased, keeping up the pressure to find out the latest news on the proposed club. Butcher Betts came home later than ever. His cleaning at the shop wasn't commenced until well after five, whereas for the previous thirty years the shop cleaning commenced an hour before closing. Usually, Henry's shop would be locked and he would be in the pub for a couple on the dot of five after five, as he would say, but that had all changed.

The club steering group was given quite a task to complete, so they met every second night to consider matters that each was researching. It was decided that, as there were three hotels in town, and as each publican was behind the formation of the club, they would hold their meetings in rotation at the pubs. The male rationale behind this needs little imagination as the grog was always available, and seeing the publicans were privy to what went on, the price was right and the precedent would be set. Maybe the girls might not join the committee if the meetings were held in these premises.

Well one could hardly believe it, but all went smoothly. The ground, belonging to St Patrick's Parish, was negotiated subject to the incumbent Monsignor and the future committee. No one proposed any new name for the club other than the one mentioned previously. All other legal or greyish areas arising were handled superbly by the lawyer, Shamus Carmody.

After a month of comings and goings, heavy meetings and long absences most evenings from their homes, much to the chagrin of their wives, the steering committee was ready to face the public. However, there was one particular point they were unable to resolve. After many discussions, it was decided to let someone else decide this potentially explosive issue. This issue would be addressed at the public meeting hopefully resolved before it became a contentious thorn in the side of the new committee.

The Public Meeting to form the 'Borderville Australian Rules Football Club' was a fiery affair. Firstly, the name was contested. Many wanted a duplicate of their favourite VFL club and this brought tempers to the boil. Then the ground on which the games would be initially played the proposed 'home ground' was in dispute. As the non-Catholics in the room tendered the Public School football oval as a contender, the Catholics won the day when it was wisely pointed out by one of their number, namely Shamus Carmody that no grog was allowed on the Public School premises.

The issues of the above and others were put aside when the ever-wise Shire President and influential landholder Albert Snape remarked that a constituted committee should be formed forthwith. In his view, they could deal with the detail. The public meeting endorsed his sentiments. So the committee was formed with the blessing of all, which included of course the three publicans, the butcher, the lawyer, the undertaker and with a few lesser mortals thrown in for good measure. Nevertheless, it is true to say that the women didn't make the grade this time around.

The first meeting of the constituted committee turned out to be the longest that would ever be held in the history of the illustrious club, possibly the lengthiest of any sporting club in Victoria. The men decided to meet every second Tuesday and rotate the meeting to give the pubs an equal share of the meeting, (and the grog sales). They would assemble at the club lounge of the Imperial at seven pm. and if the meeting went on after nine-thirty they would slip over to the Exchange Hotel and then later to the 'Railway'.

At nine thirty on the night of the first meeting the group had progressed slowly. The team's new colours, which eluded the steering committee, became a new the stumbling block, so they headed for the 'Exchange'. The 'Exchange's mine host Herb Mutton signed them in, as six o'clock closing was still the Victorian way of life, with strict licensing rules. Resilient liquor license enforcers were always lurking in the shadows of slack hotels, ready to pounce.

Choice of the Club's colours was quite important. The colours of any club often determined the 'mascot' name. For example black and yellow generally became 'The Tigers'. And the choice of their mascot was the current item for discussion. There ensued a bitter struggle, as the proponents of one or another set of colours pitched for their own idea to be selected as first choice.

As the time travelled near to one a.m., and as no decision was forthcoming, the boys decided to head for the Railway Hotel to balance the meeting. It was an opportunity to get a little fresh air as they were all determined to get the colours and the mascot selected at this meeting, come hell or high water. The success of the whole venture in the short term was the impact of the colours and the mascot. There was bound to be some dissatisfaction whatever they chose. Now, as they settled into the parlour of the third hotel, the group as a whole were quite a lot worse for wear, as they had been arguing and imbibing non-stop since seven the night before. The late hour put reason and judgement out of synch. No one in his right mind would have continued. However this was an extraordinary set of circumstances for a group of small town individuals.

Then things started to fall apart. Firstly, the publican made a crucial error when he failed to sign the troupe into the pub, then he inadvertently forgot to lock the main entrance door. The battle for the colours continued between drinks. The team was fraying at the edges then personalities came into the discussion, but no one packed it in for fear that the ' wrong' decision would be made. But in the wee small hours, near daybreak, a couple of the lesser mortals drifted to slumber in their comfortable sofas, to be ignored by the rest. The least left to argue, the more chance one's own point of view could prevail - one could espouse no doubt.

The sun rose in the heavens as the gallant Committee of the Borderville Football Club came to the realization that an agreement on the team's colours was far from them and may never be agreed upon. It was seven o'clock, breakfast time for most of them and irritation was setting in. Then a strange thing occurred. A loud noise emanating from the front of the hotel, followed by heavy footsteps in the hall signalled the arrival of trouble. Some of the delegates had feared a visit from their wives, but were not game to mention the fact. The publican of the establishment rose quickly and went to investigate. He hardly made it into the hallway when he back-pedalled into the parlour, followed by the menacing hulk of the local police sergeant.

Once he entered the room, the policeman gave a cursory glance around, running his huge left hand through his thick wavy hair, and then he boomed in a loud voice for all present to hear. "What in hells name is going on? Thirteen hours after closing time and you sods are still drinking. I've a good mind to book you all. What is going on! Can someone enlighten me?" He glared at the hotelier, who flustered and embarrassed by the lawman and bumbled a reply, "We are having a meeting and they are my guests!" he exclaimed. "Meeting! My eye. I bet if I got you all to walk the line, I could jail the lot of you, and as for guests show me the register". The policeman looked at the publican with scant regard and was about to escort him to the foyer to inspect the books, when Shamus Carmody leapt to his feet and spoke assuredly, without an impediment, unlike that of a person who had consumed as much liquor as he put away over the course of the night.

"It's like this Sergeant. We are the newly elected committee of the Borderville Aussie Rules Football Club. We are responsible with putting together the team to be available to play in the district comp next season, which isn't too far away. We have been meeting all night but cannot make a decision as to what the new clubs colours should be". He resumed his seat. The policeman, not a football sympathizer, had them in a corner and they and he knew it.

"You have broken a multitude of laws and I can't turn a blind eye to it all, but I'll tell you what I'll do. I'll pick the colours and you guys will have to abide by my decision, or I'll be forced to invoke punitive measures from the rulebook. Furthermore, the colours you choose, through me of course, will be to the ever-loving football public, the colours you chose at this so-called meeting. Am I clear?"

You could hear a pin drop. One could just about hear the grinding of the grey cells and the bobbing of Adam's apples as the men weighed up the predicament they were in. The policeman stood at attention facing them, not a glimmer of a smile or conciliation on his countenance. The assembled looked at each other and the law, then, someone among them gave a stifled groan and said quietly "Are we all agreed. Do we accept the Sergeant's offer to break our deadlock, or what's our next move?"

Not one person in the group realized the consequences of their final decision that morning in the Railway Hotel parlour. After a few minutes, the Shire President who was also the new head of the club addressed the men. "Are we all agreed? If so stand, and we will hear what the Sergeant proposes, to let us move on." They rose in unison, nodded, then sat and waited on the law to speak. "Okay, this is my call. The first person to walk into this room from now will decide the matter. What I mean is - the colouring of his or her clothes will be your beloved football club's colours for ever." They heard the last line, nodded in agreement just as the door flew open.

Standing before them in flowing attire, in her nightgown, was the lawyer's wife, Mrs Maria Carmody and no slight figure to boot. She marched up to Shamus seized him by the shoulder and rasped at him. "What do you bloody well think your doing leaving me and the kids at home all night? Get going." And she turned, glaring at the rest. Looking at the policeman, she singled him out for the final diatribe. "You should know better than this," then stomped out of the lounge with the lawyer in tow. But the others were not paying attention to her shenanigans; it was the colour of her nightgown that shocked them.

It was BRIGHT PINK.

The policeman fled.

ℰℛ

Four weeks later the undertaker and the butcher were deep in earnest conversation as to the way forward. Not one of the committee was prepared to offer the public any idea of the fiasco in the pub a month ago. The policeman had them over a barrel and they had no room to move. That's what they all thought, except the devious Carmody. The lawyer was helping his daughter mix some paint for a school assignment and he was literally hit by a thunderbolt.

That evening at the pub his second stroke of luck fell into his lap. He overheard the policeman divulging a few pointers of his private life. The lawyer was inspired. He called Henry the butcher and Uncle Boxer, the undertaker, to meet him outside his chambers at eleven thirty the next morning. Carmody advised Uncle Boxer to collect the two cretins from the stone mason's yard and bring them along as well. He hurried off to check on the policeman's moves for the next morning. He was told by the duty officer that the policeman had a 'rostered day' off and was planning to fish off the weir at the end of town. Perfect, the lawyer chortled to himself, and hurried home to his nearest and dearest.

Carmody couldn't sleep, with the expectation of a grand tomorrow lurking on the horizon and weighing heavily on him. The butcher paced his shop like a cat about to drop a litter of kittens. At ten to ten they were all there. The two boys from the mason's yard were dimwit brothers, sons of the mason Herb Dare, who was pleased to get them out of his hair for a while. Carmody explained to the four, "The Sergeant is fishing at the water hole just upstream from the causeway. I want the big boys to stand behind him when we arrive. Greet the guy but leave the talking to me. I have just found an Achilles' heel and I want to take advantage of it, okay? They nodded in approval. Let's go then, boys first."

The two brothers ambled along in front as the highly polished lawyer grinned from ear to ear like the proverbial Cheshire cat. The butcher and the undertaker fell in behind, both in contemplation. The water hole loomed up soon enough and there, as expected, was the policeman, busily attending to what appeared a tangled fishing line, much to the delight of Carmody. As they approached the embankment the lawyer cleared his throat to alert his quarry of his arrival. The policeman looked up with surprise and said "Come to assist me in untangling this mess, have you?" but noting the size of the deputation, he knew that something more pressing was at hand and he had a fair idea what it was.

Shamus Carmody, his portly frame decked with a pinstriped suit, took control of the moment. Whilst the policeman was bending to put his fishing gear on the ground, he motioned the Mason's lads to stand as close as they could at the back of their 'victim.' The lawyer's two other colleagues stood stock-still either side of Shamus as he commenced his dialogue with the Sergeant. The policeman seemed a little uncomfortable, sitting on the bank dangling his feet over the side several feet above the river, whilst five men surrounded him, hemming him in.

He spoke first and addressed the lawyer, looking directly at him as he spoke. "It's about the football thing isn't it?" Carmody nodded. "Well I'm not changing my position as it was a fair decision then you all agreed to it, so do not blame me for the end result." Carmody interjected "Well, just listen to my presentation then you can decide." Carmody ploughed on "The 'colour' has put us in an untenable position. I'm appealing to you to consider this. Pink is a product of two colours, red and white. So why not, for the sake of the people, let the colours be red and white. There's no skin off your nose and no embarrassment to anyone. Every one will be happy."

The policeman's face went a deep shade of pink, bordering purple as he struggled to contain a feeling of sudden rage. He then argued that they were forgetting his responsibility regarding the charges he was supposed to have laid aside. The committee expected him to wash all of that under the carpet. However, Carmody explained in his usual foxy manner that the policeman had left the charges too long, therefore would have to justify his laxness in dealing with the alleged offenders. The policeman pursed his lips, and then answered the lawyer curtly. "You can have the red and white but you all owe me and I won't forget, so scram and leave me to fish in peace.

The five took their leave as fast as they could. The lawyer looked behind long enough to see a large bird land close to the fisherman. He dismissed the stonemason's sons, saying, "you can go back to your work and polish tombstones or do whatever masons do, and thanks.' The hulks lumbered off with not a solitary idea what the whole thing was about. The butcher put his arm on the lawyer's shoulder, just as Uncle Boxer, having seen the white bird land on the water, exclaimed.

"Up the Swans!"

THE COPACOBANA
STRIP

Chuck Manuels literally fell out of bed in a foul mood, which didn't augur well for a good day ahead. He did not want to be in Rio de Janeiro, nor did he feel like strutting around a city he despised. He wasn't for all the humdrum associated with this place and most of all, according to his thinking; it was unfair of his editor to send him, an established crime writer, to cover an event like Carnival.

However, his editor was looking for a different angle this time and that is why Chuck was there. The other reason why Manuels was like a bear with a sore head was that the Panama hat which he had purchased at the duty free shop was a shade too small for his oversized cranium. It was his own fault; he didn't listen to the advice of the salesgirl and as usual blamed everyone else for his stupidity.

No, he had to make the most of it and work his butt off to send a damned report, as copy was expected each evening. With electronic mail these days, he had nowhere to hide as he could in the past. He grumbled over his breakfast, stumbled down to the foyer of the hotel and enquired as to the best place to meet some of the characters who present the Carnival, which was on next week. Once he received that information, he decided to explore the area for an hour or so before checking out the Carnival people after lunch..

His trained mind knew that the 'front room' hotel staff was often the best source of information when one landed in a new town for the first time. Grilling of doormen and bellboys was often a good start in his quest for solid information. And also he was a lazy sod, but a master of the written language so what he didn't get one way, he conjured up for his readers another way.

He had arrived rather late the evening before, entering the hotel from the side street after disembarking from the taxi. Therefore, he had not experienced the site of one of the world's most famous strips of sea and sand yet. Collecting a newspaper, then taking directions from the doorman, he set out to the outside world of Rio. Turning from the side street, he stepped on to the footpath that would lead him to Avenue Atlantica to get his first glimpse of Copacabana beach.

The sun was already giving a hint of what was in store for the day. It was going to be another hot one with no cloud cover. Chuck felt overdressed. He was not a beach person and the humans that were passing by him were very scantly clad indeed. Standing at the corner of the side street and the main streets, he viewed the terrain ahead. To his surprise, the picture was more pleasing to the eye than he had envisaged.

The street was in fact quite well planned. From where he was standing on the cement pavement, he had a one-way road before him, then an avenue of pleasant trees with a pedestrian path through it as well. Beyond that was another one-way road heading in the opposite direction to the first, another strip of concrete and at last the sand with the waves of the flattish sea in the distance. All very tropical and enticing, he thought. He managed to traverse the thoroughfares, and reach the sandy area, which at first glance seemed to have been raked and tidied up over night. The waters were so placid that there didn't appear to be a tide line..

The place was a hive of activity. People in all manner of attire were jogging, walking, leading dogs and chattering. The young, the old and those in between from all walks of life, from all parts of the world - white, black, wrinkled, smooth, tall, short, overweight, and some merely bones were all out walking. This was, he mused to himself the famous Copacabana beach.

He was nearly knocked off his feet when a bevy of vendors, wheeling, pushing and lifting a variety of makeshift items, descended to the beachfront. "Mind you!. Look out. Step away. F… off!" All shouted in a colourful array of Portuguese, Spanish and English. He found himself herded to the front of a kiosk, where a number of tables were assembled. A colourful assortment of umbrellas stood ready to keep the sunshine off the bodies of the patrons.

Manuels pushed his hulk into one of the chairs and sat to observe the pulsating crowd pressing its way up and down the pathways. Vehicles, and people with animals in tow, were hurrying, bustling, and noisily vying with each other for their minute piece of the fabulous 'strip.' The waiter informed him that it was ten minutes before opening but if he ordered a drink, he would be served at ten precisely. Chuck ordered a Cuban Beauty from the list not having the slightest clue what he was going to receive, perhaps something with rum in it. Did he want a cigar - best Havana? What the heck, OK. "What is all this Cuban stuff anyway?" "It's popular mister and as people can't get to Cuba easy, we fill the gap."

The reporter watched the increased to-ings and fro-ings earnestly as the opening time came closer. The waiter, an Afro-Brazilian, hovered close by, busying himself and watching for potential customers. "Over here Madam. Sir. Down here Miss." Chuck smiled, spruiking was the same the world over - drag them in, sit them down, punish their wallets and then politely shovel them out; then repeat the process. He'd seen it in every continent, time and time again.

"Sun glasses mister?" He looked up from his Cuban masterpiece. A lad, sporting a piece of cardboard about a metre long with an array of sunglasses embedded in it was holding a pair in front of his face. "Five bucks mister." The kid was polite and clean but Chuck didn't need the spectacles. He needed a story. "Kid, I'll buy a pair if you answer some questions-" The lad sat down opposite him. "What's the question man?" "Tell me son. What is the most important thing in your life?"

"FUTABUL, you know, Pele and the World Cup." "What about the big Jesus on the hill?" "You mean the Redeemer? Oh yes, he's important but the football is our life." "OK. I'll have that pair." He pointed to a large-rimmed pair. The boy handed him a pair of glasses and chuck shelled out the bucks.

Hardly had the boy moved out of sight when an elderly man plonked himself at the next table, ordered a coke, then attempted to off load a ten dollar Rolex watch. Chuck shook his head and showed his total disinterest, however, the salesman was persistent. Then Chuck turned to him and asked the man a few questions, commencing, as it turned out, to be a quite pleasant dialogue and the source of a couple of stories.

The gent had been on the beach strip for forty years plying all sorts of merchandise. He was one who had seen better times and was weary of the beach. Feeding an extended family was his lot in life and he was doomed to pound the beach for many years to come. As he talked of the old days with great nostalgia, he said nothing was ever like 'the year of the whistles' or for that matter, 'the year of the cans.'

Chuck's interest bounded and he asked the man to elaborate.

"You see," the guy explained, "there was a loose time in the nineteen sixties when the money rolled in and people began to free up a bit. We had a bit of trouble with the authorities about the drugs we used on the beach. It was like this. The folks would congregate along the beach passing around a mixture of joints, not the real hard stuff as we are a happy lot us Brazilians and don't need the heavy gear. So while we were minding our own business the police would swoop and spoil the party, so to speak."

"How to beat them was the challenge. Then someone got a bright idea. So we placed guys and girls around the beach with whistles. When a cop showed up the whistles were sounded and the pot smokers got off the sand, walked into the water then waded out to a good depth and smoked away while the cops looked on. They could not follow, because they couldn't enter the water with all their gear on. So that was good for nearly a year till some clever dick decided to get the police a couple of boats, then we were driven from here."

"What about the year of the cans?" Chuck prompted, smelling a good story floating in the air.

"Well," the old fellow replied eagerly, "'the cans,' if I recollect properly went something like this. There was quite a lot of drugs dropped off out there and brought in at night by small boats. The people who ran those operations had the authorities in their pockets and had never had any interference in years. The drugs were sealed in soft drink cans obviously in a factory built for legitimate means and used for illegal purposes as well."

"Probably the stuff was sourced in Central America or the States but that doesn't matter. What happened was that the authorities somehow decided to scuttle the big boats and mounted a massive operation. Then one night a huge load of cans were on their way, just out of Rio when the water police intercepted them and in a wild night just like you see in the movies, gun fights broke out on the ship and the police boats.

The drug people decided to jettison the cargo of cans overboard and scarper, and that's just what they did."

"For months after, people would walk along the water and pick up cans floating on the surface. There was never any idea of how many cans were collected, but almost everyone I knew got their share. Those were the days."

The old man wheezed, repeated that his health was poor, then inquired about Chuck's health. "Me, I am in good condition, I'm only forty-eight and my doctor gave me a clean bill of health before I left the States. Mind you, the editor wants me to lose a bit of weight," the reporter said patting his stomach.

"But I have to go now; I'm off to file a report. By the way, are there any bakeries?" he asked.

"Two streets behind the hotels, that's where the locals go." The man replied.

Chuck thanked the Brazilian, negotiated the street crossing with ease, and returned to his hotel to write his embellished account of 'the two years of ... ' An hour later his stomach was getting the better of him as he set out to find the bakery. As he was leaving the hotel, his phone rang. The editor was checking him out. Warning him to keep off the junk food and beware of strange women. The boss's standard line never came over to Chuck as a joke.

He noticed as he turned the corner, that the old man was watching him from across the street. "He wants to be my guardian angel." Chuck joked to himself as he kept walking on. Two streets on and Chuck was still reading the signage on the shops in quest for some mention of a bakery. He saw out of the corner of his eye, that the old man was still watching him. He became a little uneasy and kept looking for the shop. Then he saw the awning with the pictures of 'doughy things' he was not supposed to eat.

His legs moved to cross the road when all of a sudden a vehicle blocked his path. Before he could fathom what was happening, he was shoved into the car and it sped off. He found himself jammed between two determined looking and menacing beings. The one on his left had a hand gun pointed at his stomach; the other held his right shoulder in a vice like grip. Manuels' temperature was rising and he was dead scared.

He made a muffled protest which only increased the pressure on his shoulder. "Don't speak man and you won't be hurt. Look at the floor!" He did what he was told as the car weaved around several corners before came to a halt." Get out! Look down and don't speak!" the man with the weapon barked. Chuck was literally dragged from the car into a foyer of a dilapidated building. His heart was beating so fast, it could have driven an army tank. He was sweating profusely and in need of a toilet stop. He was ushered into a dingy room, still keeping his head down.

Chuck was looking at the legs and shoes of his captives. Someone seized his arms while a brawny hand pushed a white cloth onto his face and held him in a grip of steel. Instantly he smelled chloroform and drifted off into an abyss without another thought.

Dim light greeted Chuck Manuels as he woke from the enforced sleep. He lay inert for sometime before looking around. His head ached and his stomach had an excruciating pain running down through it. His left hand and his two legs were fastened with cable ties. Strangely, they had left his right untied, but then he saw the reason. A chair was placed beside the iron bed on which he was laying; his phone was on it. There was a note beside the phone. His brain was not functioning with clarity, so he didn't attempt to reach the items on the chair at that time.

Manuels drifted for a while in the gloom of his despair and the agony of his traumatised body. Eventually he was sufficiently awake and aware of things around him to make a clear decision. He grasped the phone, placed it on his chest along with the note. Just as he was about to read the note, the phone rang.

"Chuck! Good stories! They'll hit the papers tonight. Remember to lose a little weight mate, ha-ha." Chuck didn't answer and switched the phone off, screaming, "Bastard! You should be here, not me!"

He reached for the note and found that it had a phone number and an address on it. He thought it sounded like an Emergency Services number along with the address where he was incarcerated. And that's what they turned out to be.

The official who removed the ties told Chuck not to move until the ambulance personnel had attended to him. Then it hit the newspaper man like a ton of bricks. He hazily remembered the old man with the ill health and the stories of the 'years.'

"They've taken me bloody kidney! I'll kill that ##**## if I get my hands on him.

I'll give him the bloody 'year of the kidney.'"

He passed out.

UNDYING DEVOTION

Over there is a small village separated by a highway which runs by a river. The river is of such importance, in fact the lifeblood of this valley. The beauty of the landscape conjures up mixed emotions in the matters of love and to some passion. As you walk away from the village, its ancient castle casts a shadow across the market- square and the rows of houses and tourist shops. You must carefully traverse the main road to stand on the high embankment of the Loire River and view the extensive panorama.

This was a place of battles, high intrigue (also of peace and solitude). A habitation of many great farms and shall we say;- a peasant tradition and of course, much wealth. Where there is wealth there is class, as well as the impoverished. All things that could possibly happen to men, good or evil, fortune or misfortune have happened in this valley during in its long history. Many writers have related stories of these things.

Downstream, some distance from the village of Ambois, there is story of Charlotte and her friend Henri. On a narrow, but trafficable lane way to the left, just off the main road several kilometres west of the village, is the track where Henri, his parents and his two brothers lived. In a tiny cottage on the manor farm they spent most of their lives. Henri's father was the overseer for the Chateau. Henri's mother also worked on the farm

Further along the lane way, situated on a slight rise, standing majestically by itself, is the Chateau. It is set apart from an extensive expanse of arable terrain. Enough land to enable robust living for the nobility and their entourage, and to support the families of the workers, who were accommodated on the grounds. The grand- villa bears all the hallmarks of bygone aristocracy. The Chateau is set out of the way from passers by, ensuring peace and tranquility and also security for its inhabitants. The landlord, from his lofty perch, could cast his eye in all directions to control his vast holdings. This was the home of Charlotte, the only daughter of, the landlord.

Charlotte and Henri were born within the Chateau grounds, but though in entirely differing circumstances. Each would live according to their respective stations in life. In fact they were born on the opposite sides of the road.

One area of commonality the two children had was that they were able to play together. Henri's mother assisted Charlotte's mum with domestic duties. During their early infancy they played together at the big home. Once they reached school age plans were made toward their education. The only school that they could attend conveniently at that time was a short distance away. They were as close as 'two peas in a pod', inseparable. Neither mother felt uncomfortable with their children spending so much time together. However the demarcation line was drawn in certain circumstances. Civic functions and church attendance, (where the each wealthy family had their own special pews, whilst the poorer and servants where allotted separate sections). Henri never understood the separation, as he and Charlotte played together but were not allowed to enjoy the fun together at other times.

School came for them both and they attended the village school in the town. It was a walk of four kilometres and they managed that watched by their chaperones, who allowed them no frivolity. The little ones walked in twos. Charlotte always walked beside Henri until they reached his front gate. She would meet him as she passed on her way each morning, under the watchful eye of the guardians of the young. She would always pat him on the arm when they greeted or departed from each other.

This was the way it went each week day but at the weekends, when permitted, they enjoyed time playing in the fields or climbing the hay-loft when the working people were absent.

Henri saw Charlotte and treated her as a sister. He wished that they would never grow up so they could always be together. He loved the way she always patted his arm when they parted, the sound of her voice, but most of all to see her beautiful golden hair. He could see her from a long way off, her golden tresses flowing behind her. As he grew older Henri began to feel his closeness to her as the most important thing in his life.

Although he did mix with other boys and girls, it was never the same as being with Charlotte. Henri began to intellectualize that he could never be separated from her. This reasoning would take control for the rest of his life and would no doubt give him much pain and misery in his undying devotion to her. He would be unable to comprehend the difficulties that would emerge over his lifetime, through his infatuation with her. In his own quiet way he would reconcile himself with seclusion to cover his loss.

Their early school years moved albeit too swiftly for Henri, whose pre-occupation with his relationship kept him from noticing changes in Charlotte whom he regarded as a 'signed, sealed and delivered commodity.' When the higher schooling emerged on the calendar, Charlotte's parents announced that their daughter was to attend a ladies College in Paris. At this news Henri's life pattern took a turn for the worse. He began to seclude himself from those who were close to him. Charlotte explained that she would be home at the holiday season each term. This news gave him hope, but when she finally left for Paris, he switched off from his family, drifting into melancholy. He became morbid and insular.

No amount of encouragement either from his family, or from his teachers could extricate him from the condition. Charlotte returned each holiday for the first two years, but after that her visits became less frequent. His schoolwork deteriorated, so on his sixteenth birthday, his father completely at the end of his tether offered him a job on the farm in the fields. Henri accepted and went to work for Charlotte's family.

During the early visits to her home Charlotte would meet Henri when she was allowed. Henri lived in a small world and now Charlotte was spreading her wings and the social divide between them began to rear its ugly head. They held their friendship together, but their differences were definitely showing more and more with each encounter.

Then one morning the landlord announced that he had disposed of his holdings and was moving to a larger Chateau some distance from his present abode. The sale included the retention of the staff, under the new ownership. Henri and his family decided to stay on. With Charlotte out of the scene Henri went deeper into depression. This was further exacerbated when Henri visiting the village to attend some chores for his aunty, was told that Charlotte was to be married in the town where her parents had recently settled.

Everyone around Henri noticed the change in his whole being. He drifted to despair and was totally non- communicative. Then he disappeared one night.

The night before Henri went missing, he made up his mind to leave home unannounced.

The next morning, (the day that Henri was to celebrate his eighteenth birthday), he failed to show up to attend his work in the fields. His belongings had gone from his room. He completely vanished and no amount of searching could locate him. His family grew in fear that he may do something rash, but they would never lay eyes on him again.

At darkness when the family had retired early for the evening, (not unusual for rural folk), Henri waited for his brothers to go to sleep then left, carrying only the bare necessities for the travel he was to embark upon, and moving as swiftly as he could, he set out towards Charlotte's home. It would be a few days walk and he wished to progress without detection or interference.

The night was as still as the desert. and cold with the moon lying hidden behind the high winter clouds. He kept to the road, moving to the verges, which were densely populated with shrubbery. That evening through to the early dawn he managed to cover about a third of the distance it would take to reach Charlotte's village. Once at the village he would find out where the Chateau was.

The going was more strenuous than he had imagined. The rain set in on the third day, causing him to find shelter in a farm barn. His attire was soaking wet and he was in a wretched state, mentally and physically. He moved on as soon as he could muster his strength. The third night gave him no comfort. The weather was foul, and his shoes let in the water. He was down to the last of his rations that he had so meticulously planned b. The travelling became tougher as the night wore on. The lack of moonlight and the constant rain harassed him all the way. Early on the fourth morning he stumbled across a farm worker who told him he was only a few hours from his target. This gave him heart so he pushed on. He was completely exhausted and emotionally drained. The rain abated, allowing him to dry out some of his clothes.

He was now a stranger in a new district. With the small amount of money and his meagre belongings, was now completely on his own.

He had grown a beard, allowed his hair to go uncut and done much to disguise his appearance as possible. The marks from a severe bout of chicken pox had slightly disfigured his face. Henri had planned to find a place as close as he could to Charlotte. In his tiny mind, he believed that his love for her was sacrosanct and that he and only he should take guardianship over her well being. Henri sought out a little café to have his first decent meal in four days, and asked if there was any rural employment in the vicinity. The café proprietor advised him to go to the Chateau beyond the village. Henri was in a hurry to get to his appointed goal; Charlotte's home.

He came to the perimeter of the Chateau's grounds just as the winter sun was reaching its zenith and Henri was in unusually high spirits.

He engaged in conversation with a farm hand and learned that the farm was expanding its acreage. The foreman had mentioned only yesterday that he would need extra hands come spring.

The man directed Henri to the lane he was to travel in order to find the foreman. The foreman was at home as it was Sunday, had just returned from Mass and was in a congenial mood. Henri found himself in a friendly environment from the outset. Henri's self confidence rose in him and when the foreman said he could use help with weeding during the winter spell, then sent him to the barn, which had a habitable loft.

Henri settled into the loft that day. The loft was more of an attic. It consisted of two rooms, furnished with an iron bunk and a small bureau with drawers an assortment of oddments such as a small stove, some cooking utensils a table and two ancient chairs made up the second room. The loft had one window which was situated in the wall at the other end of the room. This window gave him a view of the northern aspect of the manor. He was delighted to see the Chateau was directly in his vision, some three hundred metres from the barn.

The first evening he went to the window and watched the large home, it's lights beaming through the windows. Henri's gaze became transfixed on the Chateau. His attention was on the windows. He knew that somewhere Charlotte was within, and he was now here to watch over her foreever. Henri prepared to make this place his home.

His boss allowed him to reside in the barn loft as long as he wished. Henri did not object. He never told a soul about his relationship with the employer's wife, Charlotte. Months passed. Winter dissipated. Spring came, his jobs changed according to the seasons. He was content, and at the end of each day went to his solitary perch at his window and surveyed the house where Charlotte lived, happy in the knowledge that he was near her. Each evening he watched from the window. He would go to his bed content that she was okay. He fell into a pattern and did not engage in activities with the other farm hands. He refrained from strong drink, merriment and the like; so much was the obsession that preoccupied him.

When he saw Charlotte walking through the gardens, alone or accompanied, he kept at a distance, watching her every movement. When she and her husband were absent from the Chateau, he would saunter up to the garden and sit in her favorite seat for awhile daydreaming fantasies of the early times of their childhood. He then returned to his loft and the solitude, drifting into an evening of melancholia. Sometimes in the darkness he ventured toward the Chateau, wandering aimlessly, slipping behind shrubbery or some hiding place, and scrutinizing the visitors but keeping a watchful eye on his lady.

The seasons passed swiftly.

Children were born to Charlotte and her husband, but Henri paid scant attention to them. He only kept his heart and soul for her. Thus the days slid into month, the months to years and the charade went on. His own family had all but given him up- lost to misadventure. He never contacted them from the moment he left them to his death.

Thirteen years Henri, who was not known as Henri, but his assumed name kept his lone vigil, never once touching or speaking to Charlotte, keeping her ignorant of his existence throughout his tenure at the farm. He had reached his early thirties but appeared much older.

Henri's health took a turn for the worse during the following winter. He fell ill with an incurable chest ailment and lingered a few weeks. He succumbed to the disease and died in his secluded loft undisturbed and without a single person to mourn him.

The priest came and gave Henri his last rites. Then noticing a large box placed near the end of the bed, opened it. To his surprise he found all of the dead man's earthly savings. Henri had spent hardly a franc in the days of his existence at the farm. The priest stuffed the money into his pockets, mumbling to himself that the cash would pay the church for the burial and the remainder would help refurbish the church altar. This was his lucky day.

A few of Henri's acquaintances turned out for the funeral along with the landlord. The remains were interred in the cemetery adjacent the churchyard. The miserly undertaker taking advantage of the situation built Henri's coffin from inferior materials. He covered the coffin with woven cloth to conceal his shoddy handiwork.

As the landlord bid farewell to the priest, he requested that as his family were permanent residents of the Parish, it would be prudent to have two plots set aside for his wife and himself. The priest agreed. Once the burial was out of the way he would speak to the undertaker and advise him accordingly. This matter was attended to immediately.

The cemetery was located on the side of a hill as was the church. The undertaker and the priest selected a couple of plots for the landlord next to Henri's.

Time rolled on and Henri was forgotten, weeds soon overtook his burial site and it was concealed under a mass of greenery. The family at the Chateau prospered. Life carried on as usual in the valley. The children matured and departed the area, as is the norm in rural communities. Charlotte continued her lot in life, occasionally thinking back to her childhood and wondered what became of Henri and his family.

A brutal winter brought calamity to the district a few years later; Charlotte was struck down, and passed away after a short battle with pneumonia. Her husband followed soon after. Some said this was from depression over his wife's death. They were buried in the church graveyard side by side according to the landlord's wishes.

The unusual feature of the interment was that Charlotte was placed next to Henri. In fact they were not more than a metre apart and were the closest Henri had been to her since they were children.

In the passage of time the Chateau fell into disrepair and the people moved to the nearer towns or far off cities. The church was forced to close. The church and the cemetery fell into dilapidation. Heavy rains eroded the soil around the graves and the grave sites sank into the ground, whilst the stonework cracked and decayed. All in all, the place was a sorry sight.

Many years later a descendent of Charlotte's family, searching for her ancestors was directed to the small and uninviting churchyard. With garden implements in hand, she set about to clean up her kin's last resting-place and glean as much as she could from the headstones. As she was removing the undergrowth from around the stone slabs, she came to the side where Henri and Charlotte lay side by side. When she pulled the greenery from between the two sets of stones she let out a gasp and fell back on to a grave stone directly behind her.

What she saw seemed at first bizarre. The bones of Henri's arm had fallen out of the eroded coffin and lay toward Charlotte's coffin while Charlotte's hand had fallen onto Henri's; just like old days when she touched his arm as each time they parted.

SOPHIE AND THE EGG MAN

Sophie disliked the old man who brought the eggs to her house. She hid from view every time he called to see her Mother. Sophie could not pin point the reason for her aversion to the man. So she was glad that it was her Mum who collected and paid for the produce and not her. Sophie often thought about the old man when she saw the eggs on the kitchen table, and wondered why he dressed so shabbily. Tomorrow she was to sit for her mid year examinations.

She needed to spend this evening preparing for the next day, especially for mathematics, as she was lagging behind her class in this subject. The reason for her poor math's scores was that, she devoted more time to her sport and much less time to her homework. You see Sophie was the School's best Netball player. She spent most of her spare time at the court practicing, which in the long run, was detrimental to her main studies. Sophie knew this, and it vexed her no end, as she wished to be a Vet and was torn between the two, sport and study.

That evening at dinner Sophie's Mum told her that she was going into town early in the morning. Her mum asked her to remain home, to collect the eggs and pay Mr. Walton. He would come a little earlier than usual to allow Sophie to make it to School on time. Sophie was horrified. However she did not raise an objection, feeling, that she only had to grab the eggs, hand him the money and that was that. But she wasn't looking forward to the encounter one little bit.

The next morning came. Sophie rose from her sleep. Bleary eyed and very tired she staggered out of bed. She had read through her mathematics books until she fell asleep, some time after midnight. Then the significance of the morning came upon her. Eggs, the Egg man, Mr. Walton. Oh Dear. She dressed, washed and went into the kitchen to attack the refrigerator, as she was ravenously hungry. Then she saw the empty egg containers on the table. Her heart sank. She still did not understand the fear that she had of meeting the old man.

There was a gentle tap on the front door. She ignored it. There was a second, a more definite rap this time. She collected the cartons and the money from the table, then approached the door through the hallway, with some trepidation. She tentatively turned the handle and peaked out to the veranda. It was Mr Walton alright. He wore that old khaki coat, which seemed to be a part of him. His head was covered with that funny black knitted beanie that he always wore. She opened the door, deposited the packets on the chair by the door, handed him the money and took the box of eggs.

He spoke first. "So you're Sophie. How old are you lassie?" he actually smiled.

"I'm thirteen." She stammered.

"Well good for you. Suppose I'll see you some more then. Well goodbye for now girlie, must be off then." He pocketed the money and strode down the path and out of the gate as Sophie stared after him deep in thought. She went off to school, became busy in her world. The meeting with the egg man floated far from her mind. That was until the next week, when Sophie's Mum was to be away early again and she would have to confront the man again.

The night before the egg man was to call on Sophie's home she had a dream. This dream was to assist to change Sophie attitude to the egg man. She went to bed that evening, her mind in turmoil over a conflict with one of her friends. She resolved the matter in her own thinking, and then went off to sleep.

Slumber took hold of her as a rainbow mist swirled all around her. A light breeze lifted her blowing gently on her body as it carried out of her bedroom through the window and away into a weird valley. The valley was covered in plantations of what appeared at first to be an amazing variety of trees. Then she noticed that the trees, were not trees in the true sense, but rows of straight trunked structures with horizontal branches, not dissimilar to ship's masts. It seemed an illusion but it was not.

Some of these gigantic plants carried five or six branches, all bearing different types of Sophie's favourite fruits, bananas, paw paws, apples, oranges, pears, plums, however they had no leaves to shade them. They appeared to be beckoning her to taste them. She was sorely tempted to reach out to them, lift the fruit from the branches and sample them. Soon she summoned courage to take the food as she wished, first tearing an apple down and biting it greedily.

At the first bite, the apple exploded into a black powdery and gaseous substance, which a foul smelling odour that forced her to drop the fruit to the ground. Sophie was coughing and cursing, as she wiped her face and spat out the terrible flesh. Maybe it was a bad one she mused as she was determined to try again. She grabbed a banana, but a similar result occurred again. She ran around the trees sampling the different fruits only to find that they all had the same vile fillings.

Sophie exhausted sat under a tree to regain her composure. She surveyed the weird orchard, watching the trees for a while. Then she saw that some of the trees were different they had darker trunks than the ones from which she had taken the fruit earlier. The fruit on these trees were of a vague form, such as triangular, square, round and many unusual diametrical patterns, unlike any thing that she had ever seen in her life. The skins of the fruit casings were all a drab brown, and some black, like the way bananas become after they over ripen.

Sophie looked through the multi-colored fog, and decided that she had nothing to lose in trying the funny looking fruit, her curiosity getting the better of her. She made her way to one of the trees, but stepped back as a horrible scent assailed her nostrils. The air around the tree was revolting and had the stench of rotting vegetation. Not to be deterred, she seized one of the three-sided fruit and broke it open. To her astonishment, the centre was the color of rock melon and when she took a bite, the flavour was exquisite.

She dropped the left over piece and tried another shape, the same again. The amazing thing was that the fruit from all of the drab trees, the trees which smelt the most terrible, was the real thing. She was so elated she tore several different pieces of the strange fruits and ate lustily. She was so busy and happy that the odour that was all around her was forgotten. Sophie bit into the last piece of fruit she had selected. Without warning, a large gust of wind swept her off her feet and lifted her from the orchard returning her to her home.

She awoke in her warm, comfortable bed, with the fog still around her. Her Mother shaking her, explaining, that it was time to get up, and not to forget the eggs. The eggs and the man in the old coat again, Oh no. She sort of fell out of bed with part of the dream still lodged in her subconscious. Her Mother went out leaving Sophie day dreaming over her breakfast. After a while a rap on the door moved Sophie to action. She took the money and the cartons to the front door, then opened the door. Mr. Walton was standing with the eggs in one hand and a large brown paper bag in the other.

She put the cartons down and relieved him of the eggs, handed him the money and was about to close the door when the old man coughed. She stopped as he spoke softly to her. "You said that you are thirteen years old. I wonder if you would accept these things. They were my daughter's, but I lost her when she was thirteen, your age, and her mother also. I have not quite known what to do with them since. You would make me happy if you would have them. She saw tears welling in his eyes. She excused herself, took the eggs into the kitchen, then returning to his presence collected the bag, thanked him and closed the door.

Sophie went to the window and watched the old man trudge away from the house. She took the bag and put on her bed. Whatever is in there will be a surprise when I return from school, she said to herself, as she closed the door and headed off to the School. She had a special warm feeling about the egg man now. His coat reminded her of the drab fruit in her dream.

THE STORE OF
SOULS

The Grim Reaper adjusted his black cape. As he pulled the hood back a little, he peered into the mirror. He couldn't see a thing as usual. There was absolutely no reflection, which caused a sigh to slip from within the hood. The eternal executioner reached for his sickle, smiling inwardly, as he ran his 'ever-sharp-stone' along the instrument of death. "My, I could do with a break, but that's not in my contract".

The Almighty put his head around the corner, the radiance of his presence, catching the shrouded figure by surprise. The reaper raised his sleeve to cut the glare emanating from the Almighty's closeness, then spoke quietly, with a trembling voice, that, of a servant being. "You startled me!" he said without facing the Creator.

"You certainly have a motley lot today, but that is the way it goes, I'll check through them whilst I'm about. The Angels will collect them in due course." "Please yourself", the underling replied with indifference. "I need a holiday as I'm very tired these days. Maybe the number of conflicts on this planet is getting to me?" he grumbled. The Creator cast a cursory glance over the assortment of souls, selected a few, mumbled quietly to himself about the Eternal Pit. God Almighty finally turned to look upon the hooded one, gazing into the sockets beneath the sombre black mantle. "You have queries to pose to me I believe?" The Ancient of Days queried.

"Sir I have always wondered why it is, that you only select a few souls when you call and he, the other, gets a much larger number?" "Ah that is my prerogative. You see I have a certain standard that mortals need to meet, but it saddens me that they are never prepared for their next journey." The Grim Reaper raised his hand to scratch his head, but realised that there was nothing to scratch, so dropped his arm to his side, then said. "Please explain so that I can understand clearly, the reasons that a great number of souls do not make it to your Heaven."

"Sure I will do that. Firstly, you must have noticed the special marks that my chosen have upon their foreheads. These are the ones who have, through being obedient to me have prepared themselves to make the journey. Then 'The Prince of Darkness' removes the others-those too proud, or stubborn or just too lazy to do my will. They are his after I shut the gate." The Harvester of Death frowned, obviously lost in thought as the Master of the Universe continued his explanation.

"The few I select are they who from the beginning, wisely listened, understood and followed my Ten Principals as the remainder fell away. "But why so few?" the Reaper interjected. "Remember in the beginning, when I commissioned you to collect the souls for me, it was then I gave the mortals the short list of requirements, to assist them to make ready for the journey. I supplied the Ten, but alas most stumbled at Number One, whilst many others fell at Number Four or a later Number, so I had a plan to give them a chance to finish the journey."

"What did you do?" the gleaner of 'the passing' asked, showing some semblance of understanding. "I gave the world all I had, but still only a few of those you collect will ever make the final step." "But why do you take all of the scarred and damaged ones, leaving the perfect souls for im?" "Don't you see, the damaged ones, the poorer souls prepare themselves selflessly, it is their spirit that binds them to my Spirit. Believe me, the more battered the Souls the more prepared for me they are." "Oh."

PARADISE FARM

The train lumbered towards its destination, the short toots disrupting the still night air. Scott sat upright in his seat by the window, clutching the ticket in his right hand. His face was pressed against the window of number-two carriage. He was staring into the darkness. His thirteen-year old heart was pounding, not with fear, but a sense of the unknown. He had never met the family he'd be staying with. It was his mother's idea that he should to go to the country for part of the school holidays.

The train was now slowing slightly. Scott held the ticket more tightly, as if it would try to separate itself from his grasp. He knew that his relatives would collect him when he reached Dubbo. They lived three hours from Dubbo, somewhere near the Queensland/New South Wales border. He saw lights in the distance. The carriage was swaying gently. He held a large blue canvas duffle bag, which carried his clothes for the holiday. He had never been further than Newcastle or Wollongong before, so this, according to his mum, was to be an adventure, just like the stories he read about; heroes conquering the outback in times long gone.

Lights were appearing in ever-increasing numbers. The intercom said that the next stop would be Dubbo. That was his cue to prepare for disembarkation when the train stopped at the station. It came to a halt and Scott, along with many others, climbed down from the passenger car and stood on the Dubbo station platform. He looked around him to get a feeling of this strange place. The porter asked him to move quickly to the waiting room as this part of the station was about to close owing to the lateness of the hour. He obliged and started toward the sign, which said 'Waiting Room'.

Just as he reached the door, a hand seized his arm and a voice said kindly, "Scott." He turned around and looked up. A plump round face with eyes that sparkled was gazing upon him. "I am Aunt Bev, welcome to the bush, son." Scott put his hand out to shake hers, but was overtaken by two huge arms that embraced him with a crush. He felt the warmth of the woman, and all his anxieties of the trip evaporated in an instant. No sooner had she released him from the bear hug, than she said that they had better get a move on. She lifted the bag from his grasp as though it were filled with air, slung it over her shoulder and led him to the car park.

The car was his first shock. It was a Holden, a nineteen sixty-four model. Aunt Bev opened the trunk and deposited the duffle bag into it, then reached for an old box. She withdrew a bottle and a pack of sandwiches. She offered him a drink, explaining that it was a four-hour drive to the farm and there would be absolutely no opportunity to find a place to buy something. He accepted the food and drink gratefully. His head was still spinning with the realisation that he was now light years from home.

His aunt opened the passenger side door and bade him to take a seat. Little did he know of the adventure he was about to have. He fastened his seatbelt as she got in and sat beside him, then prepared to drive off. Scott noticed a few unusual things about the car. There was only one seat in the front of the car. The seat was hard, and the gear stick was in a different place to those cars his family owned. The dashboard was made of metal and there was no sign of air-conditioning, a radio or cassette player in the car.

Aunt Bev was driving the vehicle through the streets of the large town like it was a toy. As soon as they were out on the open road, she put her foot down. Occasionally, she would look at him and ask about the family, but mostly she concentrated on the road. Scott received his next surprise that evening when he noticed the speedometer registering one hundred. He commented to his aunt, that he thought that the old car could not reach such a speed. He sat back quickly when she replied that the speedometer was marked in miles per hour not kilometres. Phew, we are doing one hundred and sixty. He hung tightly to the seatbelt. The momentum of the car gradually made him drowsy and he slept until the car finally stopped at the farmhouse.

Aunt Bev led the still drowsy lad into the house, then to the bedroom where she lifted back the bedcovers and left him to get into bed. She said good night and left the room. Scott tumbled into the bed half clothed, as he was worn out from the long journey. He slept until the sun came up, waking with a start, wondering where he was. It came back to him as he stared at the ceiling. The young man looked over the side of the bed to the floor. There was no carpeting, the floor was timber, unpolished and with cracks large enough to put your hand into. Suddenly he noticed a strange thing. It appeared that two eyes were gazing at him from beneath the floor, through one of the slits. He watched. The pair of eyes kept their vigil. Scott was staring with intensity.

He kept one eye on the floor as he began to take in the rest of the room. The room was sparse, the walls were unlined and the window was covered with a thin curtain. There was only a small wardrobe, which had a mirror attached, with three drawers beneath the mirrored side. The ceiling was covered with a patterned material, the type of which he had observed in some of the older buildings in Sydney. His bed was an unusual one to say the least. The bed had carved wooden ends. The middle of the mattress area sagged. So he felt he was in some kind of hammock. Regardless, it was quite cosy. He peered at the floor. The eyes were still there. He rolled over and curled up and tried to drift off again. He was very tired.

He awoke with a start. Some one was standing beside him. He opened his eyes and saw a big man watching. "You certainly slept quite a long time young fellow," the man spoke softly. "I am your uncle, you can call me Ray." The man reached out and shook his hand. "We may as well have our lunch since you dreamed the morning away."

Scott replied courteously, "Hello, nice to meet you Uncle Ray." After the formalities, the man turned and left the bedroom. He fell out of bed and put some clothes on, then found his way down the hall to the kitchen. This was not hard to do; he just followed the smell of the cooking.

The kitchen was out of an old black and white movie. The floor consisted of red and white linoleum tiles, which must have been pulled out of the Ark. The benches were also ancient, according to Scott's knowledge of such things, which was very limited to say the least. There in one corner sat a large fuel stove, the likes of which he had never set eyes on before. A monstrous, unpainted wooden table surrounded by ten upholstered high-backed chairs filled the spacious room. There were two windows, one set above the sink, the other adjacent. A kitchen dresser, displaying an array of cooking utensils, filled the space between the windows.

His aunt, who was bending over the sink, turned to face him when she heard him approaching. "I trust you slept well my lad" she grinned, then motioned him to be seated at the table. "Yes, thank you I did." Then he paused, "Can I ask you a question?" She told him to ask anything he wished. He told her about the eyes. To which she explained "It's probably the goanna that lives under the house. Its name is Joanna" she said. He chuckled to himself at the reply. Then Uncle Ray walked in, all hundred and ten kilos of him, squashing the padding on the chair as he sat at the end of the table facing Scott. The big man smiled at him then spoke, "Once we've had lunch I'll show you around the place, that is, the area near the house."

Then lunch was served without much chatter, except for a few questions from his uncle about the trip and the weather. The array of food that landed on the table surface was beyond Scott's wildest dreams. Home made scones nicely browned, a meat dish which aunt called shepherd's pie, followed by potatoes, peas, beans and other vegetables that he was not game to ask about covered the table. When that was devoured, mostly by Uncle Ray, the dessert made its entry. Jelly in three colours, custard, fruit and cream, plus a bowl of fresh fruit, touched down for the taking. He found out in due course that the food was prepared and cooked by his aunt, that very morning. His mum always bought the sweets ready-made and he could not remember very much cooking in the house as his mum and dad were always on the run to this and to that.

After lunch, Uncle Ray introduced him to the house and its surrounds. There were important matters to consider, such that water was a scarce commodity and must be spared at all times. Only drink water prepared by the woman of the house, or you could become very ill. There were no showers, so each evening after dinner, the tub would be filled. The bath had its own protocol, Uncle first then Aunt followed by the guest. All would use the same water, which came from an underground bore. The inside toilet was for night use and the outside one for daytime. The day 'loo' was only fifty metres behind the house.

His uncle excused himself and drove off to look at some cattle, promising to take him out tomorrow to inspect another part of his empire. After that, his aunt took him to show him around the house, explaining things and fielding his numerous list of questions. He was warming to her. She was so different to her sister, his mother. He was storing up questions to ask his mother when he returned home. Scott asked his aunt why she came to the bush, and did she like living out here. She told him that she was a trained nurse and met his uncle whilst working in the area, and she was very happy living in the country. Scott could not see his mother existing in this environment. She didn't even like dust on her shoes. He doubted that his mum would enjoy cooking like his aunt.

Aunt Bev told him that she was going to kill a couple of roosters this afternoon. He could assist her if he wished, but he did not have to. He said he would help. That was the next experience for him. Aunt Bev rounded up the two victims and put them into separate hessian bags after tying their legs. She collected the axe from the shed, which was next to the outside toilet, and placed it beside the chopping block. Scott watched all of this with great interest. "You can hold the legs" his aunt told him. With that, he stepped closer as she extricated a bird from the bag and untied its legs.

Scott held the wriggling chook by the legs as it lay, waiting its fate. Aunt straddled the bird across the block, holding the head in one hand, swung the razor-sharp instrument with the other. Scott had turned his head away, unable to look at the fatal blow. Then he let go the legs of the dead creature, expecting it to flop onto the ground after the blow. But it didn't, the headless thing leapt off the block and bolted around the yard. His first reaction was to go after it. Anticipating this, his aunt restrained him by holding his arm. He watched in amazement as the bird's nervous system kept it running for a short while. Then it fell over, and his aunt took hold of it.

After the second bird was disposed of, his aunt sat down with him, poured him a drink and explained the art of killing and plucking chickens. Then she showed him how to remove the feathers by using boiling water. Scott took it all in and confessed to her that he had never thought of killing and preparing chooks before, because they came frozen in packages at his home. That night, he dreamed that he was being pursued by a headless chicken which was as big as a camel. He woke in a sweat, and sat thinking of the day that had just passed, and of his mum. Mum certainly could not hack it in the bush: neither would his dad, he felt.

The next two days for Scott drifted by speedily, as he watched, listened and participated with his quaint relatives at their daily activities. He was a quick learner. He began to enjoy the array of jobs and compared them with his life in the city. The fourth day was shopping day, and the time to collect the mail from the small town, which was some two hours drive. He went with his aunt in the old vehicle, keeping his eye on the speedometer all the time.

This was another mini adventure. The town was something else again. Tighue's General Store was the post office, newsagent and liquor store all rolled into one. Three houses lined the only street. Petrol could also be purchased at the General Store. Inside the shop, Scott noted the amazing array of goods that were on display. Many items were unfamiliar to him and his aunt explained that the shop kept only essential items, as there were few people in the area. People went to the provincial cities for their big shopping, about once a month.

That afternoon, as he was carrying the wood into the shed, he felt that someone was watching him. He looked all around him. There did not seem to be anyone about, but a rustle in the grass nearby made him turn around. Those eyes were staring directly at him. Joanna had revealed herself at last. A thrill went down his spine as he returned its gaze. It was dark and prehistoric, he thought. It stared at him for a while, then loped off towards the veranda, and disappeared from his view. He ran to the house, and informed Aunt Bev, who was pleased for him. She told him not to get too close to the goanna, because, if frightened, they can attack a person. She added that she had never had any problems with goannas or snakes. Uncle Ray preferred to move them to another paddock, rather than kill them.

After that, Scott had many interesting encounters, helping his uncle and aunt. The three weeks passed so swiftly. He learnt about paddy melons, cattle, sheep, and about what certain general sayings of the bush are in the vocabulary of each of us such as 'the way the crow flies'. All this time, he was measuring in his subconscious the difference between his own home situation and that of the folk of the outback. These outer country people were taken for granted for all of his short life, and seen by most of his mates as far and away, and of little consequence in their lives. Time was nearing for him to return home.

Uncle Ray and Aunt Bev put on a party for Scott on the last evening he was there as their guest. The nearby neighbours came, and some from a long way off. He was overwhelmed, and that night shed a few tears in his room. He woke early next morning and looked for the eyes. They were there, peering through the crack in the floor. He grinned at them, and wished he could communicate with them. Then he packed his duffle bag.

After Uncle Ray said his farewells and went to tend the cattle, Aunt Bev prepared to drive him to Dubbo to catch his train home. Before they left, as he stood at the door of the homestead, half of his being wanted to stay, the other half was confused. As his aunt powered the car at great speed toward their destination, he pondered in a melancholy way the thought of returning home. The train was on time. Aunt Bev once again crushed him in her huge arms. He said to her in parting, "Watch the eyes for me." She grinned and stayed on the platform until the train was out of sight. She wiped a tear away as she walked to the car.

Scott sat in his seat by the window, a much wiser young man for the experience. The first thing I want Mum to do when I get home, is to book a ticket for me for the next holiday, he mused to himself.

STRANGE
JUDGEMENTS

His Worship landed just after dawn, hoping to peruse this week's challenges, well before the office staff would distract him. He enjoyed his monthly stint at Breadcrumb Creek. Some of the most interesting and curious cases that he had ever presided over occurred in this quaint village. By the way, there is no creek in or near the town. It is through legend or just the passage of time that these towns get their strange names, such as Wild Dog Gulch, or perhaps the title of your own insignificant little hamlet.

He managed to find his way to the courthouse office. As he approached the building, he was accosted by a relative of one of the litigants, waiting at the door. Politely fobbing off the person with a few kind words, and expressing appreciation of the good wishes she had given him during their brief exchange, he opened the door.

Justice Howlet was not the one to have his feathers ruffled. He was a straight shooter, cool as a cucumber, and an honest broker at that. His lot in life was to mediate, to bring reconciliation to the opponents whatever the dispute, and in other more serious matters, to bring the full weight of judgement for or against them.

The judge entered the courtroom by way of the rear door for which he was privy to a key. The great oak door creaked on its hinges like a badly tuned fiddle. Settling down in the hardest wooden chair one could imagine, he put his brief case on the floor beside him, picked up the bundle of papers that the clerk had left for him, and proceeded to examine them.

He had trusted that Mrs Hopper, the clerk's wife, would have a drink prepared for him, but he would wait. His eyes widened somewhat as he gazed at the array of matters he would be judging over the next few days. The list was extensive and varied. The list noted the interested parties, some of whom he had dealt with before and who appear before him, unfortunately, as repeat offenders or habitual litigants.

Time passed, the clerk knocked, entered at the reply of his superior, and placed a tray with drink and food before the judge, who showed his gratitude with a smile and a "thank you". He quizzed his subordinate about the morning's proceedings, and explained the time frames he expected most of the cases to take. The clerk left to prepare the court for the opening, whilst his honour prepared a list, mumbling to himself as he read through the sheets.

"What's this, a spider suing a drainpipe company for negligence, for failing to have warning systems in down- pipes?

Another spider arraigned for stalking and frightening a little girl!

A cow with a ruptured udder, litigating against The World Record Book for wrongful information! It appears it is related to the attempt at jumping over the moon. The organizers of the challenge failed to check which cycle the moon was in, before the event. The full moon had passed. The cow caught her udder on the sharp end of the upturned crescent, sustaining serious injuries to her body.

An old man was suing a goose for throwing him down a staircase.

An old woman is indicted with cruelty to her children. She is accused of stuffing them in a shoe, then whipping and starving them.

Another old woman charged with cruelty towards her dog, and starving him!

A young woman assaulted by a blackbird, whilst she is hanging out the washing!

There were several Jacks on the extensive list. One was suing a giant, another candle company, a third, the local council for failing to have adequate safety rails at a well plus other frivolous complaints.

A sparrow on a murder charge - killing with a bow and arrow!

It is going to be "one of those days", sighed the smallish judge.

Later as the Great Owl sat in his seat and stared at the menagerie before him, he noticed the defence team entering the court. The firm of Fox, Stoat, Weasel and Lynx were all in attendance.

No doubt, he mused to himself, these lawyers will expound a few fairy tales, and then no doubt, make a lot of excuses, all of which will be without Rhyme or Reason.

CIAO, CHIEF OLONGO. BON APPETIT

Marco Polo, the Venetian, set out on his adventures and delivered the goods. His exploits are well documented rightly or wrongly in the annals of history.

On the other hand, Alfonso Pillio the Genoan set out a few centuries later to conquer deep dark Africa. This time, no one documented his travels or his apparent lack of success.

"I'm going to Africa."

"But you can't son. Your papa needs you in the restaurant."

"I'm going mama, whatever happens."

"But this is your home lad."

At the mention of the word 'lad', he erupted. Italian mothers can't ever let their sons grow up.

"Don't you see mama, it's important to me."

"But your father - he will die a thousand deaths and the shop ..."

"He's got to manage without me a while."

Every day there was another argument. The Pillio family was at war - all because of their young pig-headed son Alfonso wanting to go to Africa.

"Mama the subjects closed. Don't you understand? There's opportunity in this. Every trader is heading there. It's the new frontier."

"But they're all cannibals; they could eat you son. Oh I'm so afraid, my son."

"Listen for once mama. Giuseppe and Lonzo have been. They took boatloads of shoes. Paoli went with millinery and Franceso has left with a boat loaded with dresses and other sorts of clothing."

"But we are not merchants, we are food people. We feed hungry people. That's our trade."

"Mama we've been feeding the overweight population of Genoa since creation." he said as he patted his large paunch, and we never venture beyond the harbour. Everyone else travels here and there. Our only travels are through the merchants' tales and the sailor's stories. Italians have just started to see the potential of the Africans. Let's get something out of it at least."

The mother flung the towel she was holding onto the pasta table and stormed out of the room. Alfonso had been doing the daily pasta preparation every day since he was twelve. He stood in exactly the same spot doing the same grind for four hours at a time. Then each evening he would assist his fat father to cook and his mother and sisters to wait on the greedy folk of the Genoa wharf precinct.

The Pillio family had traditions to uphold. There was no space in their diary for holidaying or for that matter, straying from a well-trodden path serving the finest cuisine and best home made lambrusco in the port. The family's food and wine businesses had been flourishing there for generations. The young Pillio lad worked that day in a melancholy but thoughtful temperament pounding the dough, and twisting and twirling until his task was completed.

He finally sat in the large wooden chair that was his father's seat when his dad did the early morning shift preparing the lunch pasta. Alfonso could hear the bustle of the people in the street and longed to be out in the real world doing what the merchants, travellers and the wealthy of the area were always doing, moving freely. His father would appear shortly and another row would certainly erupt.

His dad couldn't see Alfonso's argument and only saw red. The lad was off the planet and needed some discipline and straightening out. The young man cringed when he heard the footsteps of his father approaching the kitchen. He busied himself with the dried tomatoes as his father entered the doorway, filling most of the space between the door lintels with his immense bulk. The young man was leaning over the tomatoes pretending not to see his father's entry, but the old man thumped the table so hard the noise would have deafened the mice sleeping under the floorboards.

So the tirade between father and son took off again. After a few minutes, the lad strode out off the kitchen hotly pursued by the angry parent, shouting so all the neighbourhood could hear. "Have you got your head full of pumpkin seeds or just plain nothing but space between your two fat ears? You're an idiot. I've a good mind to send you to your uncle to bash some sense into your thick hide. His pig farm is always in need of help and good hard work is what you need my boy." he said with an emphasis on "my boy".

The parish priest arrived to see old man Pillio, and hopefully, to indulge in a free lunch. He always called at meal times, as did the municipal health inspector. This time he was just in time to prevent the father from braining the son with a soup ladle.

"Sit down Mr Pillio and tell me you troubles." "Troubles; I'll tell you my troubles. My nitwit of a son is showing disloyalty to his parents and driving his mother to distraction. He wants to take our stock and equipment to Africa and cook pasta in the jungle for some savages. He's got the notion from his imbecile friends who are running about all over the world like demented cockroaches, wasting their inheritances, and dabbling in foolhardy schemes. Just wait; they'll back home with the backsides out of their trousers, grovelling to their fathers, like that prodigal son. You know him padre."

The priest, Father Romani, sipped his glass of Pillio champion vino and tried to pacify the old man. "Sit and be calm and let us consider the young mans thoughts sir." The old man sat. He was visibly shaking but settled down and reached for a bottle of his favourite beverage, poured a glass for himself, and topped up the priest's glass at the same time.

"Mr Pillio! Consider your son. He's a grown man now. How old is he?" "Thirty-seven." the other replied. "He's worked with you and your wife for more than thirty years. Why not give him a little of what he wants and let him get the notion of conquering the world off his chest. When he sees the folly of his ways and returns, you and he could then return to normality." Mrs Pillio brought the food into the kitchen where it was customary for the family to eat. She nodded to the pastor and left him and her husband to arm-wrestle the dilemma away. Hopefully together they would resolve the matter and peace would once again reign where chaos and discord now abounded.

The father, cajoled by the priest and some of his friends, finally made peace with his son on the Africa issue, much to the delight of the townspeople, who had been witnessing the brawls for far too long.

So the die was cast. After a massive planning period, Master Pillio put together a sailing barque loaded with the essentials for a successful foray into Central Africa. His family footed the bill, most expecting a return on their investment, some ruing the whole silly business. Mother Pillio spent half her days reaching for the smelling salts and pining for her long lost son who had not even left the shore yet.

Among the merchants along the waterfront, there was much gossip as to how an overweight chef's assistant could achieve other than total ruin for his relatives. And let's face the fact that that's all he was - an overweight chef's assistant and an unhealthy looking one at that, the type who appeared to be consuming more than he was selling. He was undaunted by the task, although totally naïve to the outer world and unfamiliar with where he was going.

One thing that helped him to become organised was the fact that he had a few experienced assistants who just happened to bob up at the right time. The main person other than the crew was Sav Reggio, a student of African languages in the area where Pillio's destination lay. The student also spoke Latin, Spanish and English languages which would be needed for them to pass through the colonies established by these countries scattered throughout the continent of deep dark Africa. At the insistence of his father and much to his chagrin, three priests were brought along for the religious aspects of the trip, which meant extra wine rations to keep them happy, as well as out of the way. The contingent was sizeable. Just about all areas were covered with a back up crew on a second boat in case of unforseen problems.

The young Pillio man was oblivious to the comings and goings on the ships as his main concern was making sure that enough of the beloved menu was catered for. Barrels of olives, cases of herbs, spices, drying racks laden with an assortment of green and red vegetables were carried on board. One section of the hold was filled with bag upon bag of the Pillio select flour. Then with great care, barrels of pure virgin olive oil rolled onto the ship and down into the hold. The elder Pillio nearly had a stroke when the account for the ships cargo and the crew's wages was placed in his hands.

The two boats sailed out to the Mediterranean Ocean from the same wharf that formerly great explorers had used for historic voyages in the past. The Pillio youngster looked up at the flag's red, white and green, and saluted the colours. To him they were not patriotic colours as other Italians would see, but the true ensign of Italy - red for tomatoes and red peppers, green for olives and lettuce and then of course white for pasta. A true emblem of Italy one could be sure. Little did not the Genoan know what fate lay before him, nor did he care at that moment. He was on his way and rid of his entire family, as no one offered to travel with him on this journey. As the barques pulled away, he could just make out the family restaurant signage and the world famous slogan his great grandfather initiated. "Dinner without pasta is a disaster."

The voyage was uneventful except in the first weeks. While the crew 'heaved to' the chef stood by the outer rails and heaved over the side. The boats arrived and anchored at a preselected site and sheltered on the western side of Africa. On the way south, the captain called in at the Moroccan port of Tangier, that sinister place of intrigue where every thing illicit is obtainable. Here the captain brought on board a number of strange looking people. He explained that these were to be the bearers to take the barrels and merchandise through the African jungle. They, the captain added, were experienced carriers, Nubians from Lower Egypt, and would lighten the burden considerably and speed up the carriage of the goods. Young Pillio was satisfied, accepted the team, and the trip proceeded smoothly.

Two months after they had first embarked on their expedition, Pillio and his entourage arrived at Mongaloobo, the capital of a new colony in West Africa. The cargo was unloaded and all support personnel disembarked. After a few weeks, they were prepared for the arduous trek into the unknown.

Alfonso Pillio was now at the mercy of those who he had entrusted to assist him, especially the interpreter Sav Reggio, who to this time had hovered around the ship amongst the crew and the staff. He gave instructions as to how each person was to conduct them-selves when they were among the natives. As the trek to the inner region of this colony was hazardous, and the climate was different from that many of them had ever experienced, Reggio, who had been with several excursions to this place arranged all matters with the authorities. He even slipped the appropriate cash under the counter to speed things up.

The Pillio Pasta Expedition was now under way. A convey of oxen ,donkeys, horses, two mangy camels, the bearers, barrels on sleds, carts laden to the tree tops and an assortment of white, black and brown, coloured people sauntered slowly into the unknown. Each one in the caravan carried hopes for large rewards but each was also burdened with a giant load of fear in their hearts and minds.

Three weeks after they left Mongalooba, members of the 'pasta train' found themselves at their destination. All were utterly exhausted. Large canvas tents were erected to store the food and equipment and tents on a smaller scale were placed in a circle to defend the supplies. Guards were placed in appropriate spots to keep uninvited guests, both animal and human, away.

During the whole trip Sav Reggio kept a close council with his boss who was naïve to matters outside a kitchen and required a great deal of tutoring on the basic details of running the operation and keeping the team together. Sav had the job of venturing to the villages of the native tribes scattered in and around the vast forests and jungle bush. Once he negotiated the deal, the Chef and his team would step into the villages and show the leadership their culinary skills. The other side of the negotiations would be the bartering for each individual tribe's artefacts and a continuing supply of them.

Eight days later the first real test was to be undertaken by the pasta team. Any problems in a presentation and the whole venture could be a dismal failure. Of this, Alfonso was acutely aware. The first in a series of disasters struck when the first flour bag was opened. The high humidity meant that dampness had penetrated the grain. The Genoan went off his head. "One can't make pasta with inferior flour", he screamed. Although Father Romani tried to calm the waters, the young man still protested. The priest had said that the natives don't know anything about European food, so what's the worry.

Next, the interpreter returned from one of the villages only to report that Chief Olongo, the most powerful leader of all of the tribes, wanted the lion's share of the food and was offering the least in return. The only thing to do was to go and demonstrate to him the importance of the food, feed him, get his blessing and move on to the next. But it would be tricky. Sav advised that full-bellied natives tended to slow up and sleep a lot.

It was decided to head for Chief Olongo and attempt to pacify him. So pots, pans, measures of ingredients, even plates and pasta cutlery, plus a contingent of helpers followed Sav Reggio and Alfonso Pillio into the jungle. Hours later, just before dusk, the team came face to face with the tribe of Chief Olongo. To everyone's surprise the natives were very small and wiry, a delight to a pasta chef, room for improvement. Their huts were truly primitive compared with the European houses. The women and children came to greet them with great enthusiasm. They ran and touched the flabby paunch of Pillio who warmed to them in an instant, but then just as quickly, his countenance changed dramatically when a boy presented him with a shrunken head on a stick.

He nearly passed out, but the priest, who stood behind him and spoke in a whisper to him, warned that he must keep his composure. A short time later that day, two of the Nubians got into a fight between each other and caused the interpreter great concern as they both were badly hurt. They were to be assisted back to Mongalooba by two of the security men and this stretched the workload among the rest of the team who were battling other problems such as the insects and heat and the constant scrutiny by the inquisitive natives.

The Chief himself came to meet the party and get a first hand look at the Europeans. He was not what Pillio expected at all. He was a stumpy, rotund individual with long un-combed hair. He looked uncouth, as though he had fallen out of bed. He wore no adornments; no top; just a type of grass skirt with a myriad of coloured strings and beads dangling from it, nearly touching the ground. The black leader embraced Sav Reggie like a long lost brother, ignoring for the moment the expectant pasta master. The chief and Sav talked together for quite some time while the cook just stood and waited. Though naïve, he started to feel that there was more to the relationship with the chief and Reggio than he was led to believe. Reggio seemed to be working a deal that Alfonso was not privy to.

At last, Reggio introduced the chief, but instead of the embrace he gave Reggio, Alfonso received only a nod of recognition that would be normally reserved for underlings. He was livid, feeling that he, the master, was being sold short.

Then the interpreter spoke to Alfonso on behalf of the Chief Olongo.

"The chief is expecting to eat your pasta tonight after dark. He demands that his wives and assistants be taught how to cook the dishes and you're not to be late. Alfonso broke out in a cold sweat. No chef of note would dare allow people to watch as he prepared food. But he was not in his domain and knew he was being held over a barrel that definitely was not filled with olives. He graciously consented and called his team together for the preparation. The day was hot and steamy, not ideal for cooking. But he had made his bed and now he must lay in it and not complain. He now questioned his own stupidity for forcing the issue and coming here in the first place. He was at the point of no return and this was his show. He must succeed.

All went well on the first night. The food passed the chief's expectations. Then the interpreter told Alfonso that the chief wished that the same meal be repeated for the next four nights except that on the fourth night, his wives, under the eye of the chef were to prepare the meal. The Genoan had little choice; so it was arranged. On the last evening, the moon was full and yellow; the air was stuffy and clammy whilst the wives of Chief Olongo served their master his food along with the elders of the tribe.

The chief, up to this time, had never shown interest in Alfonso. However, he summoned the Italian to his table at the conclusion of the meal. He asked him to sit down on the ground and drink the native liquor with him. Alfonso accepted eagerly, feeling overawed by the occasion and expecting a deal with the chief so he could meet and treat other African leaders in the near future. The drink tasted dreadful and Alfonso gagged as he drunk but showed his host no outward sign of disapproval. That was the last time Alfonso was to see the chief.

Alfonso awoke in a dark room. He did not know where he was. He couldn't move and his head was thumping as though he was being hit by a thousand hammers. All he remembered was the drink. He had been drugged, bound, and thrown into this place. Then he remembered Sav Reggio, the interpreter. He thought about the way that the chief and Sav were pally and that he was rarely consulted over any matter and only ordered to perform, although it was Pillio's enterprise. He had been taken for a ride.

As he languished in the prison in the dark, and far from home, Alfonso regretted every move he had made to defy his family and venture to a place he did not know nor understand.

He was awakened from his grief when an opening appeared in the room and a woman, obviously one of the chief's wives, came in and placed a large wooden bowl at his feet. She squatted in front of him, picked up an amount of food from the plate and began to feed him. At first, he refused the food. Then he realised that she wouldn't go away until he had eaten, so he consented and tasted the food. The meal was his pasta and it was cooked well. After he had emptied the plate of all of its contents, the woman stood up and undid a piece of something that resembled rope and pulled it around him. She took it, tying a knot in the section that gave his waist measurement.

Then a feeling of utter hopelessness and fear swept over him as it suddenly dawned on him that he, who introduced pasta to Africa, would be the Chief's next course.

IT'S MINE IT'S MINE.

Maria Lazlo, over loaded with packages and standing on the pavement impatiently yelled at her son Janos who was as usual fiddling with the decrepit locks on the front door of the shop. Above the roller door, the signage said 'Lazlo Delicatessen Since 1918.' Maria's late husband's great-grandfather had built the business just a few doors from Budapest famous Astoria hotel. The hotel had that famous mirrored dining room, where one could watch the local aristocracy eating and be in another part of the same grand room, more or less out of sight. The head chef of the Astoria also purchased the finest delicacies from the Lazlo shop. Though tiny the shop was a virtual Aladdin's cave for gourmets.

"Hurry up son, my arms feel like they are ready to fall off." the mother begged. But the locks were always like this. They did not yield for the first few attempts with the keys.

"You will be late for the Castle delivery again you delinquent child."

The final lock opened. The wheezing 'boy'- man lifted the roller door, and then unlocked the sliding glass door. But that was only the beginning of each morning's ritual. A pushbike with a carry basket attached to the handle bars was in the way. The cycle was blocking the entrance along with three tables, six café chairs and the signboards which all had to finish on the footpath outside before any work could commence inside. The old lady struggled inside, put down the merchandise and switched on the electricity to the coffee machine and the stove.

"Take this list and get all the items for the Castle Janos."

She barked and he obediently moved around the shop with a basket, collecting the items listed. When he had completed the task, he wrote a docket from a pad, in the same style his great grandfather had used seventy years ago, and placed the goods into the basket of his bicycle. He then let his mother know that he was off to make the delivery. He was pleased that Josef Attila Street was very quiet this particular morning. He was concentrating on his cycling so he could reach the bridge over the Danube in quick time then cycle up the steep hill to the Castle district of Buda.

He had done this grind four days a week since he was twelve. Still, he was mother's little boy at forty-seven. He was the last of the Lazlo dynasty in a changing world. Janos just floated along with his mother day in day out, except Sundays. The grind was boring and repetitive but mum and son didn't complain. Mother Lazlo dragged the tables and seats into their appointed positions then she placed flowery patterned table-cloths over the table tops and went back into the shop to commence making the famous Lazlo apple strudel and beef goulash for the lunch menu.

Janos plugged away on his cycle toward the Castle region. Once he had reached the bottom of the hill, he dismounted and pushed his bike up the seventy metre steep incline. He didn't mind that because he could return down the hill at a whirlwind pace. He reached the Castle and took the merchandise to the back, through the gate clearly marked 'tradesmen's entrance.' He found the maid, who diligently marked off everything then went to get him the money.

Jonas knew every square inch of the Castle area. It was one of the most frequented places in Budapest by the locals and tourists alike.

Maria Lazlo in the meantime was her usual self cooking the lunch serving the clients and stacking the shelves. Being busy was her stock in trade and the time just flew. That's the way she liked. Since her husband, 'may he rest in peace,' departed this world, she and her son ran the place. Maria and her boy were very accommodating and delivered excellent service and commanded a clientele from the best houses of Budapest.

She was stirring a concoction at the stove when the front door bell announced that a customer was present. She hurriedly switched the stove down and went to serve her client. The person on the opposite side of the counter was a very large visitor. The man was wearing a heavy drab overcoat which was open at the front and a cap covering his largish head. He was a person of grubby appearance- a person she really did not wish to be acquainted with. A Romany; she thought to herself. He was a northern gypsy. a thieving, stinking gypsy. She would serve him, but she would watch him all the time.

He asked for a carton of cigarettes. This meant that he would move out of her line of sight while she collected the cigarettes. She returned to the counter. He requested a different brand. Back she went to the cupboard and once more to the counter. He was satisfied. "Anything else?" she asked him.

"Yes. A lighter as well." He replied. She placed the lighter on the counter in front of him.

"Is that all?"

"Yes."

'Gosh; he stinks.' she thought to herself.

"Is that the lot?" she said again to the gypsy, looking him straight in the eye.

"Yes." he replied.

She walked around the counter and faced the tall man. She leaned forward and pulled his coat open and retrieved the bottle of whisky he had purloined whilst she was absent from the counter.

The tiny woman of Budapest stared the scruffy man from where she was standing.

The uncouth apparition bolted from her presence, out into the street.

The little woman put the unsold goods back in their rightful places. She pulled out a can of scented air-freshener from a cupboard then she sprayed the area in the shop where the man had stood. She went back to preparing the lunch meals as if nothing untoward had happened.

Janos cycled back to the shop and parked his ancient bicycle in its normal spot near the tables. He went in to the kitchen to see how lunch was proceeding. His mother still leaning over the stove related her story to him in great detail. To him it sounded of little consequence to her what had happened that morning. Janos who was quite taken aback by his mother's apparent lack of awareness to the possible consequences of her actions said. He growled "Mum, He could have assaulted you. He might have killed you. Why worry about a bottle of whisky worth twenty forint. Mum! Don't do that again, hear me."

The loving mother kept mixing the ingredients for the strudel and indignantly raised her voice at him. "He did not want to pay for it. DON'T YOU SEE JANOS? THE WHISKY!

IT'S MINE, IT'SMINE."

CATCHING THE MOMENT

THE PUB LOUNGE WAS FILLED TO CAPACITY. Saturday lunches were the thing. The Paragon and White Rose cafes were also open, but they couldn't add a glass of liquor with the meals, whilst the hotel could. The tables were all taken; Joe Small felt he was out of luck till he spied a vacant seat. He walked towards it and noted with a cursory glance that it was a party setting. He counted the number settled around the table. There were ten ruddy, genial and happy faces, all animated and talking about all manner of things.

Joe, angling for an invite to the last chair, sidled up to the extended table. He attempted to try out his humour on the boys and to wheedle his way into their company. "Hi guys! Looks like it's the old cricket team having a party, ha-ha! "he chortled

To his surprise the man seated close to where he was standing replied with a wave of his hand, "You struck the nail right on the head digger. We are the Bongo Creek nineteen-fifty-one cricket club, just having a reunion. We haven't played together for thirty years, so now it's all off the field. Sit down cobber and have a drink. Where are you from anyhow?" "Me! I'm from Melbourne; just moved into town with The Bank. I called in for a meal but the place is buzzing. I was hard to find a place to sit."

"Well, you are sitting in the seat of our recently departed wicket keeper Jolly Rhodes. He passed on a couple of years ago poor bloke. Otherwise we are all intact."

Joe's drink arrived and he was so pleased that he was getting along famously with the old chap. "By the way you must have had some interesting things happen in those days?" Joe said. "You guys must often talk about them." "Well, its funny you asked because we've just been talking about Johnny Nesbitt and the antics he could get up to. I'll tell you a beauty if you want listen." Joe nodded eagerly. Then he told Joe the story.

"It's like this. There was only one moment in Johnny Nesbit's life in which he stole the limelight. That occurred, it seems, a long, long time ago. Johnny, himself, did not know that he had done anything significant that day in February, nineteen-fifty-eight. The reason of his unawareness was, to tell you the truth, that he was 'blotto.' He was blind drunk. Inebriated completely! The story runs this way, allowing for recollection as our memories fade years after the fact."

"It's all about bush cricket, that institution which pervaded most backyards in our youth and which surreptitiously spilled into the neighbourhood's sports arenas.

It was better known as District cricket. The season's fixture was embedded on the calendar, cricket to be played from the first day of October until the thirty first of March each season. Six months for cricket, then six months for football was the general rule of thumb. As soon as the last week passed, the cricket pitches were torn up or covered. Then the goal posts were erected and training commenced for the winter sport."

"Speaking of training, there was no training for cricket in our village, just the learning imparted to one through participating in the match. Furthermore getting a team of eleven together was a task in itself, which usually meant spending a fair bit of time at the local pub 'recruiting.' On the day of the game, there was a flurry of activity to make sure that there were at least eleven able to play. Sometimes a sister or mother would be called on to 'carry the drinks' or maybe take on the task of recording the scores. Umpires were also difficult to find, let alone entice to officiate."

"Well there were two teams in Bongo Creek. One for the 'toffee nosed' and one for the ordinary folk, like us. The elite brigade always had a full complement and a couple of extras as well. We poor blighters usually scraped up about nine if we were lucky and then spent a lot of time trying to make up the numbers, which meant a trawl of the town each Saturday to catch a couple of extras to swell the numbers."

"On this particular weekend the Bongo Club 'A' were to play the Bongo Creek team in the usual local grudge match. The Bongo Creek team had not beaten 'A' for decades, and as they struggled to field a full team most weeks, they may never get the opportunity to do so ever. This never perturbed 'Creek' in the least because just merely playing, was the fun of it all.

"'A' had a masterly line up and batted first, posting a goodly score of three hundred and twenty for three when the compulsory time was declared. This was done to allow a possible two innings each side per two day match.

"The 'Creek' responded with one hundred and sixty five all out - well within their allotted time. This gave the opposition a distinct advantage, seeing that they were already lead on the first innings. Creek were sent in to 'follow on' according to the rules of the game. They were forced to bat for the second time. All those with local knowledge expected a quick and decisive end to the 'Creek's' aspirations. One hour into the second day, Creek were at the crease but still with only ten men. They could have used another player.

"They gave it all they could. The opposition was ruthless in its attack. Creek stuck to the task, putting together a stubborn two hundred and sixty five all out. This gave the 'A' team a paltry one hundred and ten runs to clean up the match.

"The 'Creek' recruiter was struggling to fill the eleventh spot. In desperation he grabbed Johnny Nesbitt from the pub and dragged him to the ground. He installed him on the boundary with instructions to go after the ball when it came his way. Several brown bottles of beer were placed along the fence for Johnny; to keep him from dehydrating during the game.

The 'A' had an unusually poor start to the second innings losing their two openers for only three a piece. The next man in, the town's Solicitor, Robert Mack was a potent batsman and thrashed every side during the 'comp'. His partner at the other end was just as good. Unfortunately for the 'Creek' team, their replacement fieldsman was hardly in a fit state to be counted, so a hiding was on the cards.

"Sensing quick victory, the lawyer stepped down to flog the first ball over in the direction of the drunken fielder believing that there may as well be no fieldsman there at all. As soon as the ball left the bat the fieldsmen all yelled fervently to Johnny "Catch it boy! Catch it." Nesbitt ran as he was told, fell, staggered up, stumbled but kept his feet. Vaguely sensing that the ball was somewhere above him, he grabbed at the base of his jumper and pulled it out in front of him.

"Plop. The ball dropped slap bang into his jumper. He reflexly folded his arms with ball firmly enclosed in the pullover across his belly. The umpire signaled "OUT", as Johnny went to the fence to open a bottle. His awestruck team mates clapped him as the angry batsman exited the arena. Someone decided they had better retrieve the ball from Johnny, who was totally unaware what was going on; he already had the bottle to his lips. The wickets fell as 'A' struggled to reach the required number of runs. With three balls left and three runs to get and the last man in, both sides were sweating on a miracle.

"The incident which happened on the delivery of the very next ball was to make the annals of local cricket folklore.

"The next three deliveries were vital to the pride, the status, and the future bragging rights of both teams. The last 'A' batsman was at the crease. Nesbitt was still rocking to and fro on the boundary line. The batsman, a fast bowler with no batting ability, stepped forward to the second ball he received. It was a rather slow one and he did his cool. He belted the ball so high out toward Nesbitt in the expectation that the ball would clear the over weight, inebriated fielder.

"Nesbitt, egged on by the boisterous urging of his team mates, ran blindly without thinking in the direction he was called to go. He was quite the worse for wear this day, so anything could happen. He fell over and landed on his back just as the ball plummeted into his midriff. Instinctively his hands went around the ball.

"OUT", called the umpire. 'Out cold' was Johnny Nesbitt. 'Out cold.'

He was a legend.

FOUR OF A KIND

Maria stepped from the Gynaecologist's consulting rooms, and then leant against the railing, to get her composure back. A tear trickled slowly down her cheek. She reached for a handkerchief from her handbag, and settled for the first thing her hand touched, a tissue, and wiped her moist eyes. Then as she went to leave the doctor's premises, her legs became unsteady, so she sat down in a seat that was vacant. Her head was swimming with a myriad of thoughts. Maria had never in her wildest dreams expected the outcome of this morning's check up to be so devastating. It was not the end of the world, but it would change their whole lives.

A lady that Maria judged to be in her forties, a bearer of a few children, she thought, leaned across toward her, and smiling, kindly asked her, "Is this your first, my dear?" Maria gazed at her through the fogginess in her mind, and replied, that it was. "Well, I've had seven so far, and they're all just fine. Keep your pecker up and everything will be all right, I can assure you." Maria stood up and in an outburst of indignant fury, yelled at the woman. "How would you know?" Then, she turned and stormed out of the building into the street.

She drove her car to the parking lot that served her apartment, then after locking the vehicle, took the elevator up to her unit. Once safely inside her room, she closed the door and went to the couch, sat down, then burst into tears. She curled up on the couch, and cried, until she fell asleep. It was quite some time before she awoke. She suddenly realised that she had not organized the evening meal, and that her husband of three years, Ben, would be home soon. How was she going to approach him? She had settled down a little in her mind, since she had rested, and was amazed at how calm she was feeling at this point.

Her husband worked for a large printing business, down town. His main duties were in the area of creating calendars. He had held this position for five years. Ben was considered by his employers and, also by his peers, to be the best in the industry. He was, at that very time battling with his superiors to have his views regarding the next calendar, brought to fruition. His vision was for a new, innovative, circular style of calendar with iridescent script that people could read in poor lighting. He had floated most of his ideas with mixed results, but since none were rejected outright, that pleased him. He would return them back to the drawing board when he felt the time was right.

He knew that his wife was visiting the doctor today, so he hurried homewards, as soon as he could free himself from the constraints of the office. It was only four thirty, so he might take her out, if she was feeling in the mood. In his work, he was able to plan and execute his ideas with a predictable outcome most of the time. However, the thought of raising a child, was another matter completely. He couldn't see much simplicity in the idea, of irregular feed times, and of course, diapers. He cringed at the very thought of them. His home was only a few blocks away. Most days he walked to allow Maria the use of the car.

Maria was not in the frame of mind, to think of, let alone, cook the dinner. Just contemplating the task made her feel ill. It would be difficult enough to explain the test results to Ben. She felt much better than she did a few hours ago, and was thinking through their situation, especially regarding the lack of space available in the unit they presently occupied. The elevator bell rang. She stood by the door, ready to receive him, the moment that he stepped into the room. When he saw the look on her face, he said to her compassionately. "You look tired, would you prefer to eat out, instead of worrying about the preparation of our food? Then you can tell me the news from the doctor." She did not take her gaze from Ben, and replied to him in a calm tone. "You should hear what I have to say, before we go out, my dear."

She motioned him to be seated, so he sat down. Then Maria put her hand on his, and uttered a phrase that he would never forget. "There's more than one, Ben." "Oh! Two, twins?" "No, more, she stammered," "Three, triplets?" "No. More." "What? Four? Qu-, qu-, quads." "Yes, Ben, and they all will be girls. The Doctor confirmed that, from the Ultrasound, I think they call it." "What are we going to do? Where will we live, What are we going to tell our parents? How will I cope?"

It all flooded out and continued, as Ben sat holding her, He was still in absolute shock himself

Then after a few minutes, he said whatever any expectant father of quads probably would have said. "We'll cope dear". Then he sank deeper into the lounge chair, to concentrate on a further reply. Maria had ceased the tears and lifted herself from the couch, straightened her attire, and went to find herself a drink in the kitchen. He rose and followed her. He stood, looking out the window, cogitating, while she was still smoothing her dress, as if it would never straighten out. "Ok, let's talk about it over dinner. Maria, you pick the place, Ill drive." She gave him her preference. He drove and they made the restaurant in good time. She commented to him that a jar of pickles would go well. He grinned, and then they ordered their meals.

Maria had decided not to advise both of their mothers for a few days. Ben went along with her idea, as the mothers would want to suggest a lot of solutions, well before he and Maria had time to pass base one first. Also, the whole new ball game required a lot of careful thought and planning. That night after they had arrived home from the restaurant, Maria told him that she would prefer to settle on the babies' names before their parents were informed. When Ben agreed, she said that he could pick the names, as he had a very creative mind. She added that the due date for the multiple births was March 31st.

The next morning, the father to be explained to his colleagues of his pending initiation into parenthood. He told them that he could use them as his Calendar Girls, at a later date in their lives. Little did he know, as he joked about the girls, what impact that statement would have in the near future, as he set about in selecting their names. He was pouring over the work for the day and attempting to find suitable photographs for the latest calendar, when something caught his attention.

He dropped his work immediately and went to the phone. He called Maria, and asked her to meet him at the Coffee-house, the one near to his work place. She accepted his invitation, and went immediately to the parking lot. Maria watched as he arrived, then he came and sat opposite her. They ordered their drinks. He told her that the names came to him while he was collating the latest calendar.

He believed that the names he had selected would be perfect choices. Ben noted that the expected time of arrival was, as she had previously advised him, March 31ˢᵗ. Being in the calendar industry, he selected names for their four children and hoped she would approve. She was watching him with interest as he told her his choices. "I would like our four daughters to be named, April, May, June, and Julie, depending on their order of arrival. She smiled lovingly at him.

FRAU BRUNNER
AND THE SNOW

"Why am I here?" Steve thought, as he stared into the remains of his last drink. It was a very late evening, or early morning. The group he was spending the late hours with had departed one by one to their respective abodes. Steve dragged his weary body from the bar table and lumbered towards the front door. Older Austrians sitting together in their well-accustomed place by the entrance, and none the worse for their evening's heavy imbibing, chuckled as the young and rather naïve Australian fumbled his way to the exit.

"He will learn in time" one mused. "Or die in the process" another remarked light- heartedly. They all agreed and with a nod or a wink left it at that.

This was the time of the year when expatriates came from every corner of the globe to test their skills at the innumerable ski resorts in the Alps of Europe. Some found the going to their liking. Others fell by the wayside, and invariably onto hard times.

Steve was at the crossroads of his life in the skiing industry. Having muffed a few good chances early on in his career, through his older brother Rod he had at last found a door open where he had least expected it, here in Austria. It was the time of the year in Australia when he would be cooling his heels on the Gold Coast, surfing and generally loafing, passing the time until the next ski season. Last season was a disaster with little or no snow in the Australian Alps, so funds were tight to say the least.

Innsbruck had just a few years previously hosted the Winter Olympics and the industry was hitting the big time. The amenities were the state of the art of that time and all the young skiers were heading there for the chance to try out the now famous slopes. Steve was one of these but, like most of the visitors, was flat broke. His aim was to become a qualified ski instructor, then to travel wherever the sport would lead him.

Rod allowed Steve to bunk down with him and his mates for the time being, but then he would have to manage for himself. This seemed a fair and reasonable idea at the time. However, there were one, or perhaps two small difficulties to overcome, namely, Steve couldn't speak Austrian nor would he have any money until snow fell in the area.

Steve's main job was to find accommodation as soon as possible. This he set out to do once his hangover had abated somewhat that third day. The advice given to him by the seasoned campaigners was to commence to knock on doors in small hamlets near and around the Innsbruck region so as to be close to ski transport. The door knocking commenced, and as Steve drifted from house-to-house, he couldn't help but notice the orderliness of the homes and the abundance of flowers which surrounded each one.

It certainly was tougher than he had expected. He tramped all of the first day with no affirmatives, and not as much as a smile from most of the inhabitants. As what was left of the day petered into evening, his spirits were at quite a low ebb. It was a mite cool at that. He was just about to throw in the towel, so to speak, when his eye caught sight of a rather imposing two-storey villa set apart from the rest of the street. It looked a bit out of his league but he thought that he might as well give it a try.

Steve's spirit was flagging, and although he could feel the pull of the village inn tugging him into submission, he resolved to check the place out. It was a gigantic house set on an immense plot of land. Gingerly he ambled towards the residence, not knowing what to expect. He nervously pressed the doorbell. Nothing happened. He tried the bell again, then turned away to leave the premises. Suddenly, from another door at the opposite end of the house, a face appeared.

A round plumpish face with rosy cheeks peered at him without speaking. He made the first move, clearing his throat and mumbling in his native tongue something that resembled a stutter or a cry for help. "Please can you help me, I am looking for a place to stay for the winter." (The dialogue, which follows, actually was a mix of poor English and Austrian, depending on their understanding of the other sentences, but somehow they managed to communicate with each other.)

She stepped out of the doorway summing him up. "Australian?" She pondered the question to him. "Yes madam, I'm in Innsbruck for the season." He pointed to the high ski slopes awaiting the first gasps of the frigid conditions, which season by season, summon the hordes to the Alps.

"Yes" she interjected, "The young ones wanting to break the limbs. I have one room. Come in. What is your name?"

"Steven." "Ah Stefan that is easy, just one minute."

She turned, then led him into what appeared to be the dining room. To Steve, whose family lived in a small three-bedroom Australian home, this was something out of the box. There seemed to be rooms leading from just about every corner of the building, more like a private hotel than a home for an old lady. She returned a minute later, tray in hand. Placing the tray on the table, she offered him a portion of a very dark cake plus a glass of schnapps. She then explained that this was her own recipe, the schnapps of course.

"I have one space. After you eat this food we will look."

"Thank you madam" Steve replied.

"Anna Brunner " she spoke with a smile, which seemed as large as a full moon.

"Anna Brunner?" He questioned.

"That's my name."

"Oh! I see."

"Now we see the space for you for sleeping."

Steve was warming to her, but his guess as to the price of such a place was not allowing him to feel at ease at this point. He followed her through a labyrinth of hallways and rooms to a small doorway painted bright green. Here she stopped, inserted a key in the lock and flung the door open. In two steps Steve found himself in one of the smallest rooms he had ever been in his life. A small single iron frame bunk filled half of the entire floor space whilst the wardrobe occupied a fair portion of the rest. There was a tiny window covered with a heavy dingy drape and that was all.

It was already dark outside and very cold. Well, beggars can't be choosers, his mum had often said, so he turned to the stocky Frau and said.

"It seems all right. But how much do you expect me to pay weekly?"

"It would be just a little Stefan. Eleven American Dollars each week, and one more thing."

"That seems very cheap, Frau Brunner. What else do you require?"

"You are to keep the snow from the front of the house each day you stay here, and for that I give you small rent. Yes?"

"That seems reasonable" Steve replied.

"I cook breakfast each day, but you must find the other food."

"That is fine by me." Here ended the first encounter between Steve and Frau Brunner. He bid her good evening and departed satisfied with the arrangements.

Needless to say he moved in. Things moved along smoothly for the time being. As the winter snow had commenced its precipitation on the hills, Steve had plenty of work with the team preparing for the inevitable influx of patrons from the four-corners of the earth. The attraction to the former Winter Olympics venue would make the area a hive of industry, not to mention the injection of funds, which Steve and his mates required.

As the days drifted on and the snow hadn't fallen in great quantities, the staff of the lift and lodges found themselves indulging in frightfully long evenings at the local inns. One problem with this was that the amount of schnapps imbibed along with other drinks, were starting to take their toll, especially on the less seasoned drinkers of the troupe. After the heaviest evening binge he had undertaken since his arrival, and much worse for wear, Steve found his bed at two thirty am. What he was apparently unaware of at the time, was that the sleet and snow were intensifying during the early morning darkness.

Steve lay on the bed totally debilitated, still dressed in his day attire and unable to raise himself. Even if a catastrophe were to befall him at that moment, he would sleep the sleep of one who didn't wish to be woken. There was a thunderous din thumping through Steve's inert brain as though a thousand drums and cymbals were booming and clanging simultaneously. He staggered out, or fell, onto the floor. The racket was coming from the door and his name was being called out. He finally opened the door. Frau Brunner, standing without a smile, but with a solemn countenance, spoke quietly. "Much snow Stefan." then she disappeared down the hallway from where she came.

"Oh no", Steve grumbled, his head like a lead balloon "It's four-thirty." However, he did manage to stagger down the stairs. He greeted his work, without much relish. He didn't really have much of a choice. The tools were at the front door. He forced the door open and commenced to shovel the snow, whilst cursing under his breath. The drift was only a foot high, so he felt it would not take long, and it didn't. He put the gear away and returned upstairs. He was greeted warmly by her ladyship. This time she smiled and held out a mug full of hot drinking chocolate, which he accepted gratefully finding a seat to rest and consume the drink, as if it were to be his last.

His next day at the slopes was a tough one. Steve wished he could fall into any crevice, bury himself under the snow and die for he was so tired.

Winter then progressed as normal in the Austrian Alps. Skiers were in abundance and Steve managed through frugal living, which also meant less drinking to save a few dollars. The snow was not the heaviest seen for many years but all got by despite the difficulty. One evening deep in the winter, Steve received his greatest test. One of the Australians was leaving and the farewell party went into the wee hours of the morning. It was very late when Steve and some of the others, who also boarded at Frau's residence, finally hit their respective beds. An immense storm hammered the village, dumping copious quantities of snow in every nook and cranny.

Then at four that morning, the Frau was banging on his door. " Stefan the big snow. Hurry then." He could not believe his eyes. The snow was as high as his body height. He shoveled and cursed, toiled and grumbled, shoveled and raked, but the snow kept falling. He began to despair at the contract he had made, not ever thinking of the consequences at the time. Frau brought drinks from time to time but the job just didn't ever seem to finish. Finally he had cleared the front of the house and turned towards the door to put away the tools when the local snowplow passed by, dumping more snow onto the driveway. This was the last straw, he felt. He cleaned it up, then moved to enter the house to place the tools in their rightful position. It was not his night.

A great chunk of snow cascaded from the roof, landing on the driveway and creating more havoc for the young man. However, he put his shoulder to the task, finished the job and finally got a reprieve in the villa, exhausted but thankful to have gotten over the task. His landlady had brewed coffee, and food was laid before him as a kind of thanks. The snow continued in the same manner for three months solid and Steve was the fittest guy on the circuit.

From the first of the heavy snows, the Frau attended to whatever meals he required and a great friendship developed between them - not to mention that the following ski season when Frau Brunner nursed him through the misfortune of a broken left leg. She became his mother away from home. One thing the Australian learnt and he will say it with a broad grin, "I will never take on any contract without first reading the small print; and I'll never allow myself to be snowed under again."

THE THREE
COFFINS

These were unusual times in the west. Cactus Springs was an unusual town to say the least. Three coffins stood side by side against the livery stable fence. Their lids lay on the ground, where the carpenter had left them the day before. A door banged nearby, as the town's only law stepped onto the veranda. A mangy dog scurried across the street, getting out of the way pronto. The law was about to light his pipe when the livery attendant came into view. The law tapped his hickory pipe against the railing and waited. "What's the news Wal?" He said casually. "Three graves are dug on the hill Bart, side by side. Call me when the site is to be filled in."

Bart McIvor stepped down from the veranda, fiddling with his pipe as he sauntered across the street. He stopped outside the jail, called to Hank the overnight watch, to see if all was well. Hank yelled back that all was well, and that he had let the drunks out at six, to save having to feed them. It was now seven a.m. and the sun was asserting itself on the horizon. Tumbleweed drifted past him as he finally lit his pipe. Satisfied with all that he saw and heard, he walked to the law office and opened the door to collect his whip.

Bart McIvor had drifted into Cactus Springs a few years before, penniless after the Civil War. Fate had shone on him due to the fact that the law was non-existent, the town was desperate to keep itself to itself and resist the hoodlums and carpetbaggers drifting on to the scene from the East. The other problem facing small towns was itinerant thugs called 'Cowboys' trying to push out the established farmers. These brought hired gunmen with them and generally took control of the territory, pressing their law onto the unfortunate communities.

Not so far in this town! This was an unusual small settlement. This was a 'no gun' town. The Sheriff was an enigma of his time, and dealt the law with a range of measures unheard of in the west, perhaps even in the rest of civilisation. Today was to be one of those days.

The Winslow Brothers were on their way. Their aim was to take out the Sheriff, to end a long- standing grievance against the unarmed lawman. How he dealt his cards today would be an affair to behold. Bart took his favourite whip down from its place above his desk. He dusted it against his trousers, then laid it down, curled up, on his desk. He opened the top drawer of the desk, withdrew three long pieces of rope and placed them beside the whip.

The Winslow brothers lived in Silver Rapids, sixty miles beyond Cactus Springs. The Sheriff of that town had sent a messenger to advise Bart that the trio had left after a drinking binge. They had made it known publicly, that they were going to settle a score with the law. Every man and his coyote knew of the vendetta and its origins. The three brothers were not quite the threat to society that they wished to portray. However, the lawmen in each territory kept them under control and stood for no nonsense. The Winslows were petty criminals, who rustled a steer here and there, broke a few windows when they were drunk, or perpetrated a string of larcenies from time to time.

The Winslows, Henri and Luke were twins twenty-three years old, a year and a half older than Ben, who followed them around like a puppy ever since he could crawl. Most folks who knew them agreed, that if they could take the younger away from the other two's company, then he would develop into a nice young guy. Their mother despaired of them, knowing deep in her heart, that they could only finish up one way in the west.

The boys left home early that morning, just as the sun rose, reckoning on resting at Dry Gulch Bend. They had stuffed their saddlebags full of supplies, rifles swung from the leather straps attached to the saddles. Six shooters were on each hip, not that they were crack shots, but they thought they were. They would make the sheriff's town in about five hours. They planned to surround his office, and then call him out. That's about as far as their thinking went. They were not the brightest opponents the sheriff had to face in his time. However, no one needed to be a victim of stray bullets.

Doc Summers watched from his second storey window as the law walked towards the stables. He knew that trouble was in the air. He also had no idea what was in the Sheriff's mind this time. He had witnessed some strange capers in his time as medico in the town, but never before that had he seen such as Bart could conjure up. Once, Bart cleaned out a whole gang of hoodlums by taking Doc with him. After approaching the gang leader who was itching for a fight, Bart pointed to the doctor, then told the gangsters that a plague had broken out in the town, that they needed to be checked out, and possibly quarantined. They couldn't get on their mounts quick enough. Nobody has seen them in these parts since. This was the way of the Sheriff of Cactus Springs.

The law rode out of town in the direction of Silver Rapids, with his whip and three pieces of rope, his poker face concealing his emotions. The doctor knew that this was to be a tough day for the Sheriff. He also knew the Winslow boys and their mother. He decided to see to the ill and to attend to his other chores around town before the inevitable battle would happen. He wished he was privy to the lawman's inner thoughts, but he wasn't. He went downstairs, took his coat and medical suitcase, then left the house. He strolled past the livery stable. Three coffins stood side by side at the stable fence, their lids below them on the ground. He grimaced and walked on.

The Winslows travelled as they always did when up to no good. They rode single file, about three hundred yards apart. This was the brainchild of Luke, who felt, that, if they were bushwhacked, they stood a better chance than if they were side-by-side. Maybe he would live to regret his one flash of inspiration. The boys reached Dry Gulch Bend in good time. They had a bite to eat and moved on to the Cactus Springs road. It could hardly be called a road, just a track through the low hills - narrow and winding, through stunted growth and cacti. It was a great place for an ambush. The boys, moving in single file lost sight of each other from time to time.

Bart McIvor reached the point where he could watch proceedings with safety. He tethered his horse to a tree some way from the road, sat and waited. It was not more than half an hour later that he caught a glimpse of Luke, high in the saddle, riding at a fair pace. However, a rider had to slow to a walking pace to negotiate the rivulet, which crossed the road at this point. The law sat motionless as Luke passed by. Then Henri came and went, but the law sat inert. Henri moved on.

Ben appeared and slowed his steed. He didn't hear it, but he felt it. It knocked him out cold. The big man emerged from the shrubbery and dragged Ben from the water.

Ben Winslow was trussed up like a Thanksgiving turkey, then strapped to his horse. The lawman waited for the inevitable after moving Ben's horse out of sight. He didn't have long to wait. Luke, noticing his younger brother hadn't appeared, sent Henri back to check on him. Luke followed behind Henri to the water, then sent him down the track beyond the crossing to find Ben. Luke let his horse drink from the stream as he listened for Henri's call. It did not come in time. Luke didn't hear the swish, nor did he know what hit him.

The law attended to the leader of the trio in a similar manner to that of the younger boy. "Two out of three, means three out of three", he mused to himself. He climbed on his horse, then led the other animals, with their cargo, onto the road by the water. It was only a matter of time. He heard Henri call and gave a shrill whistle. Henri came into view. Before he had a chance to utter a word, he was dragged from his horse and deposited, in great dismay upon the earth. The lawman, an expert with the whip, had captured the trio without an angry shot being discharged.

Sheriff McIvor escorted the young miscreants to Cactus Springs without incident. The trip ensued without a whimper from any of them. They were so overwhelmed that each was speechless, but recriminations against each other were going on in their puny minds. The doctor was at the jail when McIvor deposited the lads in the safekeeping of the warder. "Don't waste too much food on them", he said with a wry smile, when he was out of their sight, but close enough for them to hear. "Hanging on a full stomach ain't too good for the constitution, and it puts extra pressure on the rope".

The Sheriff, the Doctor and the Bank Manager played cards that evening with no mention of the day's events. That's how the lawman wanted it and that suited the town. Talk too much about trouble and it follows you around. In fact, the lawman had a sign above his desk, and it read NEVER TROUBLE, TROUBLE, TILL TROUBLE TROUBLES YOU.

The next morning was Sunday. No hanging on Sunday, it spoilt lunch. Seeing there was no judge or court in the area, this being in lawless times, so to speak, the Sheriff got to make up the rules on the spot. Each case was treated on its merit, but most of the misdemeanours were punishable by hanging anyway, so it was sort of simplified for the lawman. Everything that related to the trio, except food, was put on hold till Monday.

Sheriff Bart McIvor was up bright and early on Monday, ready to carry out the law. His first task, that is, after lighting his beloved pipe, was to visit the incarcerated men. He went to the jail via the livery stable, where he asked the attendant to go with him to the jail. The attendant was an expert on nooses, hanging nooses. After greeting the jailer, Bart turned his attention to the gaoled, three of them. They were not in good spirits, so he dispensed with the humour that he planned to use on them. He handed the three pieces of rope to the livery attendant, then turned and faced his captives.

"Boys, this is a self help institution, this here guy is going to teach you some craft that will help get you out of this jail. Now, you're all for that I suppose?" They nodded in unison. "Now here's the drill. You will learn very quickly how to make a noose. In fact, each of you will make a noose. This will save me a lot of time. Then we will go over there". He pointed to the huge tree in the distant. " See it through the window, yes that's the tree, a nice solid tree. Notice that it has a thick bough coming away out from the trunk. That's where we will head a little later, after you have finished your craft, and Doc checks your hearts. We don't want you swinging unhealthy like." He turned and walked out, leaving the livery attendant to the task of educating the brothers in their new craft.

The Doctor met the Sheriff at the saloon, Arrangements for the rest of the day were decided upon. McIvor called on the Bank Manager, asked him to witness events as they unfolded during the day, then sat on the chair outside his office in deep thought, puffing on his pipe. It was past noon when the Sheriff led the trio out of the gaol house, across the road from the livery stable. The Doctor, the Banker, the Liveryman were assembled to witness. "All right boys, put your nooses in the coffins". Ropes left the boys hands as if they were the deadliest serpents on God's earth. The boys seemed relieved for the moment. But the release was short lived. "Pick up the coffins one each, we're off to the cemetery, … on the double".

The procession to the cemetery was all of ten minutes. The sheriff told the three men to place the coffins in the recently dug grave holes, then lie in the wooden boxes themselves. The men yelled, tried to resist the proposal, but succumbed after the threat of the sheriff's whip. Then he ordered them out and asked the doctor to examine them. With little ado, the doctor gave the green light and McIvor marched the hapless group towards the tree.

The hanging tree was half a mile from the cemetery, making executions and funerals easy to coordinate. Under the tree, directly beneath the bough, a large bench, about five feet by eight feet long was standing. There was about nine feet distance in height between the bench and the bough, plenty for a hanging and room for sag. "Now boys it's time to finish this business, so I can get an afternoon nap. Get up on the bench. I want you twins on one side, facing in, and the young one on the other side, facing them." The boys were struggling but Bart threatened to shoot them with the Banker's gun and they scrambled up. The banker did not have a weapon, but they were completely demoralized to comprehend. Their resistance had ebbed, leaving them void of thought, and their body language gave the hint of total resignation to their grisly fate.

The lawman barked his commands "Well now here's the pitch. The two on one side can kick the bench, thus hanging the young one, then you two will swing second. But if the younger kicks the bench, you two go before him, I told you this was a self-help institution, and it is. Now we'll have these nooses tightened, tied to the rail over here and all will be ready". He checked the ropes, threw the ropes over the limb, around the men's necks, then looked at the three hapless men. They were not faring very well.

The young man began to whimper. "What about Ma?" "You should have thought of her more often," the lawman yelled at him giving the rope a tug.

"Okay Doc, you preside over the end, then call me later. I've got to attend to another matter." The 'other matter' was that he needed a puff on his beloved pipe. Nothing came between McIvor and his confounded pipe, the Doc thought to himself knowingly. The Banker shivered uncomfortably, not knowing what to expect from the unorthodox law enforcer. However, his better judgment kept him from asking questions. He stood, with mouth open waiting for the next surprise, which he was certain would transpire at any moment.

During the next several minutes, which seemed an eternity to the onlookers, the trio of brothers just exchanged looks, each crying in their own way, making no effort to dislodge the bench that would send them to certain oblivion. The doctor stood, head bowed, expecting to hear the noise of the bench when it fell. Nothing happened. Doc watched the expressions on the faces of the doomed, a flurry of compassion swept over him for a moment. If he could terminate proceedings, he would. But he would not. He knew the Sheriff, he knew the boys and he knew their mother. It would be him the Family Doctor, who would convey to her the final message and make the necessary arrangements.

Sheriff Bart McIvor came back to the pitiful scene and stood beside the Doctor. "I knew you boys couldn't arrange your own breakfast, let alone kill each other. Cut them down boys, so I can read their sentences. Here's the story so far boys. You have saved yourselves from the noose today, but you're only reprieved, I'm telling you. You are guilty as hell of thieving, carousing, general drunkenness, assorted other crimes, not to mention stealing cattle, which is a hanging offence. So here's the sentence passed on the three of you.

You will get on those varmints that resemble horses, high tail it back to your town, then hand in the nooses to the Sheriff, who will notify me in due course of your movements. Then, the three of you will sign up at the Mine outside town and support your mother, till she departs this earth. Now get out of here and never set foot in this place again. Remember, there are three coffins and the three nooses awaiting three brothers if they ever as much as steal a piece of corn from a prairie dog".

The boys scurried towards their steeds faster than a dog with its tail on fire. They were mounted and gone out of sight before the Sheriff reached the livery stable. "Bring the coffins back and the bench, son. I doubt if those coyotes will ever show up again". He fetched his pipe and tobacco out of his coat pocket. He slowly and deliberately loped towards the saloon, mumbling something about his mother.

The Banker was puzzled. The Doctor recognised his agitation and inquired as to what worried him. The Banker said that he could not understand what had happened. Why the Sheriff went to so much trouble then let those evil fellows off.

The Doctor eyeballed the man and said in quiet tone voice. "You see it's like this. The Sheriff's mother and their mother are the same. However, the Sheriff's father and their father are not the same. Furthermore, the three boys don't know that".

'THERES CONDITIONS MISTER'

He pulled the car to a halt and opened the driver's side door and stepped onto the gravel surface of the roadway. Clearly, he contemplated he was lost. The map, as he had read it didn't indicate that. He was deep in the bush country of the old mining district, but he couldn't ascertain where. Leaning into the car he retrieved the map and spread it on the roof of the car. Being a sizable chap, Will Roberts was able to spread the paper out and get a good look at it from where he had placed it. The breeze of that afternoon made it a little more difficult.

Studying the map and tracing on it with his finger where he thought that he had driven that afternoon, he soon discovered his miscalculation. The error of judgement had taken him more than ninety kilometres away form his intended route. He was beyond Logan Forest and in the scrub area where life as he knew it could not be found. Except for a few dingos and the odd kangaroo that happened to get lost like him, no one in their right mind would attempt to live here. The map legend indicated harsh terrain and displayed locations of old mineral and gold mines, (long since abandoned and forgotten) with a caution that sink-holes and shafts lay scattered throughout the region rendering the land an unfriendly friendly zone for travellers.

Will checked his road options and realized that with nightfall not too far distant he needed to make tracks as soon as possible. He put the map into the vehicle and went to the rear of the car to take a bottle of water from his cool pack. While he was drinking from the bottle he walked around stepped off the verges of the road to examine some of the flora. There was a shrub that he had never seen before. It had soft leaves and small pink berries' so he snapped off a small piece of the branch. He was about to turn and go back to the car when something caught his eye.

He stepped closer and noted that a sign-post, many years old by its appearance was half buried in the dirt and vegetation but the writing was still legible.

"CHEEKY LODE MINE.PROS 9m" it read.

Interesting he thought his mind taken from his immediate predicament. The word pros would have meant prospectors something or other. Looking up from sign he noticed that there was a track, not a very good one heading to the west. The track appeared to have been abandoned along time past. It would be a challenge to his four wheel drive vehicle but that's what he purchased it for. When he returned to his car he sat and contemplated his next move. He was four hours at least from a small town which would put him there in darkness and possibly no chance of accommodation. He had enough food and a blanket and a weather-proof vehicle.

Will Roberts then made the poorest decision of his twenty six year life. He decided to venture into the unknown a man of no bush experience. He tried to use his phone but there was no signal. He started the engine and reversed the car for a few metres then turned and headed the vehicle onto the overgrown track. At first the track yield to the cars energetic push but as he reached about eight kilometres he found the track had given way to huge holes and soft sand.

The vehicle lurched and pushed on. Will sweated and cursed both his own stupidity and the roads poor surface. After all why would a full grown man tackle a pursuit such as this without at least a little investigation and research which he could have done. Curiosity killed the cat, it is said, but it could do untold damage to Will Roberts as well. He read the mileage indicator and calculated that he was three kilometres from the min area according tho the sign-post. The track was getting easier to navigate and the surface was now shale and small rocks. He saw the site from about a kilometre away and his heart leapt with anticipation. During the flurry to get here he had not once considered his actual position once he found the place. Of course he did not expect to find what he was about to stumble upon.

He had driven into what appeared to be a abandoned town .A ghost town to be exact. He brought the vehicle to a stand still in what must have been the main street. Several dilapidated buildings with their once grandiose verandas fallen off, fronts of the structures completely devoid of paint, doors off hinges, laying on the veranda floors and grass two metres high along the street. He imagined himself to be in the American wild west of the movies-some bygone era far from reality of his day, expecting a team of miners trudging home from work, to come around the corner of the street. That wouldn't happen, this was Australia and this was an ancient place that was a part of history books and the fantasy of ones imagination.

He was Will Roberts from Sydney and this was the twenty- first century where only dreams of the past were recreated to teach young enthusiasts to appreciate their past.

He decided to explore the ruins and see what these oldies left behind so he stepped up to the building that no doubt was the saloon or pub in those times it had shape and appearance that he connected with old hotels and he was proved to be correct once stepped into its interior. The building once had a spacious lounge and foyer area. There was what was left for a hallway with eight door lintels still standing, suggesting the accommodation section, beyond that a collapsed section of what could be explained as a kitchen and laundry section.

He found himself outside at the rear or the home of the not so recently departed and was staring at a strange looking building. It was shaped like a rotunda several sided and there were hooks hanging from the rafters which were the only pieces of the building still standing. A sort of butchery he thought to himself. It was into dusk now so Will decided to sleep in the car and get back to civilisation as soon as the dawn appeared the next day.

He hovered about the ruins drifting from one building to another until he felt a little spooked from the whole weird event. One thing he didn't do was to venture a little further and investigate a couple of dwellings on the fringe of the ghost town. He'd look in the morning.

He decided to walk across a small paddock behind the hotel and peruse an old barn type structure he had seen from the pub. The grass was quite thick and the ground rough. As stepped past shrub he tripped and fell he put his hands out to save himself and landed without injuring himself. As he stood up he felt a presence around him and thought he'd caught a shadow passing on his immediate right. He turned quickly but then convinced himself it was due to the unexpected fall. He was still quite jittery. He jumped when a stray rabbit bolted from the thicket beside where he was standing. Now he was not sure that staying close to here for the night was such a good idea after all.

Will Robert, a Sydneysider and not a bushman at heart settled down to endure the evening in the strangest place he could have found himself in .He had laid the back seat down and stretched out under the blanket. It was not comfortable as he was a large person and was not able lay full length as he would have hoped to .anyway he would be gone from here in a few hours and that was that. Fortunately the night was a pleasant one with little or no wind. The stars put on their usual clear sky panorama and Will drifted to slumber.

It was a horrendous bang which threw Will Roberts from sleep to total awareness. It was pitch dark and the sky had given way to dark clouds and wind had replaced calm and panic had replaced Robert's composure. A gunshot he was sure it was a discharge of a firearm. Then he saw that the side window was broken. This was the end of a pleasant sleep to wake to a living nightmare. He literally sprung from the car and landed onto the grass. Taking a swift look around could not see any one or anything for that matter

"Who's out there" he half choked as he spoke.

"Just sit on the ground sonny" a voice from behind him said in a menacing voice.

Will did just that and dropped to the ground. Yokels from deserted outback places weren't too friendly he had read a few stories about people who strayed onto places similar to this and fell foul of local woodsmen.

He shrank to half his size, wished he was dreaming tucked up snugly in his warm bed at home. However, he was he was staring down the barrel. Staring down the barrel of a monster shot gun, the size of which he had never seen before. In fact he hated guns and war, therefore weaponry didn't interest him one bit. At the end of the gun was a leering face at the top of a short hunched body. The body displayed short arms and legs, head partly balding at the hairline and a scar across the left cheek. The man was dressed in very old worn-out attire. It looked to Will Roberts that this apparition had been in the wilds a heck of along time.

The man with the scar stood stock still and looked the traveller over for a few minutes he then checked out the vehicle the returned to Will who had not moved a muscle since he hit the ground. The man stood about five metres from him still training the weapon on him .he beckoned the young man to get up and turn around. Will did as he was told in fear for his life He heard footsteps emanate from another area. Soon a solid darkish woman came into the dim light and stared at Will. After a short while, another woman, short, grisly faced with an uncouth air about her, stepped up near him. Goodness, there could be a clan of these he thought despondently.

The next thing certainly put the frighteners on him. The man handed the tall woman the gun and pulled what looked like a candle from his back pocket. It was no candle will guessed it was dynamite. The second woman took the dynamite and told Will to sit on the ground. He did just that, realizing he had really two choices live or die. The man rummaged around in the car and then having found the keys climbed in and started the motor the drove away around the corner on the hotel will could hear the motor as the car disappeared then the motor stopped and there was a silent pause.

A heavy grating sound came to his ears then not a movement. A few minutes later the man returned on foot and took the gun from the woman but left the other holding the explosives.

All manner of scenarios came to Roberts head but he dismissed them as distractions. His main concern was to stay alive and try to escape the ordeal. His biggest challenge at present was to find out how many protagonists were in his way and how to exit without causing him to be badly damaged or worst of die in the process. The weather was on the brink of changing for the worst a trickle of misty rain came and went intermittently making his sitting on the ground most uncomfortable. Suddenly the man came close to Will and said "Get up boy: we're gonner give you a party." With that he was herded along a path which he noticed was well worn and down a slight incline to a hut one of those he saw from the hotel earlier in the evening. The larger woman who had about two teeth pushed him to be seated on the floor of the hut then she closed the door.

"Son you created a problem for us by trespassing, so you got to pay restitution,"

"Sir I am sorry if I made a misjudgement and I don't mind paying my fine if that satisfies you." Will's words tumbled out and he was relieved to have been allowed to speak. "Well, son ain't that simple.

There's conditions, Mister, on being on our land-our folk's land. They dug it and perished on it and we are the guardians and our folks don't like to be walked over.

Will was about to ask a few questions but held back.

"We got rules here son so you gotta know the conditions. First there's drivin' cars and the like on this land, so your car is now ours. Your jalopy has gone to a good purpose. It's in our conditions

"What did you do to the car?" The traveller yelled.

"In the Cheeky Shaft with the others." The old man replied." Won't be long before we fill the shaft up, jest a few more trespassers." He grinned. 'Maybe another five or so." He added.

"Now we gotta sort you out." The man sneered and simultaneously wiped his nose on the sleeve of his grubby coat as he picked up the gun and motioned the women to leave the room.

The man grabbed at the young man's belt and poked the gun in his ribs. All the time Will was trying to search for a sign of weakness in the situation, something to exploit and to find a break for freedom. His car was his life blood. His only way out it seemed so he would see how the next few minutes pan out.

The scar faced man pushed Will Roberts along a path similar to the one that lead to the hut, but this one went in another direction. Soon they came to a clearing and the two women were standing, waiting.

Then he saw the hole and the man pushed him close to it. The man stopped at the edge and the young man knew why. It was a shaft, the Cheeky Shaft. His car was about six metres down in the hole. The young guy almost wretched his pride ad joy the money he saved to get that. The sacrifices he had to make and hard work all gone in a stupid error on his part. It was wilful and reckless.

Then he was pushed on from his vehicles grave to a further part of the paddock. They stopped and he saw the reason another shaft.

The man pushed him to the edge and he saw that the shaft, unlike the other one was narrower and deeper, perhaps twelve metres deep.

Suddenly the man whacked Will with the firearm taking him off guard then pushing the boy fiercely. Will Roberts temporally lost control of his legs, flying out then uncontrollably downwards. He hit the side before he hit the bottom of the pit. A piece of timber protruding out half way down slowed his downward spiral. Nevertheless he hit the floor hard which shook his whole body. He lay dazed, trying to summon wind to his lungs.

They watched with no outward emotion showing. A short time later the man noting that Roberts was sitting up but not looking too good leaned over the side of the defunct mining pit.

He was still leering as he addressed the hapless prisoner.

"You gotta kill yourself and bury your self son. It's the conditions you see. Don't you?"

The pitiless moaning ceased from below, as the stunned man tried to reply. "Why don't you just shoot me now and get it over with."

"Can't, got no ammo." and he let of a devilish shriek.

At the base of the shaft the prisoner screamed he could have bluffed or done something earlier. But he did not, and he did not know about the gun.

He was in such pain aching all over "How do I kill my self and bury myself smart arse?" the boy screamed from the bowels of the pit.

"It's easy as jumping off a cliff son!" With that statement the tall lady as if playing a theatre role, stepped to the rim and threw down the stick of dynamite then a box containing three matches.

"You see kid you can end it and bury yourself at the same time, save us the work."

"What if I don't do it? He yelled back.

After that a few minutes elapsed.

"Hurry up boy we haven't all night." the old man yelled.

"I'm not doing it I'll rot here instead," were the boy's last words.

Two minutes later the tall woman appeared at the rim of the shaft. She threw a stick that resembled a candle with the wick alight and spluttering.

"All present and buried." she said to the other two

It was their conditions.

LOVE'S
ENDURANCE

Alena Saranova stoked the ancient receptacle which doubled as a cooking stove and a heater. Her aged grandmother was crouching closely, half seated on a decrepit wooden fruit case trying to draw as much of the heat from the fire as she could, whilst stirring an iron pot containing the remnants of yesterday's meal plus a few new additions.

The old fruit case was a permanent part of Anna s home as long as she could remember. The old lady, dressed in outmoded attire, was staring into the fire, her tired old frame rocking from side to side as she watched the coals and the pot.

Alena moved around the room tidying the house in a manner any observer could note as suggesting urgency. He is coming today, she spoke to herself. Today is Saturday. He always came on Saturdays, about lunchtime and stayed but a short time - too short a time she thought. All too brief were his visits but they were like a charge of electricity to her soul. Though transitory, his manner toward her was as transparent as crystal and with a tranquillity that lifted her being, and held her aloft until the next encounter.

Ivan Petrovich closed the grey unpainted slab of timber that was called a door, after nodding a silent farewell to his mother, he then stepped out into the snow-covered street. The winter wind which bore down from the Urals was not present so early today - at least at this time he could set out without the immediate sting of cold. He knew from bitter experience that its presence was not far distant, so he must move with haste.

It was a presumption to call the track a road; it was slush and mud with anything that the winter storms threw onto the ground. There were ice-covered puddles that stretched across the entire width of the track.

Ivan dressed as he normally did, wearing three layers of clothing, a pair of heavy army boots, a scarf plus an old balaclava headpiece pulled tight over his ears and his blonde hair.

His clothes had a saga of their own, as could the entire attire of his village. Ivan's boots were found on the feet of an unfortunate Russian soldier who failed to conquer the utter desolation of this part of the frozen wastelands of this god-forsaken territory of the former Soviets.

His clothes either were all hand-me-downs or pilfered from here and there; as were most of the meagre possessions of the small forgotten village he called home.

He pulled the scarf tighter around his neck so that all that was visible to the onlooker were his two eyes. He commenced his customary walk, a trip that would make the hardiest westerner falter. With large strides, Ivan moved along as the bell of the church clanged midday, less one hour. He gazed toward the old building, the place where all of his family past and present were wedded and buried; it must have been a magnificent church once, he thought sadly. Everything in his life was once full of hope, but the hopes of these communities, flung far and away, had become only despair.

The bells hardly echoed over the land; their aged and worn parts refused to sound out any anticipation or expectancy. He walked on past the school. It also had a forlorn aspect about it. Yes, once it was something important, Ivan thought again, as he dodged a large tract of half-frozen water. The breeze rose stealthily, and this found him pulling his clothing more closely about him. He walked on, buoyed with the expectation of his meeting with Alena. Snowflakes slithered from the trees and floated down upon him like dancing ballerinas putting on a special show for him.

Ivan Petrovich heard the bells once more. The noise of the bell would have called the people out in the golden days, but, alas there were too few who listened with eagerness or cared or who even believed anymore. Years of communism, of lies and betrayal, and lost causes, had broken their spirit. With little to look forward to except bitter memories, and with young families moving to the west, nobody cared any more, even for their own sakes.

The makeshift snowplough, an ancient army vehicle with a blade attached, pushed past him, making a bigger mess of the way he was going. Lonely snowflakes jostled for a spot on his nose, he tightened his scarf once again and kept moving. He passed the cemetery which was deep under the snow, the headstones jutting out, as though they were grey stumps floating in a sea of glittering white brine. He glanced as he went on his way thinking of the remains of those lying below, whose souls having long gone to their appointed destinies.

The wind grew stronger and so did the resolve of Ivan Petrovich, his whole being focused on his mission, his thoughts were centred on Alena. It was thirty-five degrees below freezing, yet he knew that in a few weeks time it would reach over minus fifty degrees. Then, not even a bird would attempt to fly, or it would drop from the heavens like a stone.

Ivan knew the landscape and the risks. He was familiar with the potholes, the undulations of the road, every tree and hillock on the route. Although he was aware of all of this, he knew there were possibilities that a tragedy could always occur. He understood the dangers of stepping into a puddle which would allow the perishing cold to enter his footwear and freeze him to the very marrow of his bones.

Snow could precipitate at any time; wind may gather strength without warning, while sleet and rain could fall in copious quantities. He kept to the road, mindful of the ice holes and the shrubbery jutting out from the sides of the road.

As he walked on, the road's direction changed and the wind was at his left side, not directly in front of him as before. He was thankful that the wind would be at his back on the return journey. He arrived at the heavily wooded section of his trip where the kiss of winter had removed the foliage, and the defrocked trees stood and waved their branches in a type of salute, wishing him well or harm. Which, he did not know; nor did he ponder on it.

Ivan Petrovich walked on. The clouds were bleak and solemn, grey and intimidating, and appeared to fairly lap the treetops as snowflakes in ever increasing numbers tumbled to greet the young Russian travelling to meet his beloved. Again, he tightened his flimsy apparel. He was walking as fast as he could, hoping that the canvas coverings on his boots were holding the water out. Although he was feeling the frigid air on his face, his feet were still warmish. For this, he was thankful. He tramped onwards boldly as he passed the old abandoned factories, their forms appearing as spectres of white against grim shadows forsaken by idealists fleeing not from an army in pursuit, but to a better life in the west, or abroad, to relatives in far away places.

A steeple tower appeared away in the distance. This he discerned was his destination, only one hour to go, he said to himself. This is the home of Alena Saranova, whom he had courted for as long as he could remember. For nine years, every Saturday, Ivan walked to her village and then home again, never complaining; always cheerful. How could a man so in love dare to complain? Russians were born into hardship after all, as were the Tartars and Cossacks before them. But that was once, and that once was gone forever.

The town was someway off as he came across an abandoned Jewish shetl, a small impoverished hamlet long emptied when the inhabitants sought the will of God and then emigrated to Israel; or wherever a benevolent relative could support them. They were wise he thought, getting out when they could; but us - oh well someday I suppose.

The town seemed to move quickly toward him and his body forgot the extreme cold as he strode at a fast pace. At the outskirts of the town, he noticed a few mortals trudging around, and paying no attention to the young person moving among them, as they searched for the necessities of life in the freezing temperature of the day. Ivan knew this small place sought comfort from their misfortunes through slivervitch, schnapps, and any other remedy that could keep the freezing cold away and numb the brain. So it is, and so it will always be.

This town is a shell of its past, Glasnost and Perestroika passing them by, a community hovering on the brink of nothingness. Ivan was now only five hundred metres from Alena's house, his heart pounding, his countenance lifted with expectancy and confidence.

Ivan Petrovich was standing at the front door now, raising his hand to announce his arrival. He knocks just as the door is flung open. Once again, he beholds the woman he has cherished for so long.

Alena Saranova smiled at him, the only way an impoverished thirty-year-old Russian could in these circumstances. She motioned him to enter, taking his ragged mittens and his scarf. He did not remove his coat, for even in the presence of a heated room, the chill of the sub-Arctic was pressing through the shallow walls threatening to penetrate them with every thrust of wind.

She reached for his hand. He extended it and she shook it, and smiled at him then led him a few steps to an old-fashioned lounge chair, beckoning him to be seated. She did not sit nor speak during this early part of his visit. Her mother spoke first, welcoming him to their humble home. Then turning to the fireplace, she reached for the teapot which was lodged on the top of the samovar, from which she poured a small portion of black tea into a chipped, white china cup. During this ritual, there was silence. The mother handed him the drink as Alena passed the sugar cubes and a spoon. In other times, the Cossacks would place the cubes in their mouths and let the tea flow through them but this was now, and Ivan stirred his tea and sipped slowly as he glanced around him.

After the tea was consumed, Ivan took a small parcel from the left hand pocket of his coat, handed it to the mother, explaining that it was all his mother could proffer, and to please accept it with her love.

The older woman opened the newspaper wrapping to find, to her delight, a piece of uncooked chicken, a thigh.

She looked to Ivan with warmth, saying this would enhance the soup at lunch. She knew he would be staying to enjoy the meal with them, and the newspaper was the first she had seen in a month so it was a double blessing. Ivan was pleased. He turned to Alena, who suddenly became animated and gushed out the news of the week to him, then offered him another cup of tea which he accepted with a smile, and bowed his head respectfully. Ivan turned toward the fire casting his eyes over the ancient being who was attending to the soup - Alena's grandmother, who was gnarled and wrinkled with decades of severe living conditions. She never uttered a word throughout any of Ivan's visits, but he did not see this as a rebuttal, but just an old lady keeping her own counsel. Russia was a country, endowed with millions of grandmothers who have witnessed a generation disappear. Maybe they will never be in the presence of their offspring again. This is a time of great bitterness for the old.

Alena stood up suddenly from where she was sitting, moved to the end of the lounge, and seated herself next to Ivan. She looked into his eyes with both love and despair, they had been courting for many years but neither could extricate themselves from their immediate family predicaments. Both had the older women to care for. Ivan was the only male member of either family left in the district. Regardless, they would continue this courtship for a very long time into the future, unless a miracle was to come upon them that would allow them to have a life of their own.

Ivan wished he could take her out from this place for just a short while today, but the weather was brutal and was just not worth the risk. Lunchtime arrived. The soup was tendered to Ivan along with a small piece of black bread, which was as hard as a brick and the only way to eat was to dip it in the watery soup.

Time passed quickly for Ivan and Alena. It was imperative that he return home before dark to avoid the possibility of a perilous trip, for no one would go out to look for him if he failed to reach home in such treacherous conditions.

Ivan stood up to take his leave. The mother bade him god-speed, cursed the incumbent government, and then requested him to convey her good wishes to his mother.

Alena accompanied Ivan to the door, assisting him to set his scarf and returned the mittens. She embraced him in front of the older woman. This was the first time she had done that. Ivan was not only surprised but he was thrilled at her uninhibited approach. She opened the door; he hastily said his farewells and turned out towards the direction of the road for his return journey. He quickly looked back, then waved to her as she was about to close the door. She returned his gesture, and then disappeared into the warmth of the dwelling as Ivan moved briskly along the walkway that led to the road.

Ivan Petrovich turned his collar up, placed his mittened hands into his old coat and commenced to stretch his legs for home .The lonely church bell tolled as he set out for his village, his stride increased in tempo as his spirit lifted by the events of the day. The snow was falling gently, the wind at his back, and the sky dismal and foreboding.

Ivan Petrovich strode smartly along the way, deep in the knowledge that come what may, he would go through the next six days waiting with great eagerness for Saturday to arrive again. He would do it all again, so great was his love for Alena Saranova.

THE WAY OF
THINGS

He told me about the tragedy, how it came about, and the end result as we sat on Mc Ginty's veranda. I was shocked at first, but soon realised how people in authority thought in those days. It was the mindset of the times - the eighteen nineties. Misfortune had befallen the mailman, William Gifford during a very hot and sultry summer, with heavy downpours making life very difficult for the folk in his neck of the woods.

The storyteller was an old bloke, well into his eighties. He was the local history guru and people out there swear that his recollection of the events was spot on. The old man was a skin trader, and in those days, both rabbit and foxes out numbered the humans profusely. A quick way to earn cash was by contracting to cull these creatures. But foxes brought a higher bounty than rabbits. The old man gleaned his information from many sources around the traps and the record sheets as well. He remembered reading the letter after the unfortunate event, so here is his version. As I said, it was a sticky summer and the watercourses were all running a banker.

Bill Gifford saddled his pony and went to collect the mail before riding to Bongall Creek homestead. The day was a stinker, at its worst, the type of humidity that drove people to be miserable, to cursing and to irritability. As he rode out he would have felt the danger of travelling in such boggy conditions, but he was an experienced bushman and his work was on the trail. The incessant rain in the past weeks had made the land impossible to work, and forced those with grazing stock to move their animals to higher ground.

William Gifford was a robust sort of chap. He needed to be, to withstand the pressures of the bush along with the isolation. He'd ridden the mail run ever since it was introduced to the area. He had intended to farm the land but found the going tough. However, his good wife suggested to him to apply for the new service that was being initiated throughout the country. So he did, and started the only general store for miles around. According to the locals, he and Henrietta made a good fist of it. He was a soul who possessed integrity and ingenuity, and was always welcome at any home in the district. It seemed that little could stem his enthusiasm and zeal for the profession he had undertaken with the Postmaster Generals Department.

On that fateful day, Bill rode his faithful horse, a bay of several years to the main creek crossing. He had a string of horses and alternated them and also employed their strength to bring supplies from the larger towns. Sometimes his wife or an employee travelled to collect the merchandise. He did not ford the water at the usual spot but rode south, past his family's favourite picnic spot to the shallower, but rocky track which often was more accessible. Here he met and chatted with Eddie Fowler the drover before crossing to head for Bongall.

Then, it's recorded, that Bill spent a few minutes in conversation with two stockmen who were attempting to move a herd of cattle to higher ground, about a mile before he reached the homestead,. Bill made the pickup at Bongall cattle station, exchanged pleasantries and departed at about the time he always did heading back to the store. That was the last time anyone saw him alive.

His horse found its way home that night. The rain bucketed down as the search party was assembled and went off to find the mailman. The women stayed to prepare food and to give comfort to Bill's wife and family. They retrieved the body well down the creek a few days later. The mailbag was intact and the authorities notified. Gloom settled over the district as word spread of the death of the good and faithful servant.

The events of those tragic few days were swallowed up in the tales of the bush over time, lost among those of further tragedies of fire, flood and drought that followed for over half a century of progressive settlement in the area.

Years later a diligent individual unearthed a document regarding the tragic death of William Gifford. It caused great consternation and anger throughout the area. The communiqué sent to the Governor by a menial clerk, read as follows …

"In February this year there was a misadventure at Cooper's Crossing near Bongall homestead. It appears a mailman was drowned attempting to cross a swollen waterway, however, I am pleased to advise that the mail was saved intact."

THE COIN OF
CONTENTMENT

The habit of tossing the coin came from his grandfather, an old Irish immigrant, who in his latter years moved in with Will's mum and Will's two sisters Kate and Mary. The ancient, grisly- and gnarled-faced man, his countenance weather worn through being at sea for more than half his eighty years, was the teller of tales and folklore that stretched one's imagination, as he carelessly handled the truth.

Will often watched with utter awe, as the antiquated specimen he knew only as 'Pop', conjured looks of wonderment from his listeners. "Tell us another Joe."

He would, and another plus another half dozen. Will would sit silently and endure the repetition day after day, noting how the stories took on a different slant each time they were told. He took a mental note of how the narrative became more manipulated, depending on the makeup of Pop's audience.

However, it was not so much the storytelling but a strange habit of the old sea dog that arrested Will's attention time and time again. Before he made a move of any sort, Pop would retrieve a coin from his baggy trousers, place it in his right hand then flick it with his thumb into the air, catch it on the way down in his left palm, then examine the result. According to the fall of the coin, he would often scratch his balding cranium or clap his hands, mumble to himself then proceed to do whatever he was going to do before the coin was tossed. This strange action of his grandfather puzzled Will no end.

Will's mum always looked across at her father with a wry smile, knowing him and his antics only too well, but wisely kept her counsel. Pop was well respected in the pubs around the Eastern Suburbs of Sydney, but some did not hang so close to his yarns, because they knew and understood the embellishments undertaken by the old sailor. They did however share Will's amusement at the antics with the coin. But they never inquired as to the reason for the strange behaviour.

Will turned fourteen on the day his grandfather was placed in a nursing home. The old guy was frail but had not lost his marbles at this point. Will, with his mother, and accompanied by his two younger sisters, drove to the facility to assist the elderly man to settle in. They brought Will's birthday cake along to celebrate in his company. Pop asked his daughter if Will could stay a while and be picked up a little later. She agreed. Pop instructed the lad to pull up a chair and sit close to him. When the boy was near and attentive, Pop pulled the coin from his pocket, spinning it around, flipping and catching it as he always did in the past.

"Son, I want you to take this here lucky silver coin, and follow my fortunate ways

by using it. Every time you are ready to make a decision in your future, do what you've seen me do. Flip the coin. It'll make your decision making easy and take the pressure off your mind. I've had this shiny piece for nigh on sixty-five years. It served me well. But remember the trick. Whenever you need to make up your mind about anything, then toss for it. Only move forward when the heads come up."

"That's the trick! Heads - you go ahead with the thing you wish to achieve! No heads - no go!" He looked at the boy, then at the coin with a wily grin, flicked the silver piece again, and then handed it to the young man.

Will left his grandfather that afternoon pleased as punch. Never in his wildest dreams did he contemplate being the recipient of such a valuable piece of his grandfather's heritage. When his mother collected him, he told her what her father had done. She concealed her inner apprehension and outwardly commended her dad for considering Will for an heirloom, which was always a part of him. In fact, she couldn't remember ever seeing her father without it, flicking, tossing it, guffawing over it. It also occurred to her that she had never been allowed to handle it.

Now as time progressed in the life of Will O'Hagen, his 'coin of contentment' controlled his every move. People around him were amazed at the young man's progress in his ambitions. Will and his lucky coin never parted company, that is, not until he was appointed to the Bar as a Barrister in law. Will's judgment was, some would say, uncanny. Sifting through his cases and placing his clients into winning positions, he became the most sort-after 'legal eagle' in the land.

Then as most fairy stories have it, a nasty blow befell Will. He misplaced his coin. Just like his grandfather before him, he had had a magnificent run with his coin of contentment. Now, faced with the toughest decision of his career that morning, 'promptly at ten' as the presiding judge had coined it, he was frantic.

Somehow, somewhere, he had lost his faithful servant the coin. Every day since he inherited the coin it had controlled his world. Decisions about this, determinations about that, so on and so forth. He had been resolute, firm, determined, and above all, he always showed a positive attitude.

But now his shoulders were slumped, his demeanour perplexed, and his mind fragmented. How would he cope without his backstop, his most valued asset?

Try as he may, it was to no avail, it was lost. He didn't front for his meal at the 'Lawyers Bar' as usual. He had never missed a meal there for years and he was always the life of the party with lots of budding 'fledgling eagles' to rub shoulders with.

He went back to his home, to his aging mother and straight to his bedroom. His mother, hearing his approach but not his customary greeting, did what all caring mums would do. She went to his room to find out what ailed him. As she neared his door, she heard a sound that she hadn't heard since he was a little lad. He was crying. Sobbing in fact, and beating his pillow. She knocked on the door then entered his room. He was sitting on the bed with his hands pressed across his face, a grown man crying, his face pressed into his chubby hands.

She spoke quietly to him, like only mothers can do, when calming a storm in youngsters, although he was not young anymore. He told her what was tearing him apart. He had lost his 'safety blanket', and he was devastated. The woman sat by her son knowing well that this was to happen at some time. It had happened to her father once, and her mother found the lost item, just in time to save her husband from one of the worst drinking binges of his life. She left Will shortly after, then returning with a drink and in a quiet manner, she said.

"Is this what you had lost?" She held the coin up towards him. He took it from her hand and embracing her, said, "You have saved my life."

She sat there looking at her only son, pleased with him, but at the same time saddened, that his attitude to decisions in life, that same attitude of her father's, was totally controlled by the coin that had taken control of him. She would never tell him that when she found the coin on the floor of the bathroom, it was the first time she had ever held it in her life. She would never disclose to a living soul that, when she examined the coin of contentment, she discovered its secret. It was engraved "HEADS" on both sides.

BONFIRES

Who would have thought that the days of the bonfires on the fifth of November would disappear from sight, just to be a fleeting memory of ones' youthful days? There is little wonder that they did cease however, when one traces the antics of small boys, enthralled with and armed with lethal implements of encased gunpowder, wicks and matches.

However, the bonfires did disappear, much to the chagrin of the Quarry St Gang of Old Alderton. There were four urchins in the group; Henri Wilks, Joey Abra, Ken Flynn and the runt of the pack, Billy Lightfoot.

The boys were all aged eleven when they inaugurated their secret club and set out to terrorise the neighbourhood, especially the elder members of the town. Guy Fawke's intentions to blow up a few Englishmen and their parliament gave inspiration for these youngsters to dream up a few stints of their own.

Being able to elude detection was high on their agenda when they planned their capers. For instance, rendering a few letterboxes inoperable by means of a quantity of double bungers stuffed in them, and then setting them off as the kids scurried for cover in South St, had the locals up in arms. But the boys held their ground and maintained their innocence under heavy questioning from the authorities.

Billy's dad was Shire President and organized the town bonfire each year, so Billy boasted to his class mates that he would have the privilege to set off the bonfire. He was always telling the gang that this year he would be 'it' but he never got the chance. This is what happened, according to one of the boys.

The lads had a marvellous hideout. The local sawmill accumulated a huge mound of sawdust over the years which covered nearly half an acre. The gang managed to burrow their way into a section at the end, away from the mill and made it their clandestine abode.

On weekends, and virtually any time they were available to liaise with each other, that's where they rendezvoused. The other hide-away they had found, was at Minton's farm and not far from the sawmill. Cyprus trees surrounded it, and the boys found it a comfortable retreat. High in the branches of one tree they built a shelter, enough to enable them to weather the elements and have a discreet meeting place.

Early October each year, the fireworks started to appear in the shops around town. The hardware store packed a large array of the much sought after devices. Their showcase window was decked out with just about everything a budding Guy Fawkes would require. Lay-bys were accepted by the management to assure that everyone got their share.

One morning that October, just after the milkman disappeared off the scene, Henri Wilks, armed with a large magnifying glass that he had purloined from the science room at school, headed for the hardware store with minor criminal intent in mind. The sun was shining directly at the showcase window of the shop.

Henri, applying skills he had acquired from torturing ants and other creeping things on their mounds, went to work to set the skyrockets and roulette wheels ablaze. He succeeded in launching three rockets before people began appearing on the streets, lost his nerve and scarpered home. Unfortunately, he was observed by the postmistress, a prude. After that, his father gave him the thrashing of his life.

Ken Flynn, in the spirit of the time, stole his dad's gun belt for devious purposes. He placed four-penny bungers in the loops usually used for cartridges and set off around the neighbourhood. In one evening's escapade he single-handedly terrorised thirty letter boxes, by tying three of the large bungers together for maximum collateral damage. He wasn't caught however, but a great amount of suspicion was floating around the community that he was one of the culprits.

Whilst all sorts of pranks were being played out, the serious task of building the fifth of November bonfire in the centre of the showgrounds had begun. Billy's father was the one who organised the dads and lads to move great quantities of combustible material to the site, then erect a frame to build the bonfire around. The energy expended in building a monstrosity that would eventually be destroyed, was amazing. No one cared; they just wanted the biggest blaze ever.

As that work was proceeding along with due diligence, Joey Abra had a plan of his own. The plan had filtered through his fertile brain once or twice in the past few months.

A derelict gent who hovered around the village from time to time was back in the vicinity. He had taken up residence in the main park, on a bench, under a huge spreading oak tree which assisted in keeping most of the frost and rain off his person. It also made him generally less conspicuous.

On this particular day after school, Joey kept a close watch on the man. Then when he was satisfied that the derelict had dozed off after draining the contents of a one gallon flagon of 'five bob bombo', he moved in.

The sleeping man had a pair of socks on, without any toe coverings attached to them. Joey carefully slid penny bungers between each toe. He had, beforehand, lengthened some of the wicks and shortened others so the fireworks would blast off simultaneously. Joey lit them and ran to the nearest hide-away - an elm tree opposite, to watch.

The poor being reacted by leaping up and off the seat cursing and grabbing at his lower limbs in a half stupor. Joey couldn't find a laugh within himself. What he thought was fun didn't finish up that way, it was so undignified. He waited a while, and then disappeared back to his home.

Being able to get to the shops early to reserve ones individual selection of fireworks was difficult, as the store owners would, rightly so, allow the grown ups to purchase the goods. This didn't please the kids, as their parents often procrastinated until only the 'rubbish' was left in the stores.

One way the kids overcame this impediment to their impending enjoyment, was to raise as much cash as they could, then ask an older boy to purchase fireworks on their behalf. Thus they were able to perpetrate their 'dirty deeds' on the public well before the big day.

Collecting soft drink bottles, then selling them to the shops, which paid a bounty for the returns, was the normal thing to do. If they were still short of cash, they would steal over the shop fences under cover of darkness, take the bottles back and sell them the next day to another unsuspecting merchant at the other end of town.

With the big day not far away, the boys had an immediate problem to overcome. Billy had become morose and difficult to work with, so much so that the other three wished to expel him from their ranks.

It all began a couple of years before with Billy. It was his desire to light the town bonfire, but every year his mother intervened and Billy's wish seemed be doomed, never to eventuate and he became, as the boys would say, a pain in the 'proverbial'.

The usual annual ritual for the opening of the bonfire evening was in the hands of the incumbent Shire President, who was in this instant, Billy's father. The townsfolk with their offspring in tow complete with selected weapons, double bungers, sky rockets, Catherine wheels, all types of sparklers, jumping jacks, and for the docile at heart, roman fountains, were moving towards the showgrounds.

Adorned in their oldest attire, in case of burn holes in their clothes, they stepped into the showgrounds precinct, eyeing greedily the stalls laden with food, drink and any paraphernalia that could be passed on to gullible, unsuspected party-goers. Parent's warnings and threats about behaviour would go unheeded as the children ran rampant through the throng of revellers.

Then came the moment that all assembled were waiting for. Precisely at the stroke of seven pm, the Shire President and his wife, with Billy eagerly following behind them, stepped onto the dais to carry out the much awaited deed; the igniting of the bonfire. Then there would be three hours of mayhem to follow.

The huge stack was ready for the matches. Billy's dad, with Billy right beside him, went forward to strike the match. Billy pleaded with his dad to let him do it. His dad looked at Billy, then Billy's mother. Just as one thought Billy was to take the match and assist his dad, his mother seized Billy by the arm and escorted him to the back of the crowd.

Billy was humiliated, for he had boasted to his classmates that he would set the heap ablaze, but this was not to be. He yelled and squirmed and played up for a bit, then, resigned to his fate, settled down, after his mother had swept him off balance with a swift whack to his backside.

Nobody crossed Mrs Lightfoot. She wore the pants in that household. She never smiled and when she opened her mouth she displayed a set of crooked teeth that resembled that of a chainsaw. She had a ferocious temper to boot.

Once the fire was lit and well ablaze and the real partying was under way, Billy was temporarily forgotten. The young boys set out to chase the girls to toss fireworks at them, and to generally be a nuisance until they were hauled home by their weary parents.

No one had noticed that Billy had slipped away from the gathering, much less his parents, who were too busy playing 'mine host' to the multitudes. There was to be a display by the local volunteer fire brigade who were there for good measure any way.

An hour or so had passed since the lighting. The fire was still burning brightly as the sound of the fire sirens split the night air, which, to all gathered, meant the display was to get under way. However, to the crowd's utter amazement, the two fire tenders with full compliment of firemen and women turned full circle and exited the grounds. People were agog with anticipation. What's happening?

Many people seemed to be attracted to the excitement of following the fire trucks and ran after the vehicles as if possessed. The fire fighting machinery appeared to be stationary outside the Lightfoot family residence. The double storey building, the pride of its owners and envy of the town, was well ablaze. It appeared that nothing could be salvaged from the inferno.

A huge crowd had gathered, all awestruck by this experience. The three gang boys stood watching as the police sergeant was attending to Billy who was sitting on the grass outside his former home. He was holding an empty four gallon drum which had the words on the side 'Kerosene'.

HAND OF FATE

The rope flew over the branch of the tree. Both ends were now dangling a few feet from the ground. Two muscular wrists sporting strong dirtied hands seized the rope ends. A slip knot was made on one end and the other end of the rope was pushed through it and the knot slid up until the rope was firmly fastened to the branch. The young man grinned. So far so good he thought to himself.

He began to pull himself up toward the limb. When he reached it, he grabbed hold a piece of wood which had been leaning against the tree trunk and slowly lifted it to the limb. There were two limbs forking out. The piece of loose timber was straddled across them which made a position to sit on. He repeated the task and soon a second lump of wood was positioned beside the other.

"That will keep me from the dogs." the boy muttered to himself. He went down the rope again and retrieved a bundle wrapped in a grey blanket.

The dusk had merged into night with a cool breeze floating through the tree, as the man unwrapped the motley blanket and put the assortment of goods carefully beside him on the makeshift hide away floor. Se stuffed his pockets with oddments he had collected for his journey. Night life was waking around him. Nocturnal bird calls and the rustle of the grasses made him suddenly feel the loneliness and apprehension of the hour.

He listened intently for the sound of the dogs. No such sound came. He wrapped the blanket around himself covering his back and chest, but his legs would stay cold all night.

Still, there was no sound of dogs yelping about the place. It won't be long, he thought before a group of searchers would be upon the area, hunting for him. All was so still and peaceful. It was too still and peaceful for his liking. He shifted a little as the cramped manner in which he had placed himself at the beginning was now creating soreness in his back. Then he heard the crackling of twigs not far from his tree. He shut his eyes pull he blanket over his head and sat as still as he could. Yes, they were here by the sound of it.

He couldn't ascertain how many by listening; but there seemed to be at least three by the direction from which the movements were coming from.

Somebody was whispering then another replied but he could not make out the content of the conversation. He sat and sweated in the cold night air-sweated for his freedom. His life now depended on his diligence and restraint. He had to outsit the adversary hoping that they would move on and leave him to see the night out and then to escape to another place in the dawn. The rustling of the undergrowth continued for some time, vexing him no end. After what seemed an eternity there was no noise at all. He waited another short while then slowly slid down the rope to stretch his legs for awhile.

Satisfied that they had left the area he walked furtively around the tree. Not even a bird stirred at this time. Soon he retuned to his hideout and settled down to sleep the rest of the night away. He drifted off for a short time awoke, then drifted again. He woke with a start when a shrill voice not far from the tree was calling to someone apparently on the other side of the tree. He understood what was happening the two men were gathering wood to light a camp fire. They apparently planned to stay near the tree until sunrise at least he fathomed by the backchat. He became terribly frightened. He would be in grave danger if he made one wrong move, sneezed or coughed; both which were possible in the cool night air.

He was at his wits end

A coyote howled in the distant, reminding him that other creatures out there in the desert could railroad his plans as well. He shivered, pulled the blanket tighter around him and sat uncomfortably in the tree waiting the next drama.

The men below seemed to have settled down around their fire. Then another variable reared its ugly head. Smoke from the fire drifted upward and passed through the tree top, engulfing his hideout with a pungent odour. He was becoming deeply distressed covering his eyes which were watering and keeping his mouth tightly closed. The breeze swung away slightly and eased his plight after an indeterminable time, much to his relief.

Then a strange thing happened. The two men doused the fire, walked away into the darkness. Soon the sound of horses hoof beats strayed into the night air. The young man literally leaped down from the tree limb and went to the fireplace to see if any food or drink was left. During their haste to depart they had just kicked at the embers and carelessly let the dying fire and left to burn it self out. There were no remnants left so he would have to wait until his luck changed, when ever that would be.

Disconsolately he dragged himself back up to the limb and perched his weary body on the logs that straddled the limbs. Tucking up in the blanket tried to get a little sleep as the night would soon move into the early predawn facet and there would be a lot of walking tomorrow. No sleep would come- his mind wandered here and there among the events of the past weeks leading up to this sorry state of affairs he now found himself in.

His name was Clive Robbins, orphan and roustabout on Hector Climas, cattle property. That was until three years ago. During a drunken brawl in a far away saloon he caused grievous injuries to a man he did not even know. These careless actions lead the hard nosed magistrate to place him away in jail for eight long years. Three years had passed being an exemplary inmate he was then sent to Hoxton Springs, a low security institution for the duration of his custodial sentence. That was three months ago.

Robbins couldn't hack the restrained life and the prison culture and had spent all of his time plotting a way out. He well knew the consequences of his actions if he were caught. He saw the results of those who had failed before him. What he didn't under stand was how easy his escape was earlier today. He did not expect to make the break so soon but a series of unexplained events gave him an opportunity too good to pass up.

Firstly, the warden, Sam Gaites sent him to assist the cook, a Chinaman named Win Yu. Win Yu was employed to feed the inmates and the staff and was given 'low risk' men as helpers from day to day. Any problems and the prisoner went back to the rock heap or to work in the prisons vegetable patch, which was overseen by a rigorous taskmaster named Alby Sawyer. Sawyer was a brutal man with a temper to match. He kept his charges working the full day with little rest. The staff and the prisoners alike hated Alby Sawyer.

Warden Gaites was a quietly spoken man and treated all the men under him with respect. However if anyone would put a foot wrong intentionally, a load of bricks would tumble down upon him.

The young man remembered that that morning the Saddler, Yates from Spring Waters arrived to collect some dilapidated horse gear. Robbins overheard the warden say that only two horses would be available till the saddler returned the repaired gear. That meant that less people would be able to follow after him. At the same time as the saddler arrived, the cook complained of a stomach ailment and left the prisoner to his own devices, whilst he went out to find the prison doctor.

As all this was happening the young man noticed that there was no guard at the gate as the time the saddler was leaving. He decided to make a dash for it.

The saddler had placed the leather work that he was taking back to town, on the buckboard, in a heap, and then climbed aboard the driver's seat. The seat had a back rest which was about three feet high and it obscured the driver's vision to the rear of the wagon. This was perfect for the prisoner who, after grabbing the blanket which belonged to Win Yu, and a few pieces of cooked meat as well and high-tailed it to the wagon, which was by then nearing the gate of the prison.

The warden was out of site, arguing with an officer, so Robbins leapt into the back of the wagon without being spotted by Mr Yates who was preoccupied with the horses. The disappearing act worked to a treat.

An hour down the track Robbins saw the clump of trees and decided to slip out as the wagon turned towards the town, which was still twenty miles away. He managed to disengage himself and left the unsuspecting driver and ran to the cover of the bushes. Things happened so fast that he did not really think it all through but acted on instinct and raw nerve. He still could not believe his good luck.

There was along way to go and with little food and an aching body plus lack of sleep his task was foreboding to say the least.

Young Robbins finally drifted off to sleep. The air was still and cold the first trappings of dawn were present. A night owl broke the silence

He woke with a start as the purplish tinges of morning pushed the night aside. He was dreadfully tired, dishevelled and extremely hungry.

Here in the desert country he had no means of foraging for food. In his haste to escape the prison he did not consider this matter. Now in the predicament that he was in, the folly of his ways had come home to roost. Down from the tree he dropped after untying the rope and collecting the blanket, his only possessions in life.

He had no idea of time or direction he had just run out climbed into the wagon then leapt from the cart finishing up a tree in the middle of nowhere.

He shivered in the cool morning air, feeling depressed and lethargic. He wrapped the blanket into a manageable size, tied the rope around it and stared at the panorama around him. The wooded area to his back faced a wide plain in his front on his left a rocky outcrop of a mesa was the predominant vista. At his right side a copse of brush trees a feature of the area and blocked his view. It seemed deep and uninviting.

He contemplated his plight a while then, with a renewed purpose he turned to move away from the treed area which he held his night vigil.

A twig snapped.

Something fell at his feet.

A voice spoke softly. He cringed, but didn't look around. He knew the voice. He bent down and retrieved the object at his feet, a water pouch; he opened the lid and started to drink its contents. Then he stopped and slowly turned to see if he was correct. Yes he was right.

The form of the warden Gaites stood about ten paces away. He was holding a double barrelled gun of some sort, but he was not pointing it at the escaped convict as Robbins expected he would. It was pointing at the ground. Robbins took another gulp of the water then eyeballed the man, with fear in his eyes. The other stood stock still, a wry expression on his face. The boy closed the lid on the water container then bent slowly reached out and placed it on a rock.

The prisoner's eyes were insolently fixed onto his captor's face. Minutes had elapsed since he had heard the twig snap neither had attempted to commence a dialogue. Warden Gaites walked toward the place where Robbins stood, bent down and collected the empty water vessel without looking in the direction of the lad, although he passed within a few feet of him.

"Well, what is the next move on your agenda young fella?" the lawman said quietly as he fastened the water bottle onto his belt.

"Back to jail I suppose," the younger replied in a trembling voice.

"What made you do a silly thing like that son?"

"I was thinkin' of gettin' a new start and the next five years is so far off, sir."

"Lifes tough boy but you gotter hang in and take the good with the bad."

Then the warden smiled and sat down on a felled tree trunk then motioned to the other to sit down too.

"Did it ever occur to you that certain things happened in a strange sequence yesterday?"

"I thought it weird but sometimes things go like that I suppose."

The older man smiled at the other then said "I've had my eye on you son, ever since you came to this here penitentiary. You see you suit my purpose."

He then pulled out a tobacco pipe and tapped it on the log whist he continued talking. "You can get on the horse I have brought for you." pointing to the copse beyond. "Or you can do a favour for me and get away to where it's comparatively safe. There a little employment on offer. If you like the challenge, that is."

He started to stoke the pipe not looking at the man.

Robbins, not sure what to make of this commentary, stuttered his reply. "Course I don't want to go back to prison, but I don't understand what you mean. But I'll do any thin' to keep me out of jail."

"Good son, then this is the deal, take it or leave it. But if one word ever reaches my ear that you have told another living soul of this conversation I'll personally bury you so deep that the fires of hell will be in the next chamber."

"What do you want of me?" The boy stammered."

"Past that mesa there." he pointed. "Its twenty or so miles to the Montana border and there's no extradition treaty. So you're safe if you keep your nose clean. Get my drift? Then a couple of miles to the town of Crowded Springs, after that another thirty miles to Pleasant Sands. That's where you're going.

You see, my kid sister Maybelle lives several miles on the Forked Canyon road. She is a widder with two young ones, but no help, and winter will see her with out wood and feed, so that's where you come in, so to speak."

The warden went on. "You are to find my sister and tell her that you will cut her a mountain of wood and dig the biggest vegetable patch known to mankind. Now that's an easy task to save your hide ain't it kid?" he lit the pipe took a puff or two and stared at the other man. "Is it a deal boy or shall I truss you up like a Thanksgiving turkey, drag your hide back to the barracks then let my counterpart Alby Sawyer spend a time with you?"

Robbins, at the very thought of the warden's threat to place him under Sawyer was the catalyst.

He couldn't move faster if his pants were on fire. "I'll go. It would be a pleasure to help your family Mr Gaites, yes sir, but it is a long walk."

"I'll get you to the border and then you are on your own. But remember kid you'll be housed in the barn and just your keep. No extras, no frills understand?"

The young man nodded. The warden motioned for him to follow him to the wooded spot. When they reached the clearing, there were two horses. Gaites mounted one and then assisted the other to the saddle of the second horse. Then young Robbins realized that these were the only saddles left at the compound as rest had gone with Yates-so no one could leave the compound except Gaites and an extra.

Gaites dispatched the man at the border, returned to the prison declaring that the prisoner had eluded him. The escapee must have made it to the border. Then he wrote the same account in his journal just for the record.

Warden Gaites poured himself a whisky, thought of his ever loving sister- a girl he really detested. "That should get the whinging bitch off my back." he thought to himself as he puffed steadily on his pipe.

CROWDED NIGHT
UPON A HILL

The moon was shrouded by wintry clouds on the high plateau. Pine and cypress trees were bending under the influence of a strong breeze putting the policeman's expectations at risk. The smell of the pine trees caused him to fantasize that the fragrance was that of Sandra his latest girlfriend. She was probably watching television in the comfortable surrounds of her lounge, he thought, while he was witnessing the end of winter from a lofty plantation. His expectations were high but he needed the breaks that would come from diligent planning and careful monitoring of the criminals who were cleverly controlling their illicit trade.

His assistants Croad and Beecroft had worked tirelessly to bring this operation to an end. Unlike the 'movie cops' they were very human and needed to get home to their respective families once the arrests were made.

Paul Mondale had banked on this evening to conclude the charade he had been apart of for the past months. That now may not be the case, as he required a peaceful night weather-wise to execute his warrant and of course the plane with the cash and drugs had to land unhindered. Furthermore all of the team of criminals he had been trailing for months needed to be here as well.

He was conscious all the time that he would have rather been with Sandra his girlfriend than sitting undignified in a tree in the middle of nowhere. He chanced being injured or worse, things one tries to not think of while working at this type of job. Sandra had put the hard word on him recently to give up the force and pursue a 'decent job' but he was enjoying his role. At some point of time she and he would have to make allowances with each other, or else part company. He agonised over this, because he really loved her and he felt that she in turn loved him.

Realising that the timing was the most important part of his assault on these criminals, he met with the others two hours before. They were concealed their vehicles in an adjacent wooded area with surveillance set up from both sides of the woods. They were in fact in a forest plantation owned and operated by forestry workers for a private sawmill.

Except for re-afforestation or thinning of the trees for milling it was an area seldom visited. The owner had given the law authorities full run of the place, with keys and maps to assist in the planning and executing the operation. The two main forests were separated by a strip of cleared land approximately a kilometre long and four hundred metres wide. Plenty of room to land a plane- an area had been cleared regularly to provide a buffer in case of fire.

The wind seemed to be abating and the sky was now less covered in cloud. He sensed something was afoot. It was. There was the sound of a vehicle approaching the property. He quickly climbed on to the next branch a few metres from where he was originally seated. The noise was closer so he flashed his torch in a Morse Code S.O.S signal to two other comrades perched farther away in a tree across the paddock.

They, like him were anxious to finish the surveillance and apprehend the gang who had led them a merry dance for eight months. Tying loose ends together and gathering all the facts on these people had been a trying matter for his team of three.

Their boss wanted quick results but always pleaded financial constraints as the reason for no extra support and occasionally threatening to circumvent the whole operation. They knew that this would not happen as the section to which he belonged needed a boost of confidence and those in the know backed this operation to do just that.

The policeman shifted his body so he could be in a good position to observe proceedings and make judgements, and also keep an eye on his partners some where over the way. He was so pleased that he wore coveralls as the sap was sticky and he was continually wiping his hands on his clothes.

The plane carrying the loot, and possibly more saleable illicit goods, was according to his snout, due to arrive at eight thirty and it was close to eight now. The van, which he thought he heard a few minutes before, was now pulling up near a clump of trees.

The van disgorged three hefty men when it came to a halt and the motor ceased. The first one to step out, the driver, was walking around giving the place a cursory glance. Satisfied that all was clear, he begun to direct the other two to empty the contents of the back of the van. Paul could from his vantage point see that they were moving what seemed like lanterns for the guidance of the aeroplane to land safely.

He noted that there were quite a number of lamps being lit by one of the men to disperse them around the makeshift drome. When they had completed the task they commenced to carry the illuminated lanterns along the paddock, arranging them in straight lines. After what seemed to be an eternity they completed the task. A row of green lights were obviously for the centre of the runway with two rows of red for the sides. Two blue lanterns were placed at the end to signal a stopping point for the aircraft.

Paul felt uneasy, to say the least, knowing that the variables in a job like this were always unpredictable and no matter how well planned could fragment and completely fall apart through the slightest bit of misfortune or oversight. There could even be other unknown players about.

He could still smell the fragrance wafting in the air similar to the one which Sandra wore. Cleopatra One was her favourite perfume. His imagination was running wild he mused to himself as he watched the unsuspecting men preparing for the arrival of the aircraft.

Patience was going to be the key the key to success he thought. So he sat and waited, and thought of his plan of action. As he kept silent watch on the proceedings below, he thought of the events of the past few.

He was pleased that his girl Sandra had such a fertile mind. She became involved in his case after listening to his deliberations each night. He had shared confidences with her although was normally taboo with members of law enforcement agencies and their families and relatives.

But Paul felt that as they would be together for along time, she would be more supportive if she was included in the picture. Getting some feed back from her may not be such a bad idea in the long run.

There was still no sign of the moon but patches of sky appeared in the dusky setting. The wind had abated.

The three men pulled a box from the van, put it on the ground, opened the top and withdrew some small objects. Paul watched through his night glasses. Weapons and ammunition were kept under lock and key by a very thoughtful string puller- and a safety conscious one at that. A cautious crook no doubt. A chill went through Paul as he realised the implications. His team had only a revolver each and would appear to be undermanned to say the least.

The men were apparently in no hurry to put ammo in their weapons. This gave him an idea. Surprise; utter surprise would be to his advantage. To take the three before the weapons were armed. At this, he made a decision. As he was a fair distance from his assistants, he sent text messages on his phone to his counterparts. The text read. "I am grabbing them now. Come in as soon as I blow the whistle."

Whilst planning the op, he thought that the whistle was a great idea, seeing that the trees and shrubbery would have muffled most other sound. Good old fashioned stuff.

He took the moment. Climbing down from the tree and using the darkness to his advantage he came within six metres of the trio before declaring himself. The three were so surprised that they fell flat on the ground when ordered to do so. After the whistle blew, the two policemen arrived and handcuffed the three men who were still lying on the ground. Paul's two assistants ordered the three to walk to the bushes nearest to where the van was parked.

Paul pressed the three for information and found that they were only lackeys with 'needs to know' information only. He cautioned them to remain silent or suffer the consequences. They were taken into the wooded area and handcuffed to each other around a tree trunk for the duration. They were clearly not a happy lot, but resigned to their fate.

Then the policemen checked the vehicle, disabling it for the time being, then, moved the weaponry to a safe place behind one of the trees, being careful to check that the guns were empty and the firing pins removed. All of the ammunition was locked safely in the box which they placed back in the van.

The drone of the plane became evident and one of the policemen went to take position to flag the pilot down. The information of how this was to be carried out, was revealed to them previously by interrogation of the man who had the job. Paul could swear that he could smell that familiar perfume again.

The plane hovered, and then came into land without incident on to the runway, taxiing to a halt at the blue lights. The policemen seized the pilot and his one cohort and placed them handcuffed together, in the back of the van.

'It's getting a little crowded up here. If the phones would work we could call the boss to come up." one of the lawmen said.

Paul didn't want his superintendent to interfere with his show so ignored the remarks. The head of his section had arrived the evening before, but decided that the dirty work would be left to his subordinates. Mondale instructed Beecroft to back the van up close to the nearest tree so that if its occupants got lucky couldn't get out of it.

This done, the police squad set to work on the plane, going over it thoroughly. They found a considerable number of packages containing sizable amounts of ecstasy tablets 'ice' and an assortment of hard cocaine mixes which they were familiar but not expert. There would be others to sort that out later.

Paul Mondale asked Croad to fetch the police van, put the drugs in the back and secure them.

Beecroft, who was still sniffing in and around the plane, called his boss. A large canvas bag lodged under the seat of the craft was pulled out by Beecroft. It was the money he was expecting, and lots of it. Mondale remarked that it had all been 'too easy.' The police van arrived in due course and Croad placed the drugs into it. As he bent to place the canvas money bag into the van he was stopped in his tracks by an unexpected event.

A loud voice through what seemed to be a microphone and boomed over the scene. The muffled voice called on the police to fall to the ground. The stunned lawmen hesitated. A second voice called from another direction affirming the first. The policemen realising that they may be in mortal danger if they did not obey the instructions, dropped immediately to the earth.

The first voice told them to lay face down and keep their eyes closed. A sound off feet walking slowly in the grass gave them the first contact with their hijackers. Each policeman felt the gloved hand of one of their captors pull their guns phones and handcuffs from their belts. Their belts were removed. They soon found themselves in a similar predicament as the criminals in the forest, all shackled together and grossly uncomfortable and humiliated. The person who hovered around the men did not utter a single syllable during the entire time that the assault took place.

The loudspeaker which seemed to be situated in the woods to the left made all the requests. The phantom walking around and about them prodded each of the policemen checking for keys and any thing that might be used to alert attention. Satisfied that the policemen were without any supportive gear, it walked stealthily away in the direction of the right side of the woods. Only the slight rustle of grass gave an indication of another being was hovering nearby. The night was still and chilly; not an animal groan or bird call troubled the silence.

After what appeared to be a light year of time Paul Mondale felt safe to move a muscle and utter a word. He tried to sit up but his attempt was impeded by the cuffs. He spoke quietly. "It seems as though they have gone. Let's see what we can make out of this mess. At least we are not tied to the tree. Come to think of it, the last group didn't ask about the other five. Weird isn't it?' Then together the three policemen tried to stand up. It was a matter in getting each to move carefully at the same time.

Paul shackled to his team-mates, walked slowly around the scene, trying to see what may have been left or taken by the assailants. The van was still where it was placed against the tree. They checked and found the three assistant crims still attached together 'ring- a – rosy' fashion. Paul and his entourage stumbled about for a short while trying to put two and two together, but the sums just never added up. The money was gone, the five crooks intact, unable to go anywhere, and the phantom few had disappeared into thin air.

There was on piece of good fortune- the police van was not interfered with- an oversight which gave the police a little comfort out of a night of high drama. Paul's thoughts of earlier that evening came back to him. "It was too easy."

Croad hampered by the cuffs and the other two, managed to radio to the low country, explain only what was necessary for the station staff to know, and requested back up and medical assistance. The latter was a precaution only as they did not have any idea the condition the three anchored around the tree, or the van- dwellers health condition was at this stage.

Mondale also did not want to let the five know about the hijack, as this would no doubt buoy them up and weaken the police position. It was to be harder for him facing his peers and answering their queries. That could leave more continuing doubts rather than immediate clear answers.

Paul Mondale sat down on the grass, still latched to his workmates, awaiting release by the country police sergeant who would reach him in an hour or so. Besides being hungry and disappointed he was very angry.

Beecroft, not the world's most articulate thinker or arranger of diplomatic speeches, came up with the simplistic notion that maybe this was an inside job. He espoused the theory that someone close to the gang was responsible for the hijacking proceedings and perhaps those in the van and those tied to the tree were caught in 'the line of fire' so to speak. The senior cop Mondale took in what the younger had said, and felt it was a fair way for him to evaluate the situation, given the mess that he was in.

Mondale felt much to his chagrin, that there was a simple answer to the whole debacle and that he was the dummy.

His brain told him as he sat in the paddock on the high plateau, that a small female, laced with the fragrance he had smelt had done him like a dinner, taking the cash and maybe his professional career. He remembered clearly now as he sat on the grass in his current undignified position, that was she approached him on that first day they met, and not the other way around. She was first to talk of the case, he had not introduced the subject. At that time, he was besotted with her and dropped his guard.

It was perhaps his fate to be sucked by the fragrance, but not to see the wood from the trees.

ADVERSARIAL MANAGEMENT

Frank Delaney stepped off the porch to attend to the duties of the day. He was pleased that his conscientious worker Bill Couch offered to take the calves to the saleyards. He had commenced the days work at five o'clock that morning. He was now able to go to the local school to witness the children's show his two children were taking part in. It was going to be a pleasant day - a typical Western Victorian spring day - cool early, then sunny and warm.

As he bent to retrieve a piece of paper which was floating around the yard, something caught his attention. The distraction was over at the stall where the calves were to be taken from that morning. By impulse born of years of experience, Frank walked briskly toward the spot which caught his eye. As he reached the place which took his attention, he stopped in his tracks. The movement he spied was a lonely calf, obviously missed by the farm worker. Frank was furious, but resolved that he would take the animal to the saleyards as quickly as possible so as not to miss the kids' school show. It was eight thirty, and he had two hours to get the job done.

Frank went to the garage and backed his car to the stall. He opened the boot of his EH Holden sedan, and placed a chaff bag on the floor, lifted the small calf onto it and then closed the boot lid. He briskly strode to the house to inform his wife. She told him to hurry back and not to be late.

He left the property with haste and arrived at the saleyards just in time to have the calf placed with the rest of his lot. Just as he was lifting the calf out of the boot, he felt a tap on his left shoulder. Turning his head to see who was trying to arrest his attention, he found himself staring at the grim countenance of Hazel Crunchbowl, officer of the

Respect the Animals Society. She was a large-boned formidable female. This was a woman whose stern look could cower any man at ten paces - a woman that no man dared cross, except at his own peril.

"What do you mean by conveying an unfortunate animal in the boot of your car? That's an intolerable situation. That calf could have suffocated. I will vigorously pursue you in the courts Mister Delaney sir." She turned away and strutted off to fill out a report and gloat over the predicament she had placed the farmer in. Delaney, for his part, was furious and drove home in a foul mood in time to visit the school for the show.

As soon as he arrived home from the school he rang the Department of Agriculture's local Veterinary Officer whom he had known for some time. He had always been on friendly terms with David Patricks. "David I've run into a problem. Is there any rule against carrying a calf in the boot of your car?"

"I've never heard of that before Frank. Why do you ask?" The farmer related the morning's events to the vet who reacted by saying to him, "I'll come out once I've finished my commitments here and we'll talk, okay? But I've had another thought. Before I leave, I'll phone our Legal Department and run it past them before I call out to see you. The Vet immediately called the solicitor and explained the matter - to which the solicitor replied "Be aware that if a person is convicted of cruelty to an animal it is a criminal offence and that person becomes a convicted criminal. It's a serious matter. Such a conviction could be a slur on his character for life. I would advise him to defend the case as strongly as possible." Then the lawyer outlined some ways that a defence may be worked out. After David Patricks had thanked the solicitor and satisfied himself that his desk was clear for the time being, he left his office and set out for the Delaney farm.

David explained the Solicitor's views and a plan of action they could pursue. After lunch, the Vet asked Delaney to allow him to lay in the boot of the car while Delaney drove him to the sale yards. Delaney agreed, and when they reached the sale yards, the Vet said that in his opinion that there was no problem for a person to be in the confined space. There was enough air and space for a large person, and therefore there could not be any problems for a small calf. In fact, the Vet said that it was probably better to carry a tiny calf in the boot than on the back of a truck or open trailer.

Several weeks later, the court case of the Respect of Animals Society versus Francis Mulcahy Delaney was in full swing. The legal people for the Society outlined the case against Delaney in emotive descriptive language - portraying Delaney as a callous, thoughtless, cruel and careless individual. Hazel Crunchbowl sat at the back of the court puffed up, chest out like a turkey gloating, surrounded by the ten members of the local Chapter of the Society.

The solicitor defending Delaney called the government Vet to the stand and asked him to describe his trip in Delaney's car. In a hushed Court, the animal Doctor did so graphically. As soon as the Vet completed his testimony, the defending solicitor approached the bench and with arms folded tightly across his chest, submitted that in view of the overwhelming description of the comfortable condition of the car journey from a reputable citizen that the case be dismissed.

The magistrate agreed, but with a qualification that rocked the farmers in the court. He said "I dismiss this case on the evidence submitted, but I would not like this outcome to be taken as a precedent for judging any future cases of this nature."

People milled around Delaney, congratulating him on the decision. One farmer standing back from the crowd said, "Hey fellas! Hold your horses a minute. The 'beak' virtually said that Crunchbowl could charge any of us any time in the future with similar silly matters, and that he would consider every case on its merits. Any one of us could be standing here like Frank was today with a big legal bill to prove our innocence. She's got public funding, and she can make our lives a misery depending on her whim at any time. Next time one of us could finish up in the clink or have a criminal conviction on our records for life." That was a party stopper.

The farmers were incensed.

"Let's go to the pub and talk about it." All agreed and went off in the direction of the pub. The club lounge of the pub had the atmosphere of a funeral wake once the group of farmers and their wives sat down. The publican, sensing the angst, shouted a round on the house and left the people to their discussions.

"Why don't we call Joe Lightfingers our MP. He'll know what to do." someone said, "Why not a top legal firm?" another said. "That would cost us heaps. Their fees are thousands a day." The Delaneys' lawyer replied. He was there at the request of Frank Delaney who had become melancholy over the situation.

Out of the group came a quiet bolt from the blue. Frank Davies, a dairy farmer from the other side of the district who'd been silent till now, spoke. Known for his cool approach and smart thinking, he broke into the conversation.

"Friends, we can deal with this predicament in a simple way." He paused and gazed around and noted that he had the group's undivided attention. He continued. "As I see it, there are only a dozen or so members of the local Chapter of the Respect for Animals Society. Old Crunchbowl announced to the press yesterday that she was rallying support for new members before the annual meeting next month. She said that she will try harder now that the court has left the matter in a no-win situation for us. It's a power thing. Can't you see what it's all about. So why don't we fight our antagonist with her own weapons – namely, join her society. I am sure we could swamp them and not have to face this situation again." He stopped speaking to an applause that could be heard all around the pub. "Let's go home and meet at a later date to formulate a strategy: but in the meantime let's keep it quiet. We don't want to be rumbled at this stage." They all agreed and dispersed.

Miss Tilley Lampshade was the proprietor of a small enterprise known as 'Tilley's Collectables.' She was also the able secretary of the Respect for Animals Society. She, on the request of the president of the society, called the annual general meeting for Saturday the first of October. The membership cut-off date would be one week earlier at five pm, at Tilley's shop. At precisely 4.30 pm on the final day of the membership drive, a shadow appeared on the verandah of Tilley's Collectables. It belonged to Frank Davies, who was appointed by the farmers to collect names for the memberships.

He quietly entered the store with a large brown paper envelope tucked under his arm and a wry smile on his face. "Good afternoon Miss Tilley", he said. She looked surprised to see him in the building. Usually it was his wife Angela who purchased goods from her. "What can I assist you with Mr Davies?" "It's the Society's annual meeting next week and I've some new membership applications for you." The old lady blushed. "That's good of you. Since the court case we've had an influx of new members - another four would you believe. That makes our membership sixteen. It could actually pass twenty with yours."

"I am sure it will, Miss Lampshade." He handed her the envelope "Heres another forty- eight members' applications for you to process. You were quite right when you said that the court case stirred up new member applications.

"But I'll never write the receipts out before the time." she protested.

"That's alright Miss. I have made out a list of all the new members, and a place for you to sign that you received the applications and the money. See. I've brought forty-eight pounds in single notes. She was flustered, and nodded. Frank noted that she was clearly disappointed, realising that her society was being hijacked without any recourse.

At the annual general meeting of the Society, honest, hard-working farmers and their families filled the President, Vice President, Treasurer and Public Relations Officer positions, along with those of the ten committee members. They retained Tilley as secretary.

Miss Crunchbowl wasn't pushed. She jumped, fair out of the district. Rumour has it that she is employed by a city car firm sewing car mats for car boots.

OLD HABITS DIE HARD

Mike kicked at the campfire to dislodge a half-burnt log. As the disturbed log moved closer to the centre of the fire, the embers rose upward displaying an array of red and golden radiance. The mystical glow on each face had a different effect on those who were gathered around the heat. Some had rosy faces and others were just silhouettes. The flickering light cast eerie, shadowy spectres around and about. Conversations had moved from this to that and came to a pause as Eddie returned with a bucket of water from the Jordan River, which was fifty metres from the campsite, to heat for washing the dishes. The friends were sipping tea or coffee whilst staring into the fire, watching the disrupted embers spiralling skyward.

Gaby had finished her drink of milky, sugarless tea. She then handed the part empty cup to Eddie, who had offered to wash the dirty utensils that evening. Eddie's first remark, when he took the cup was that Gaby never finished drinking the contents of her cups, always leaving an amount in the bottom. Taking her turn at fidgeting with the fire, she quickly replied that it was her mother who had instigated the habit. It was so that the tea leaves and the dregs stayed at the bottom of the cup. He nodded and said that that was fine when one uses tea leaves, but today tea bags leave practically no debris. "Well, it's a habit I just have not yet broken" she retorted. She bent down to place a piece of pitta bread on the fork for toasting. "Anyway you've probably got a habit or two to break away from".

Preparing to toss extra old branch on the fire, Mike let out a shrill laugh then entered the discussion. His face reddened from the warmth of the glowing timber. He remarked that he had similar challenge with an old habit. He found an old rock and perched on it, away from the heat, then explained his habit. For many years, he would find himself standing on the toilet seat in bathroom, and drying himself with a towel after having a shower. It perplexed him no end. He had never noticed any one else doing this same thing. So he asked his mother about it. She explained to him that as a child and being rather tiny, she would lift him onto the toilet seat to dry him. She had been unaware that he carried the habit into his teens and beyond. He very swiftly dispensed with the practice after that.

The sweets were passed around as darkness crept in under the hills. The large samovar was heating the water for the next round of tea. Gaby, a little taken back about being criticised over the cup saw an opportunity to fire a broadside at Eddie.   "Look at you, a grown man eating your sweets with a teaspoon. My kids don't even do that." She grinned in satisfaction at her perception. "Oh that. I've always done that. You see as a boy, in a family of eleven, small portions were order of the day. Even minute amounts would be all we would get if any one else sat down with the family." He tossed another piece of wood on the smouldering heap, fiddling with another and sending a shower of sparks heavenwards. He then continued.

"To drag out the minute amounts of tasty treats for the longest possible enjoyment, I used the smallest spoon I could find, and I still do." He sat back and licked the spoon while Mike attended the fire again.

A lone jackal cried in the distant Golan Heights, briefly cutting into the stillness of the night. A helicopter returning to its base, passed overhead, and then disappeared into the distance.

Hillary was dreamily poking at the fire while half listening to the dialogue. She turned to the three who were seated together, and contributed something that certainly put an end to this particular line of chatter. "When I prepare my husbands clothes for the laundry, I carefully check the pockets. He has a habit, not a bad one, but one born of bitter memory. He leaves pieces of bread in his pockets every single day. During each meal, he mechanically collects a morsel of bread, and then puts it in his pocket absent-mindedly. You see, Youpie's mum always put a piece of bread in his pocket just in case there was no further food whilst they were incarcerated in a German Concentration Camp."

OPPOSITE ENDS

The Under Twelve football game had concluded about an hour previously, which allowed the three lads to saunter home at their leisure. Their parents no doubt were already embroiled in the 'local derby' at the show grounds along the way, some two miles distant. The eleven-year olds found plenty to amuse themselves with, as they strolled by the creek, which meandered through the town. The waterway was heaven on earth to such youngsters who regularly pounded the same beat to and from their respective schools.

"Dad and mum won't be home tonight till pretty late" Joseph Monaghan quipped as he bent to adjust the laces on his black leather shoes. "Mum said that we have to go to Mass on our own, as dad would be the worse for wear if his team wins this arvo." The second boy, Joseph's brother, Michael, groaned at the thought. Michael was a year younger than Joseph, who had just attained twelve but through a quirk in the rules, was able to play in the Under Twelves. This seemed to always favour the Catholics, who bred an abundance of offspring. You could be forgiven for thinking it was their way of "stacking" the football teams.

The third boy tagging along was not a Catholic like most of the lads in the district, nor was he a Protestant. Eli was something else, but he did not quite know what. His dad, who owned the General Drapery store in the village, often went to Melbourne, to attend religious functions. It was a long journey, so he would only occasionally take his family. His mum taught him and his brother David at home on matters regarding their family religion, and about their beliefs. He attended the town public school for convenience rather than preference, for they were an isolated Jewish family.

"What about coming to Mass with us Eli?" Joseph prompted, knowing full well that he could, and most likely would, get into hot water with the priest, for bringing a stranger to church unannounced. "Don't know whether I should, Joe" Eli replied with reservation. By then, they were close to their favourite haunt, the large cypress tree at the end of Doherty's Lane. The immediate conversation dissipated. The race to be the first to climb the great tree became the centre of their thoughts and actions for the time being.

The winter afternoon was turning quickly to dusk; the sombre sky was pinking, as the urchins gave their precious tree back to nature, and scurried towards the centre of town. At Carmichael Ave, they usually parted company with Eli. However, this time he lingered on. He suggested, "Let us get some fish and chips". So they pooled their meagre resources and sent Mike to purchase the food, while they sat on the old men's seat in Parry Park chattering about everything and nothing much at all. When the fish and chips arrived, the weather was turning to wind and drizzle, which prompted Joe to suggest that they adjourn to the church, where it would at least be warm and dry.

Without too much resistance from Eli, that is just what they did. As they approached the huge brown brick construction, Eli had fears that this was not for him; but he was eleven and everything was an adventure even if it was quirky. The massive green doors were directly in front of them, as the rain commenced its heavy precipitation. The trio entered the building and slipped into the back pew more or less unnoticed, except for Mr O'Shannasy who was the church 'gatekeeper'. She was the one who, by her own authority, controlled proceedings around the church, much to the annoyance of the other members. The kids sat on the floor and the newspaper enveloping the fish and chips was removed. Eli cast his eyes around for a minute totally awestruck to what his vision was taking in.

Eli asked Mike, "What is that statue?" "Its Mary, Mother of God" he replied. "Oh! But God didn't have a mother, like Adam, my mum told me" Eli retorted.

"The priest can tell you about if you want" Mike interjected. Then he noticed the windows were curved at the top, and all had coloured glass panels, figured with images. It was the number of apparitions adorning the windows that caused him to utter a sigh. "Who are they?" "They are the twelve Apostles, and they always live there." "Oh!"

The Mass was being conducted in the front of the church. Eli noted that nobody sat down the back. He placed his hand on the back of the pew, then levered himself into a position to take in a view of the proceedings. "Who's the old man in purple?" "That's the bishop. He comes from somewhere else and bosses the priests and the nuns" Joe explained. Eli was fascinated with all of the icons and statues that adorned the interior of the church. "What's the man tied up on that mast?" "He's Jesus." "Cheeses? Why is he looking so uncomfortable?" "He's dead. They nailed him there before I was born" Mike told Eli, who shuddered and felt it was time to leave.

However, before he said a word, something began to happen up the front of the church. Eli asked Joe what it was about, and Joe whispered that they were having a parish meeting, and that the Bishop was telling the congregation to dig deep for enough money to purchase new cars for the priest and the nuns. The fish and chips had disappeared and Mike stuffed the leftover paper into a nook under the seat, out of sight. After a short while, there was a slight to do. A man came to the back of the vast room, pulled the door closed, frowned at the three, then trudged up the aisle and disappeared into the company gathered.

Eli asked Joe what was going on. The other explained that the bishop was not happy with the pledging of money for the cars, so he shut the doors and was sending the pledge cards around again. The congregation will leave when the money was promised in full. Eli then inquired as to the funny language they used in the mass. "Latin", was the older boys reply. "It was what the Pope spoke," he offered. With that, Eli responded that he thought Julius Caesar spoke Latin. Joe said that if he lived in Rome, he probably did. "Yes he did", thought Eli. Then the old man came and opened the green doors, allowing the boys to escape and bound off home.

Eli was in deep thought as he hurried home. Catholics are strange people. A dead man hanging around and people living in windows - it sure was creepy. And nuns! I'll ask mum what they are.

MISADVENTURE

The Marshalling Yard was akin to a massive cemetery. Skeletons of days long gone, littered the landscape, casting eerie shadows along the lonely steel tracks in the early morning light. A solitary figure was perched on the steps of a carriage. The carriage was standing alone looking gloomy and desolate. Men would come and rescue it from it's abandonment, They would attach it to two throbbing machines, then, after coupling it to twenty or so squeaky carriages, take it on another journey to the city, or maybe to a place far away, somewhere down the line. The man on the steps stood up and stretched his arms. He waved to a person, another male, who was approaching him from the furthermost section of the rail yard.

Carl Wilson, Crime Writer for The Star, and, as an author under pseudonym for many crime magazines, strutted toward his friend manning the empty carriage. He moved with agility, that of a tiger with prey in sight. He could smell a juicy story from a long way off. He knew that when Jon Harris called him onto a scene, the going was getting tough. Jon needed an extra set of eyes that saw, not as a policeman would, but from totally independent viewpoint. This assistance worked both ways. His help reaped its own rewards. Carl gave advice which helped the detective immensely, whilst Jon passed over tit bits of information that aided the writer to collate a source bank for his profession.

"This is a curious matter", the detective said, after they had exchanged pleasantries. Carl, leaning against the wall of the carriage, being careful not to get his clothes in contact with the sooty metal, stroked his chin in a thoughtful manner, and spoke as to himself, "I read the report you sent me. According to it, the dead man was hit on the right side of his head. He took a pretty hefty knock. No doubt about that." He extracted a sheet of paper from his trouser pocket, looked at it for a few seconds and continued to add to his opening remarks. "What I would like you to do is to arrange to have this Guard's Van attached to the next goods train that passes this station. Let me know, so I can be here to observe." He paused, folded the paper and put it in his pocket.

Jon Harris gazed at his friend and replied, "I can organise that request. We could use the eight twenty this morning. Anything else you need Carl?"

He removed the phone from his brief case and flicked the cover open. "No, that will do for now. Has the weapon been found, or a motive established for the death?"

"'Not at this point. However, the Coroner is calling loud and often, for some sort of finality on the matter." Jon sighed.

He was visibly fatigued and frustrated at the slow progress he was making. Llewellyn Davis, a well respected, diligent worker for the Rail Authority, was travelling as Guard on the Thirty Eight Class train seven days ago.

"Failing to show up for his dinner that evening, his wife called the Station Master, then the Police. Davis' body was found on the floor of the Guards Van. It appears to me, that someone had been lying in wait for him and struck him as he boarded the train. As the train was a long one this particular morning, the driver could not have seen the deceased step aboard the carriage. The Station Master said that he signalled the driver to move off when he was satisfied that Mr Davis was safely aboard. The other employees were not near the scene. Most were working several kilometres away, and all checked out squeaky-clean. The guy's wallet and other personal items were found intact. He was wearing standard issue uniform, supplied by the Railway Authority. He has left a widow and a couple of grown up kids. The young ones live interstate and have been notified. There are also Railway Dicks cruising around."

Harris asked Carl to nose around a little, which was carte blanche for a big snoop.

"Mind if I see the wife and the Station Master?" Carl inquired.

"Go for your life", said Jon Harris, as one of the Rail Detectives sauntered toward them. Carl winked at Jon and excused himself, leaving his mate to field the questions from the company rep. He found his car, checked one of the addresses Harris gave him, switched on the engine and left the crime scene. He motored to the suburb where the widow resided, and headed for the street. He located number forty-two without much trouble.

The home was modestly appointed, both outside and in. Mrs Davis was a short plump homely, kind faced lady, the stereotype of one that belongs to women's groups, or a hospital auxiliary. Carl used his usual charm, being ushered inside by the grieving woman. She kept the place spick and span with every thing in its place, and it had the hallmarks of someone with a mania for cleanliness. He introduced himself, gave his condolences at first, then asked her a few simple questions - simple for her, but important to him. "Mrs Davis, did your husband have reason to be in a hurry on that day. Also did he show any ill ease the night before, or on that day, such as impatience or anger?"

She was trembling slightly, but Carl pitied the woman having to answer questions from the police, her husband's former employer's blood hounds, now himself. She was making tea, and offered him some, which he accepted. "My husband was a punctual man and very loyal to the Authority. He never enjoyed being late, but that day, the battery played up in the car and he was about five minutes late I think. He was to go on the early train but it was slightly late. You see, he telephoned the station and advised them that he was on his way." She poured the tea and went on, "He didn't say goodbye, as he usually did, but I understood he mustn't keep his trains from their timetable" she said, almost bitterly.

That was all he got from her, but a clue dropped into his fertile brain, as he noted a magazine rack, brim with certain folders. He left her at the front door, she was muttering about the flower garden. He then went to the station, to observe the shunting and massing of the goods cars. He made it by a couple of minutes or so. Carl stood next to the Station Master, while the train staff went through the motions. During the next few minutes, he carefully noted the movements of the workers and the Master's activities. Just as the cars where being coupled together, the phone rang in the office. The Station Master dropped what he was doing, moving quickly, went to answer the telephone. Carl noted the time. Before the man returned to the platform, the convoy was joined together, ready to go.

Carl watched intently, as the re-enactment of the fatal day was carried out He wrote down pertinent events as he saw them and noted where the Station Master stood, in order to signal the driver. Then Carl thanked the Master and left the area. He needed a few small pieces of information .He called Harris and asked him to perform a duty for him and then a second favour. Jon Harris had the information within three hours. He called Carl and arranged a meeting at a convenient coffee shop.

"I checked on the betting shop, which you requested, the Station Master, Guard and the Driver. All three are regular patrons. Question one answered. Two, the train time tables were rescheduled four weeks ago, placing the early train departure one and a half hours earlier than previous. Three, The Master placed bets for himself, and on behalf of several work mates, regularly. That a little helpful?" Jon Harris grinned. "Yes". Carl slapped him on the back and added, "We would make a good team. You could pull the strings and I could write the scripts to our liking." He ordered a drink and Jon ordered one too. When the waiter moved out of hearing, he let go his thoughts.

"This is how I see it, from an outsider's perspective. The Roster was re-aligned a couple of months ago. The boss in this case had no say in it as it was a head office directive, if that's the correct word. The Station Master always placed his and his staff mate's bets at eight o'clock each morning. Being an autonomous station to a point, the Master played by his own rules. You see I think it was like this. The Station Master was to put the bets on with the betting shop at eight fifteen as usual, which was also the train's departure time. The train was slightly late that morning."

"He was used to the punctuality of the guard and the driver. So when the phone rang, he abandoned the train, went in and placed the bets, leaving the other two to go on their way. However, he did not anticipate that the guard would be running to catch the train. The driver did not know that the guard was late, so pulled the train out on the dot of eight-thirty". Carl paused then said. "Get my drift, Jon. This is a classic case of dereliction of duty; one that could cost a few heads, after the Coroner gets his pound of flesh. So the guard jumps to ride the van, but the carriage is rolling, not fast, but swiftly enough to catch the man, as he foolishly leaps to get aboard." He sipped his coffee, and then continued.

"The Station Master is right for dismissal, if the Coroner's report fingers him. Yes, it's not a murder. It is a case of neglect and the unfortunate man was hit by the door-jamb, as he made the carriage (not an assailant) and hits the floor, dead. Maybe, the blow didn't do all the damage, but sufficient. How the driver hadn't had contact with the man, is one mystery to sort out. I guess that they ran such a loose ship, that the answer is a simple one". Harris interjected, by raising a couple of questions. "Why was the body not found until the wife called the police, and who normally does the paperwork for these guys, which allows them to cheat so easy." He looked at Carl, knowing the answers, but testing him a little. "That's easy, the Station Master covers their tracks; all of the time. The next move is to sit with the Rail Authority Investigators, to explain this theory, that is, only after your men have filed their report. I think the Station Master is in a lot of hot water if the Coroner fingers him.

It's not murder; it's just a case of criminal neglect and misadventure."

THE MAIL MUST
GET THROUGH

The early morning sunlight cast striped shadows across the stables as Harry prepared his horse for the arduous task of collecting the area mail bag. He was to retrieve it from the other side of the swollen Junction River. Tropical downpours over the past days left a swell in the local tributaries, thus cutting all connection with the outside world. Trouble with a capital 'T' was ahead for Harry Barton, but it was par for the course for him- and Molly, his wife and business partner.

It was always lodged in the back of Harry's mind that some day it might be impossible to carry out the Post Master General's decree that. 'The mail must get through,' regardless of the perils encountered by the delivery men.

There were countless tales of men who fell into misadventure delivering the mail in the outback. The authorities held firm in their belief that the King's Mail was more important than the loss or injury to any menial functionary.

The horse was prepared and ready for the task. The return mailbag was strapped securely along side the saddle and water container were also in their appropriate places. If the weather held it was possible that the water flow could be moderate he should be back by sunset.

Molly was a very capable manager –a caring and loving soul who was able to supervise the store, deal with the multiple tasks of bush business and family life. Harry and Molly moved here twenty years ago. They tried to farm and graze the land and had moderate success. Then a new opportunity arose, the store and post office was commenced, and they won the first tender; that was fifteen years ago. The shire had fifty or so farms scattered and some land development workers, plus the lime mine at Walton creek which employed fifty people. The river separated the eastern hills from the western plains and travel between the two regions was severely hampered when it rained heavily.

Harry's dislike of the way the national mail business was run was well known. He was not shy as to write to his employers from time to time and vent his anger and offer solutions but it all fell on deaf ears.

He reached the river after two hours of steady riding, with intermittent rest stops for the steed and to roll a cigarette as well. The river was running a banker-a foot of water above the flood line marker. The current was strong but not unassailable according to Harry's reckoning. He worked out the spot where he would enter the water. He tied the horse to a tree. Stripped to the waist he gripped the mailbag, holding it above his head, and then started the precarious crossing of the fast moving stream. He reached the opposite bank without any difficulty. He removed the incoming mailbag from the limb of the tree that was always used for this purpose, and put the outward mail bag in its place.

The return journey was to be a strenuous affair. He planned his approach to the water expecting to be taken downstream by the current but did not worry as he would walk back to where the horse was tethered once he crossed.

He stepped into the water and started his way across. He was intent at keeping the bag dry and was facing down steam, unaware of the objects that were floating toward him as he swam.

Near the centre of the river he was hit by a tree limb, which was moving at a rapid pace; it slammed into his back. The impact forced him to let go of the mailbag which caught onto the limb. He swam after the limb and thankfully for him, it hit the embankment and was held by a tree jutting out into the water. Normally it would be on dry ground. He swam and floated until he finally touched the edge of the bank which was under water. With the aid of a young branch he dragged himself and the partially wet bag to the land. He crawled on the muddy earth until he managed to reach a patch of grass; although it was wet it was safe. He lay exhausted and thought of the possibility of both he and the mail not making it.

It was late in the evening when the mailman arrived at the post office store. Dragging his weary and sagging frame through the door of his house, which was part of the store building, he threw the mailbag on to the sorting table. Molly handed him a mug of tea assisted him to a comfortable chair. She could see by the state he was in that he had had a very close encounter. She had seen this before and held back her comment; as it would not alter anything. All she managed to say in a concerned way was. "Well, I hope it was worthwhile, dear."

After he had eaten his meal and had recovered sufficiently he opened the mailbag and spilt the contents onto the table.

There was only one letter.

It was addressed to him.

It was from the G.P.O. Head Office.

He opened the letter, and stared at its content without comment to his wife.

Harry Barton handed the letter to his wife, who after reading it threw it on the table and burst into tears.

THE LETTER READ…

"Dear Sir, I wish to bring to your attention a matter of grave concern to this establishment. It has been brought to my attention that you have been forwarding your weekly returns to the second floor of this building instead of the fourth floor. Will you please be more diligent in the future; you may be not realising the great inconvenience you cause this office, having to send one of the staff to the fourth floor each week."

DOUBLE
DISTRACTION

Sam Weeler surveyed the large house with the eye of a true professional – the eye of a professional burglar with intent to lift its most precious contents. But Sam was in for a surprise that night. He also cast an eye over it as an engineer. Every avenue of entry and escape were taken into consideration before he went over the fence later that evening. Sam, in fact, was an engineer!

There were many variables to consider; the weather, neighbours, pets, alarms, unexpected arrivals and so on. Sam was a stickler for detail; the more planning with contingencies in place the better executed would be the job at hand.

He had to study his choice of victim, examine the most effective way to enter and leave, assess risks and evaluate the worthiness of the task he had in mind.

Firstly, he knew that the inhabitants were abroad, an alarm system was non-existent and a good deal of jewellery was to be purloined for the successful burglar.

Sam was a loner. He had been successfully slowing down the wealth creation efforts of a good number of citizens in the past several years. He had certain inside knowledge because of his position with his family of architects and engineers. Being privy to old records and plans, he was able to carefully handpick his prey. He also knew some of them personally.

Business is business and Sam knew most of those he robbed did not report their tax avoidance indulgences.

It was a pleasant scene before him - a three-story home with wrought iron surrounding, wrap-around balconies on the first and second floors, verandas beneath. Bay windows on either side balanced the aspect.

The house reminded Sam of a cotton mansion in South Carolina he and his Dad visited when he was about 16 years old. There was a large staircase in the centre; this he knew that from having visited the house during its construction several years previously.

The expansive lawns held circular garden beds with all manner of shrubs and flowers adorning the extensive landscape. The owners were financiers and no expense was spared to elaborately dress up the home, both within and without.

Sam checked his watch. Time for a bite to eat! Never burgle on a full stomach. It's a bit like sport. Beforehand there are the nerves; during - the adrenalin; and at the end, loads of concentration. That would be the order of the night.

He retreated from the bus shelter under which he carried out his surveillance and crossed the park to his sports car. His mind was absorbed with all manner of questions. Occasionally doubts surfaced in most planning, but in this vocation, they were more exceptions than the rule.

He found a quiet restaurant and dined by himself, scribbling over several white serviettes the floor plans and several other ideas as they came to mind.

He left the restaurant and drove around for a while, clearing his thoughts.

Sam had planned to just open the front gate and proceed straight to the house's front door. There were verandas on the front and sides.

The sensor lights would pose little problem as he had been watching the house for the past few nights. Occasionally the light would go on, but mainly because the wind was strong or a stray cat passed by. None of these episodes produced reactions from either neighbour's house, which were both a fair distance away. The blocks of land were large and each house was set in the centre of their particular grounds.

Sam didn't wait till it was after midnight, as movie burglars seem to do. He believed that the later before midnight one carried out his job the quieter the landscape was. And whilst vehicles and music emanated from around about, sounds that may come from his enterprise would have a chance to pass unnoticed. The night was now overcast. No rain was forecast but it was a chilly July evening which kept more people inside than usual. Only the hardy, and a few forced by necessity, would venture out.

He opened the main gate and stealthily moved along the concrete path, moving between the rows of medium-sized shrubs, stopping to check his next movement, taking a few more steps, then pausing. This was repeated until he reached the veranda. The sensor light was set more for convenience to callers than for security, so Sam kept well to the left of the path. At the veranda's edge, he hugged the wall and stepped under the overhang into comparative darkness.

few butterflies spun in his stomach, but he was fully alert and advanced past the front door to a window which was obscured from both houses. He proceeded to test the window – it was not a tight fit. Putting a hand on the left side and the other hand on the right he placed a small amount of pressure to test the sash lock which was a half turn type, set in the middle of the window sash. The window was quite amiable, and invited itself to be breached. Sam was wearing a pair of overalls with extra pockets, one from which he drew a small battery-powered drill and a piece of solid wire about 20 centimetres long. The drill had a special bit to penetrate glass. It would only take a few seconds. The drill itself was small; it was covered with a rag to assist muffling the noise.

Being a little below average height, Sam had to stand on his toes to get leverage for the drill. It was child's play. The glass was penetrated; he inserted the piece of wire, pushing slowly until the locking mechanism gave way.

Returning his tools to their rightful place, Sam carefully lifted the bottom of the window. It slid up with ease. He knew by experience that the type of sash could make a lot of noise if the sash ropes were stretched or weakened. So far, so good! Once the window was opened he removed his shoes - Velcro strapped sneakers for convenience, reached over the window ledge, and placed the shoes on the floor. Climbing in with care, he pulled the window slowly down and turned the locking devise at the centre. He would leave another way out if the security alarm would allow him. Standing a metre from the window, he stood for a couple of minutes getting used to the darkness and the light, also listening for any movement in the dwelling.

He stepped a couple of paces. He discerned he was beside a large table, but kept his hands away from it until he reached into his back pocket for his light gloves – good disposable ones at that. Once they were on his hands, he stepped around the table. This was without doubt the dining room. The family and living room would be adjacent; across the hall would be the kitchen. His stockinged feet were feeling the floor, searching for squeaky boards. There seemed to be no problem in that regard here. His breath was a little faster, his pulse the same. He found his way to the door to begin exploring the very large house.

He had been in the house ten minutes or so. Now his eyes could make out the appointments in the rooms. As stealthily as he could he advanced first to one room, retreated, and then to another. He came back to the hall and foyer after he had carefully scrutinized the ground floor. The loot would be in the bedrooms, library or study. Although the house was cluttered with a myriad of classic pictures, hangings, and bric-a-brac, and the furniture was mostly oak and Jacobean, his interest was only in top quality jewellery. He gave the furniture and paintings, vases, etc a cursory glance, but nothing in that field made his heart leap or even register an interest.

The staircase was about 1200 centimetres wide, with an ornate balustrade and a Persian patterned carpet fixed with metal treads on each step. These could be dangerous for a person in unfamiliar surroundings, especially in the dark. Stairs creak at the slightest weight placement, so step by step he went upwards; pausing and listening, but only the sounds of the city broke the night air.

The first floor, with five bedrooms and three bathrooms, took a little time to examine. The safe would be in the main bedroom. He would look over the top floor then come back to the master bedroom.

The top floor surprised him. He thought it was a residential top floor but there was a study and a games room with a small theatre. The back section was a balcony which looked out over the pool and back yard area. There was no electronic alarm system within the house itself, which meant, he believed, that a substantial safe was somewhere in the dwelling. He returned to leave the landing. Carefully he commenced to make his way down the stairs, when an unfortunate incident occurred.

As he stepped on to the top step, his left sock caught in a protruding screw. When he tried to pull his foot away, he lost his balance and fell down the steps.

Rolling down, his body stalled on the first floor landing. His foot was cut and bleeding and without the sock.

"Bloody Hell" he cursed. Holding his foot with a finger on the injured part to stop the bleeding, he pulled the rag off the drill with his other hand to bandage the foot.

Suddenly he felt a chill – as if someone was watching him.

He looked up the stairs.

A dark figure was standing on the top landing, holding what appeared to be a club.

Sam was dumfounded, totally speechless.

The apparition did not move that instant. It just stood stock-still.

'The bloody thing will kill me. I've got no defence,' he thought with trepidation. The apparition moved towards him down the steps.

"Who are you?" it said-it was a woman's voice.

Sam was utterly flabbergasted.

"I, I, I lost my way! …er, who are you?"

"You sneaked up on me", Sam complained.

"What are you doing in this dwelling?" she asked.

"Are you the owner? I thought they were all abroad."

"They are! At least I hope so."

"Are you hurt badly?"

Sam had forgotten his foot and any other pain he had.

"I'm alright, I think. But, what are you doing here?" he enquired.

The woman moved a little closer, put down the club and sat on the stair.

"I'm burgling the place." she said, laughingly.

"So am I.", Sam stammered. "I can't believe this." He ran his hand through his hair, not that he had that much these days. It had receded a lot since he was a teenager.

The woman's face was visible under a hood she was wearing. She had a dark tracksuit which completely covered her, and dark gloves to match.

"I think we have to sort this out" Sam said.

"That's easy. You hobble out and let me continue with the work at hand." He thought she was grinning.

Then without a word, she bent over him to check on his injury. She wasn't very old – perhaps 30 – 35. Face looked pleasant, a bit impish he thought.

"Well, did you find the safe?" she asked.

"Not yet, it must be on this floor."

"I know where it is" she grinned. "Better clean up the blood. We don't want DNA everywhere, do we?" She tied the piece of rag around his foot, walked up the stairs, collected the sock and put it on his foot.

"Thanks" Sam said, standing up checking his limbs. "I think I'm OK."

"I'm Sam" he said, putting out his hand. She took it, shook it and said "Millie." They both sat on the steps.

"What are we going to do?" Sam posed the question.

"Let's rob the place and sort it out later." was Millie's reply.

"You're a mercenary bird! I thought you'd run once you saw me, and look at me." He pointed to his foot, and grinned.

"Well we are here; we may as well leave with our pay packets."

"What do you specialize in?"

"Jewellery – I only want the good stuff!"

"Me too! OK let's split it half 'n' half and part company! Where's the safe?"

"Where you implied – main bedroom, but not the usual wall thingo, under the bedside table; the carpet is cut to flap over the hole."

"Good, I can pick those locks." Sam smiled.

"So can I.", said Millie.

"Great, let's go! But your club -" He pointed to the top of the stairs.

"Oh that's a bottle of wine! I grabbed it when you made all the commotion."

They moved to the main bedroom, removed the bedside table, pulled back the carpet and exposed a metal safe, face up; a combination lock and a key lock beneath it.

"No problems! What tools have you got with you Millie?" He looked at her. He liked what he saw, that impish grin again.

"Just a tickling set, combo, screwdriver, pointy pliers, hammer, pinch bar, hand drill and bits."

"Regular little thief, you are."

"OK let me listen to the tumbler. By the way, see if you can find the phone number of this place just in case they are stupid. The last two used their postcode, easy as taking candy from a baby."

Click, click. He was concentrating, holding a small torch in one hand, fiddling the safe dial with the other.

Millie returned with the numbers, handed them to Sam, and then knelt down beside him to observe the delicate operation. Sam tried a few combos without success. He was now concentrating on the key lock which was also to be penetrated. It didn't take him very long; when he sat up, she leaned forward. He pulled the handle upward. The safe opened directly.

"The silly boffins only used the key lock!" he exclaimed, looking into the safe and shining the torch to get a good look.

"Hmm, not bad at all-there's a good few trinkets." Millie leaned over to get a view.

Sam pulled a bag, much like a marble bag with a drawstring, from his pocket.

"Do you trust me?" he asked as he shovelled the desirable contents of the safe into the bag.

"Well I'll have to," she answered.

"Well I cleaned out the bedroom jewellery boxes so we can sort it out once we get far from here," she whispered, then put her hand to her lips to signal silence.

He did not move as she slid without a sound out of the room.

Sam closed the safe gently, placed the carpet in its proper position, put the bedside table back where it belonged, collected his tools and the jewellery and tip toed to the bedroom door.

Millie had vanished.

He couldn't and wouldn't call out. He waited, intently focused on the silence.

No movement, noise, or anything that might resemble intrusion by a third party.

"Struth" he thought, I hope there's not another burglar in town.

Just then, Millie poked her head around the corner of the top landing.

"Cats, that's all" she said.

"OK! Let's get out of here."

"Which way did you enter?"

"By the back fence, it is darker."

"Well you go first. I'll wait for ten minutes, and then exit."

"Where will we meet?"

"Do you know the Trocadero Café in South Road?"

"Yes. I'll be there in half an hour."

"OK" she said and disappeared into the night.

Sam checked for bloodstains on the carpet. "Good thing" he thought. "The Persian carpet would hide any blood stains to a point," he mused. He cleaned a couple of spots, retrieved his boots, settled the wine bottle back into its rack and moved to the front door.

It was deadlocked. Blast!

He went to the laundry door by the side adjacent the kitchen. It was a simple motel door type with snib from inside. He exited, closing the door behind him.

Trocadero, here I come; and he too, vanished into the night.

TROCADERO BY NIGHT

The Trocadero Café was just as Millie had expected it to be - Fifties and Sixties style. Sliding open the front door she stepped into her parents' era. She remembered, as a small child eating in such places until the new vogue of fast food swept most of these establishments away. Mostly immigrant owned and managed, it wasn't uncommon to see the whole family working in the shop all at the one time. The children would be at the tables or washing dishes at the sink as soon as they arrived from school.

A long serving counter, covered with black, red and yellow laminate, dominated the left side. It seemed to go on forever, down to the far back wall. Here a small hole allowed access to and from the tables and it was the only break in the bulky servery. Opposite, on the right side, Millie noted an array of tables and chairs all with their salt, pepper and sugar receptacles neatly placed in the centre of each table. Along the wall were several booths, each with a central table and bench seating for six people. The only curios missing that would make this a café of its era were the Juke Boxes which were normally screwed above each booth. She could see the marks where they had been, her mind drifting to the Rock and Roll music she used to hear.

The booths were empty except for two. A couple occupied the one closest to the front door. Her objective, Sam, was seated in a booth at the extreme end of the building at the back wall - a good spot for an intimate chat, or in this case a late 'Business Meeting'.

She moved toward the booth, nodded to the waiter and slid her slender frame between the padded seat and the fixed table, placing her red leather purse on the table in front of her while looking directly at

Sam. She spoke naturally, as though they were acquaintances of long standing.

"Do you come here often? she asked with a smile.

"Not often, but when I happen to be in the neighbourhood. It's a good refuge after a hard evening's work, and what's more its open until 1.00 am. It's respectable and not only that, but the food's good."

The waiter hovered nearby.

"Would you like a drink? Or perhaps something to eat before we talk?" Sam asked her.

"Yes, I see they make old fashioned milk shakes in metal containers. I'll have chocolate malted and a tomato sandwich … toasted thanks."

Sam ordered a latté and fruit cake for himself, then turned back to face Millie's pleasant countenance.

"Oh such a polite burglar" she uttered.

He laughed. "Where do we start from, young woman?" he said.

"Millie" she enforced.

"Okay! Millie!"

"Well! Tonight's enterprise must be finalised to our mutual satisfaction." she noted. "Where are the goods?"

"They're in safe keeping for the time being. I'll show you later."

"Okay, let's deal with them now so we can split and go our separate ways after this." She pointed to the food arriving with the waiter. She stopped speaking.

The waiter placed the plates and drinking vessels down on the table and returned to the counter to pursue chitchat with a soupy blonde seated there.

The young man seemed to be totally engrossed in the blonde; the two burglars could have a very private conversation in peace.

"Good", Sam said. "We must now evaluate our collection. That's simple for me; I have a tried and true assessor who could do this before morning."

"Why don't we just lay them down and take one by one each. That's simple." She spoke assertively.

"If that's what you wish. They're just a few hundred metres from here and I'll go along with that. Okay?"

"Okay", Millie said.

"Now we can't proceed around these neighbourhoods falling over each other from time to time, so we need to agree to either make a territory for each of us or".…. He broke off.

"We could join together." she said with a wry smile.

Sam put his hands on his head, looked straight at her and frowned. "Two burglars in the one establishment is one too many." he quietly replied.

"Oh, I didn't mean we had to work on the same patient together. We could just say, pool ideas, dispose of our stock through the best channels, that sort of thing." She spoke with a hidden hope as she was enjoying herself, felt comfortable with her situation, and could now have a mentor to discuss her ventures or adventures with, whichever was the case at that point of time.

"Well, let's sort the goods out first and go home".

"How's your foot?" she inquired seriously.

"It's okay. I actually forgot about the evenings proceedings as I was trying to figure out where we go from here or more pertinently, where I go from here." he added.

"What do you think?"

"We are two loners, we seem to have similar clients in mind, and are professionals in our non-nocturnal activities."

"Our work! Yes, that's only a few hours away."

"Well, the right philosophy in all these matters is that the less you know the fewer problems can occur." she said.

"That's correct". Sam spoke with certainty.

"Thanks for the hospitality" she said.

"No problem! You can wash the dishes." He rose from the table.

"My car is over the road. We can divvy the spoils in there if you're happy."

"Yes, that's alright with me!" she replied.

"How did you get here?" he inquired, opening the door to let her out into the street.

"I like to walk to do my shopping." she grinned pulling her jacket on to escape the cool air the early morning brings.

"Spunky little bird, and smart also." he thought as he walked out of the café.

"My car's the red one over there," he said pointing to the small sedan across the road.

"Are you happy to finish the deal in the car?" he asked.

"There's not much option. I don't think two burglars making a split of the spoils in the main street of suburbia would get very far."

"We'll have to find a quiet spot."

"Okay". He crossed to his car, unlocked the driver's side door and sat behind the wheel as he opened the passenger side for her from the inside.

"Bachelor," she mused. "Confirmed bachelor - no doubt doesn't open doors for his women folk!" He switched the ignition on and as the motor was idling, proposed to move the car out of the area to end the liaison.

"Okay" she said with expectation and a cheeky grin on her face.

"Good."

During the short drive, Millie's attention toward Sam was a few side glances, trying to figure out what a man obviously well off, intelligent and driving a Mercedes Benz would need or want to burgle! It is a dangerous pastime.

Soon she would know.

Sam simultaneously, was trying to fathom how a bright, sensible, clever woman with good looks to boot would want to do what she does for nightlife. Maybe she has a habit to feed, he thought; or hidden kids; or gambling or he didn't know what, but he thought and saw only blanks. The thought only made him shudder. Well she'll soon be out of the way. He didn't like drugs or violence and hoped deep down, he would never encounter either of the two. He parked the car in a private area he obviously knew of, and no one else was present. Then reaching under the dashboard retrieved a small package which he handed to Millie. It was a brown paper envelope with a string tied around it.

"There are the spoils!" he indicated to the package, which Millie was quickly pulling apart.

"All present and correct", she said happily.

"You take what you wish", he said. "I'll have the rest."

"That's not fair" she exclaimed in protest.

"It is, my good woman." he said.

"Millie" she objected.

"Okay Millie. I know you would not have hit me with the wine bottle back in the house, and you did save me a lot of hardship, so take the best part as a vote of thanks and hurry up – we do not want nosey parkers looking in."

"All right." She was looking at the jewellery. "I'll take these." she said holding an emerald brooch set in gold, a diamond necklace and a cameo pendant.

"That all?"

"Yes! My fence will offload these quickly. I don't like slow sales – it's dangerous!"

"You've cheated yourself!" Sam protested.

"It's all right. I've no need for more. We're even and its been an interesting and enlightening evening and early morning, so we'll just have to keep ourselves out of each others hair from now on" she said quietly, but made no attempt to leave his presence.

"Wait", Sam said, as he looked at her with a faint smirk on his dial.

"Look, I'm intrigued as to why a woman like you is in this strange trade. It's quite obvious you are doing this for either urgent necessity or just to get a kick out of a clandestine pastime" he said. "Why have resorted to crime? Do you have a habit?"

Millie burst out laughing.

"Definitely not. No habit except burglary. No necessity. I despise drugs and have wine only on special occasions with meals."

"Well" she said, "I'll explain where I've come from and where I'm at if you will do the same. To find a second person on the same patch as me tonight was quite a shock, so here's my story."

Millie set out to explain her position as a burglar with a twinkle in her eye.

"You see, Sam" she emphasised 'Sam', "I spent my secondary schooling at a private girls' school in a provincial town. The buildings in which the dormitories were housed were three stories high and built at the end of the nineteenth century as far as I recall; hence there were staircases with large balustrades, creaky wooden floors and lots of small rooms which is where I first became acquainted with the notion of my talents as a devious young woman.

We had a very strict and domineering Madam in charge of the dorms.

She was an overbearing, sour faced old bird (no wonder she was a spinster) and there were about 50 of us girls sharing our lives in the buildings. So as you would know, girls being girls, all of us wanted freedom from the claustrophobic environment created and maintained by Miss Gregson. So every avenue of escape from the coop was devised and a sort of state of war quietly existed between us and them - especially her.

"Anti establishment behaviour was enshrined in our attitudes - so bending, twisting and occasionally breaking the rules was rife. The larger the act of defiance the stronger the bonds became among us girls.

"So one night, early in my residency, my best mate sneaked out to liaise with a boy, came home late and was unable to get back in without setting off the alarm system. I was expecting her. So I crept down the two flights of stairs, past all the offices, Dorm Mistresses and retrieved my friend from a very embarrassing situation.

"Once the matter was aired in the Dorm, I seemed to find myself the rescuer of all the stray dogs who locked themselves out or just didn't note the time or just became lazy. I began to plan new and novel ways to leave and return without detection. I became able to creep, crawl, climb and move over the entire building without detection. Then I needed to help myself. There was one time when I had a secret rendezvous in town and lost track of time, returned late, and found myself out in the cold so to speak. I was freezing in the night air. I scaled the pipes to the first floor, forced a window with a steel bar I had purloined from one of the garden sheds, held the alarm circuit from triggering the alarm, and successfully negotiated my return.

"The girls were flabbergasted when they heard the story.

Time after time, the events of an evening prompted elusive, quick thinking action to save others or myself; I just became expert at it I suppose. When graduation time came around, the girls collectively said I was the best cat burglar ever.

Since I work in the drudge of accountancy in a well established family business, I need a little thrill or two to make the days a little brighter." She paused.

"I've been ransacking the eastern and northern suburbs for nine years. I've had a few close shaves, but if any of my family even knew only one of my exploits, they'd all probably drop dead with surprise. My Uncle Roy, whom I work with closely in my day job, does allow me to commence work a little late providing all my work is up to date. So even he does not suspect anything about my nightlife alter ego. "

"How do you offload your merchandise?" Sam asked.

"Well that's where I struck gold, so to speak." Millie went on "I have an acquaintance in the industry."

"That's all I will say at present. Now it's your turn" she smiled expectantly.

"Well it's easy" Sam replied. "I'm an engineer by profession, also like you; I'm in a family business. I am often on building sites and many times I'm required to inspect the interiors. But keys are not left out for me, so I have improvised many ways of entering locked premises. Also I have a fair idea, through experience, of the layout of homes in each particular area of this city.

"I stumbled upon plans in our archives of homes built by my father and his brothers forty and fifty years ago. So why not empty them out, I thought. And I did so, one by one over a long period. When I feel the urge, I case an ideal place. When I'm satisfied 'pop goes the weasel'.

"Nowadays a lot of information about the lifestyles of our past clients is in the local papers, so it gets easier. I don't really need the money – I require a diversion from a mundane life. It's becoming a habit, and it's hard to shake off."

"Have you ever thought about the possibility of getting caught?"

"I have, but I set myself rules such as no violence, so that, if I see any sign of problems, I cancel out.

"Also I dress well. This makes it easier to talk my way out if disturbed. I always make sure of a hiding place for the goods as quickly as possible after I move away from the target area." The main rule of thumb is that I search for self employed, wealthy types. They often flaunt, but seldom insure; they have lots of tax dodge goodies so there is less chance of police or security arrangements on their premises.

"In fact, of my first five houses, only one reported the theft and even that did not make the news.

"My main 'target' is top jewellery; it's easy to offload. No watches or fancy gear – they're too easy to trace and my fence will not take them anyway. Then I have a cooling off period before the next venture.

"Anyway I'd better drop you off as its getting late. Or should I say its early morning."

Millie started in surprise "I was so absorbed in your lecture, sorry - story I mean. I've completely forgotten the time. My car is in Albert Street, Maricham. I'll show you.

"By the way, your sentiments are similar to mine. I won't risk a venture, or over indulge in knick-knacks. I also select my targets after lots of painstaking homework."

"Good girl" he said, starting the ignition.

The car slid away from the kerb and Sam proceeded to guide it to its destination, assisted by Millie's directions. Sam noted a small sports car near a row of trees. It just suited her he thought – "a little sporty type".

She left him with a goodnight after he proposed they meet for dinner one night. "But I haven't your number" he said.

"You do not write things down" she said.

"I won't", he said, reaching over the seat and colleting a set of plans from the back seat. She told him her number as he wrote it on the plan – '6984X3397M'.

He showed her. She grinned, nodded and departed. As she approached her car she turned and waved. He paused a while until she was out of sight, then turned the car around in the quiet street and sped off into the night.

Gee, 'What a night', Sam thought as he looked at the time on the dash. Two thirty; he yawned.

Millie headed for her unit, a small handful of neat jewels and a pumping heart. She felt warm all over.

'What an adventure and what results', she mused to herself.

CONTEMPLATION

Sam literally fell into bed in the early hours of the morning. He was unable to switch off from a busy and illuminating evening, in which he nearly came unstuck. In all the years he had planned and executed his jaunts, although risky, he had never been caught as short as he had been when he tripped on the stairs the night before. What if he had broken his leg or injured himself in such away that he couldn't have removed himself from the house? Pondering over the events that had passed he felt himself extremely fortunate to have escaped the situation so lightly, thanks to the woman.

However, his new acquaintance was the other source of his insomnia that morning. Had he made the correct decision to engage her and share the spoils; was that foolhardy or naive of him? Should he have aborted the show when she met him on the stairs, then cut his losses and scarpered without collecting the jewellery? The circle of events happened with such rapidity that it was mind boggling to say the least. His mind was awhirl, contemplating what might have been and where it might head now. Then there is the matter of the girl; what of her?

She seems to be 'well heeled', intelligent, not bad looking either. However, sharing such intimate matters as ones 'moonlighting escapades, is not the done thing. Once one takes in another's confidence, it weakens the defence and adds extra danger to an already tenuous situation. It could put one in mortal danger. A woman scorned and all that, if something went horribly wrong. But she didn't seem the type to run willy-nilly if things fell flat. She had as much to lose as he had, Sam figured out.

Well there was not much he that could do about it now. It was all water under the bridge and she was a reality. However, pulling off a job with her could be a tricky event, and yet it might be exciting and a bit of fun. She could be the person he could spend a bit of time with, seeing that most of his recent flames were travelling on different wave lengths than he was these days. Anyhow, he'd test the water tomorrow. For now, he just needed some sleep. Old Burton would be calling for his plans in the afternoon so a little shut-eye was needed.

Millie dived into the shower. It was past three am. She was both physically and mentally exhausted. The last few hours took her to a new high in both drama and danger. What if the bloke at the bottom of the stairs had been the owner, a relative, or perhaps an aggressive person! Maybe telling her life's story to a stranger, even if he was a 'fellow traveller' wasn't such a smart thing to do after all.

Hell, it's done and he was quite pleasant and apologetic. He did give her the chance to pocket first pick of the spoils as well. He's not such a bad looking chap either, so what's the problem. She lay on her bed staring at the ceiling and conjured up all types of fantasies that flitted through her fertile mind. Fancy knocking off a residence with him and planning the gig as a twosome, she thought. However we would have to be diligent and very careful. Perhaps, too many burglars may spoil the haul.

Maybe it wouldn't be as much fun sharing the spoils, as doing a place over alone, with only you privy to the outcome for better or worse as the case maybe. Any way she thought, I've got to get some sleep. I have a heavy day ahead. Later in the morning, Dad requires an extra assistant to sort out a few tough clients, and I'm sure he will not be expecting me to look and act as though I've been hit by a bus. She rolled over, pulled the covers over her head, and tried to doze off.

Difficulty in getting a decent amount of sleep was a problem for both of them, tossing and turning to at the point of not really resting at all. Deciding to rise early and prepare for the challenges of the day seemed to be the prudent thing to do. Millie thought to herself over breakfast that she'd never been hassled before after a job- so what's with her now?

The day, that is, the working part of it, went smoothly but the two found the need to speak to the other at the end of the day. Apprehension, coupled with a sense of inquisitiveness gave them both a little room for a further encounter for say, extra enlightenment regarding each other. There was a certain chemistry forming and it needed a little refining.

Sam made the first move and called Millie at six that evening. She answered rather promptly, which made him a little suspicious that perhaps she was about to call or was waiting in expectancy for him to ring. However, he had a line to spin and it was this.

"I was wondering if you would appreciate a further discussion regarding some mutual arrangements - maybe the possibility of a joint marketing venture could save doubling up on things, if you know what I mean."

"Yes, you wish a date that's it." She retorted.

"Well, you do know that as we work in a similar field, the pooling of resources could be beneficial."

"OK! Let's meet." she said. "But you pay and I'll choose the place."

"That's fine with me", he said. He was quite pleased with himself for getting this far so smoothly.

"What time?" He asked

"Well I have not prepared any food as yet for tonight's dinner, so a nice Rib-eye at Finnegan's Irish Pub at Boat-plaza Concourse sounds the way to go. Say seven thirty?"

"Fine. I'll pick you up."

"No. See you there. Bye."

"Bye."

Finnegan's was a general, run of the mill pub with raucous noise. It had a few discreet corners to hide away for that intimate hour or so, if one was so fortunate. The place was adorned with pseudo-Irish paraphernalia and painted in several shades of green which resembled moss on rocky ground. Bosomed girls in short dresses, incomplete with low cut tops to titillate the male patrons, swept around the place searching for those whose glasses were empty, collecting orders, whilst engaging in small unthinking chatter mostly heard in places such as these.

Millie arrived early, ordered herself a glass of 'cab sav' to steady her nerves, and found a quiet hidey hole between the lounge and the exit to the beer garden, well away from the chatter. When Sam appeared, he entered from the back door, gazed around, hoping to spot Millie and save himself any embarrassment if he erred in recognising her, as he had only met the nymph the night before.

He saw her, moved speedily to the table, smiled and said "Hi", then sat down opposite her.

"How are you this evening?" she asked.

"Well and truly beat." he said as he signalled one of the greatly endowed of the species to fetch him a drink.

"Is this where spies meet?" he joked.

She blushed, her cheeks went bright pink. "You could say that."

He ordered a light beer from a lightly clad waitress then said to her.

"Well we could order something to eat, I am famished and I don't want a late night of it."

He inquired, "Would you like another drink?" "Yes please, a Cabernet Sauvignon."

As soon as the drinks were delivered, Sam collected the menu and they settled on their respective selection of food, ordered, then sat in silence as though each was getting their thoughts together. Millie raised her glass, eyeing Sam through the wine, and grinned to herself.

Sam broke the ice, trying to be hospitable and at the same time in control. "Remember last night when you told me your story and the idea of trying a joint venture came up. I have thought that through a little today and have a few reservations about it. Each of us has run our own course to this point, except for the last evening. Either of us could have botched it through a variety of ways. It seems to me that we don't know enough about each other to be comfortable with a partnership, if that's what you call it."

"Well." Millie hesitated, laughed lightly then said, "We have a fair way to go before we tackle that sort of thing."

She went on "It was quite a shock to the system to find another person crossing my path and doing the self same thing that I was doing. Then to find that that person had a contented life, so to speak; but also needed the challenge to follow this dangerous pursuit like I have, was amazing. I suppose if we were teenagers it would have been graffiti or something akin to that."

Sam spoke and smiled "I often think of what my parents would say if they ever found out. Do you ever contemplate that sort of thing?"

"I sure do but I hope it never comes to that. By the way you could do some thing for me. I'm going a holiday to the Whitsunday Islands next week and may need to send a parcel to an address that is discreet. Get my drift Sam?"

She had finished her meal and was becoming jovial. He noticed that her reserve was removed, and to him that was a good thing.

"Yes, I'll give you a post box number for your convenience."

"By the way, I have to leave soon." Millie said. "I'm sorry but I need to call on Mum and pick up my washing."

Finally they parted both in great spirits. Millie went off to see her mother, whilst Sam drove away whistling softly to himself. He still had a small bit of skull-duggery to do before he hit the sack.

Millie lugged her washing into her apartment a few hours later. As she placed the basket on the kitchen table, she noticed a brown envelope at the other end of the table.

She opened it and to her utter surprise it contained the jade necklace that Sam received as a portion of the heist yesterday.

A WORKING HOLIDAY FOR MILLIE

Millie stepped aboard the boat, casting a glance here and there. She found that she was the only single on board. It was winter – not many tourists for the Whitsundays. Two couples sat together, the women talking rhetoric, whilst their men sat in silence. Heard it all before!

A young blonde couple were devouring each other; Scandinavians she thought. The girl was just about falling out of her clothes, whilst her partner looked as though he had slept in whatever he was wearing.

The inter-island ferry was no 'show boat'; its main task was to convey the inhabitants and daily workers to and from the islands and the mainland.

Early and late trips were generally scheduled for the locals. Most of the tourists went out on the 10.30 am which was Millie's boat, and returned no later than the 4.30 pm boat. She could do with a drink but the signs explained food and drink wouldn't be served until the cruise was underway. Ah well - she mused, this girl could wait.

Millie had dressed down for the trip; she had also shortened her hair. She wore a loose orange top with a pair of black slacks and sandals without jewellery or rings – not even a watch!

She soon lost interest in the few human beings around her and sat with eyes closed waiting for the boat to get underway. She was just about to doze off when something glittering caught her eye. She was staring with disbelief. Only a few metres away from her were a large contingent of tourists, all being disgorged from a tourist bus. Millie's thoughts of holiday came to an abrupt halt.

This was too good to be true.

These weren't the normal mix but all from the one social stock. In fact they all looked like they emanated from one large family. Greeks, definitely Greeks – maybe second generation or perhaps a mixture of new and old, all with "Golden Eggs". Millie was drooling at the prospects of the next few hours.

But it wasn't the people she was amazed at; it was what they were wearing. There were thirteen women and eleven men. The men mostly wore gold chains around their necks, rings on their fingers and handsome watches. Millie felt she could even smell a Rolex – a burglars delight. She mused. Sam will have a fit. I'm supposed to be resting.

Millie's heart pounded. The women were literally swamped with jewellery. One had four or five gold chains under her fat chin; brooches; baubles; bangles; rings on nearly every finger.

It's a wonder they could carry all that loot. Then she noted the handbags – she beamed.

Millie turned away and moved through the middle of the boat to think this out.

But as she left, 'mine host' of the boat made an announcement. She said in a loud voice "welcome aboard a touring party from Greece",

This quickly caused a stir. One of the gents corrected her by saying "Sorry Miss – we are from south of Sydney and Canberra. We are café owners on a business trip." The woman blushed, then abruptly brushed the matter aside with a mumbled apology and moved to the matters of the day, namely safety and the itinerary.

Millie grinned inwardly and mused to herself. Never receive Greeks bearing gifts, but Greeks bearing the spoils of a mountain of greasy chips and tanks of cappuccinos – that's different. She thought mischievously that if the boat came to grief it would be a bonanza for a salvage team.

The touring party obviously kept their display for travel because the Tax man had no time to holiday.

The time to observe and plan occupied Millie's mind. Sam told her not to indulge herself on the travels north. Soon he would receive a parcel, then another. He would know she enjoyed herself. She always sent mementos of her trips.

She spent the six hours of the cruise isolated behind her large sunglasses; vigilant, listening for anything that would assist in purloining the ostentatious goodies from their rightful owners.   Sam would be livid if she took too many risks but be that as it may, it looked like taking candy from a baby. After half an hour on the boat eavesdropping, she heard one of the ladies explain to an inquisitive passenger the resort and rooms the group were resting their trinkets in.

She thought of Sam and his advice to her. The first rule was never to engage the intended in conversation; show no outward interest in them, but watch, look and listen.

Millie took up her position at lunch in the midst of the café entourage.

After four couples sat down at the tables, she moved with her food and drink to the table beside them, forcing the other couples and the single women attached to the Greek party to settle in tables around her. To her relief no one asked to sit with her, allowing her to study several times, a brochure on scuba diving and abseiling. Slowly snippets of information filtered from those who spoke English to each other.

For the first time in her life, she loved the beach, the sand, the sea. She sat with absolutely no interest in anything around her – totally absorbed by the people whom she had chosen to attach herself to. So deeply was she concentrating she nearly lost her guard; several times ignoring people who spoke to her for some reason or another. The day drifted slowly. As the boat slid across the final stretch of the ocean, and farewells were being orchestrated and the cacophony of noises reached an inaudible pitch, Millie was gathering herself together preparing to move off before the crowd, to get into position for a final perusal of her intended victims. Perhaps she would tail them back to the resort.

It suddenly dawned on her that she had not made an accommodation booking for herself and smiling inwardly, she felt maybe it would be better to be miles away after the event.

The challenge in the course of events to follow would be to pick the right rooms, ascertain the whereabouts of the goods she was interested in and make herself invisible. There was, in this matter, no room for a diversion. The number of escape exits from the area was limited and the victims may carry protection. Millie felt the blood run fast in her veins. Millie moved her vehicle to a position to follow the coach carrying her 'intended'.   After three roundabouts and several kilometres of urban manoeuvring, finally the group arrived at their resort.

Millie was greatly relieved to note that the resort was merely a one storey motel complex with a large swimming pool and enclosed recreation area; the restaurant was central to the rooms, and this assisted her in keeping an eye on proceedings. Millie parked in a designated parking area, then made a few adjustments to her appearance – namely a wig, her favourite new set of spectacles and a top that contrasted totally to the one she wore earlier. "Don't panic girl", Millie thought to herself.

Millie went to the reception and found an woman behind the counter with her head in a woman's magazine. She waited and after a few minutes the lady disengaged herself from the book and gave Millie a cursory glance and mumbled that they had only one room , it was situated at the end of the corridor. She explained to Millie that tonight was 'Coach' night so there was bound to be a lot of noise. She was forewarning her so she wouldn't get complaints later. Millie was pleased that the place would be rowdy as she would blend in with the tourist and drift around more or less without being conspicuous. She took the keys and found her room placed her small case on the bed and went to park the car in a spot she felt that it would get scant attention at least.

As it was getting close to evening meal time she spruced up in her room then took a stroll around the precincts of the hotel. She had checked out the where the Greek-Australians were accommodated be by glancing at the diary on the reception desk while the receptionist was processing her booking.

The restaurant appeared to be doing brisk business. She decided to hold off for a while; give them time to relax. It was now past 7.00 pm. Oldies eat early she thought to herself; and usually retire early, but maybe these could party awhile. She would move in about 7.30 pm. Millie had no idea how the evening would pan out. She knew she was on her own - she could not afford one mistake. Better to pull out at the first hint of trouble. She didn't have Sam's backup or any contingency plan in case of calamity, and that's what it would be if she were caught. She was the cat and they the mice. She trembled with excitement but her anxiety heightened as she thought the whole thing through.

The moon was high above, and full, when she walked into the restaurant Bar. "Bacardi and coke please." Then she was seated in a spot not far from her intended victims. Her worst fear was that someone may try to engage her in conversation and that was the last thing she needed. Then she ordered her meal, pulled a book from her handbag and commenced to read and eaves drop simultaneously. She had set herself for the next phase of her 'evening out'. She took her time over the meal, concentrating on the people around her.

The café crowd was in a jovial mood; there was only herself and the holidaying café crowd.

Millie observed that the drinks they ordered were mostly red wines apart from a few mixed spirit drinks plus cocktails for a couple of the women. As the evening unfolded Millie was satisfied that the tour group would sleep soundly tonight, hopefully throughout the early morning. Her excitement was starting to mount as the night wore on.

Finishing her dining she moved to the foyer then outside into the crisp air and moonlit nightscape. The night sky was cloudless. She shivered a little. "Is it the coolness, or is it my nerves?" she mused. The good thing for her was that they were accommodated in rooms clumped together .all rooms had sliding glass doors on the outside. The best point as far as Millie was concerned is that the place seemed so layback therefore no surveillance cameras were installed

One by one and two by two the patrons settled in for the evening. Millie checked her watch. It was 17 minutes past 11 when the last patron filed to his door. The restaurant was already closed; its lights extinguished, and its staff dispersed homeward. Only the perimeter lights and essential lighting, still remained. She was amazed that no one had approached her during the evening. Perhaps they were too busy talking or going to other personal engagements. That, she would never know.

Millie went back to her room, put a dark pullover on and lay down on the bed. She waited with a trained patience born of experience in the nocturnal habits of the human race. She was relieved that there were no animals around the resort - a management directive. She pulled a blanket over her and lay quietly composed.

She waited.

Outside, the moon was hovering in a star laden sky; the air was still and cool, but not cold or unpleasant. An occasional vehicle passed by on the main road.

She waited.

There would always be an early riser, someone who needed to be on the road before sun up.

She waited.

Then at two thirty she made her move. First she quietly opened her door cautiously checked the hallway then stealthily moved toward the reception, where she could detect the sound of soft music. A young girl, obviously a family member of the Motelier, was asleep in the chair, the television and radio both switched on. Satisfied, Millie back pedalled and retuned to her room. She placed a few small objects into her slacks' pocket and left the room.

Room one was a cinch the couple were snoring their heads off and the jewellery was easy to locate she was tempted to grab the Rolex watch but cautioned herself against it. She could not access the second room so handled three and four with perfection then returned to her room.

She placed the items she had stolen in an envelope and with her gloves still on she left her room went to the rear of the motel and stashed her ill gotten gains in a small shrub. If something went pear-shaped she would not be implicated. By four thirty she had burgled five rooms and called it to a halt, safely depositing all of the gear and her tools in the bushes outside. She had also taken the precaution of settling the accounts with cash before she had retired. She was ready and to leave, collected the booty and headed for her vehicle.

The moon and the sun were both in the heavens when Millie slowly moved away from the resort. Thank goodness for that, she thought. I was beginning to wonder if they wouldn't all sleep in. I should be well away before the fun starts.

Once she proceeded through the town and headed north toward the next town it was just after 6.45 am. Turning into the small town centre some 20 kilometres away, she pulled the car to the kerb adjacent to a red post box, stepped out and with minimum movement, deposited two packages already generously stamped, into the receptacle, then climbed back into her car and sped off. The sun was now a golden balloon smiling a new days awakening. Millie placed a CD in the cars player and drove on.

Millie had no sooner returned to the northbound road after eating a small breakfast at a roadhouse, when she noticed a car a few hundred metres behind her. Her heart missed a beat or two. A police car had pulled out from behind the trees and was fast approaching. Butterflies bounced in her stomach.

Blast, what did I do wrong? She thought. Keep cool; drive carefully.

The patrol car overtook her, then its flashing lights indicated to her to pull over. She did. The officer, a young man walked slowly to the car, glanced at the front of her car and then proceeded to the rear. She smiled at him. "I've not gone over the limit officer."

"Madam you have only one number plate on your car."

"Oh I must have lost it. Which one is it?"

"You need a new one at the rear."

"Okay, I'll get it done when I return to Sydney." She replied with a cheesy smile.

"Drive carefully. Good day Madam."

The police car moved away. Millie sat motionless, thinking "I hope it didn't fall off at the resort." She was visibly and inwardly shaken. Should she go back and look for the number plate. She decided not to; too risky.

A short time later, after her nerves settled, she recommenced her journey northward. "No, I'm going back" she said to herself, "and check." She drove back to the motel and pulled up at the spot where she parked the car earlier. The plate was on the ground. She collected it and drove off- not a sole was paying her any attention, she observed. The discipline she and Sam had always applied to all the 'business deals' could come unstuck through the merest misfortune.

Three days later Sam received the small parcels, made himself a coffee and sat down to open the packages.

He spilt their contents on the table and was pleasantly surprised.

Several gold necklaces, three pearl necklaces, six bracelets and a small assortment of rings.

"O! sod", he mused, "this woman will never give up. Always on a working holiday." He picked up his telephone and dialled a set of numbers-the phone number of his 'fence'.

"Hello Trojan Horse." Sam grinned inwardly.

RICKETY KATE

The three Aces were standing side by side. Each one of them was ill at ease. This came about because of the strange manner in which this meeting was hastily arranged. The fourth ace had not yet shown up. It was the fourth who had called the others stipulated the place and time of the rendezvous. Not one of the trio was in the habit of being summoned by any other mortal, let alone the person whom they considered the weakest link in their Cartel.

The men standing together on the patio were the most ruthless of the international drug, protection and smuggling syndicates. Each man headed large family concerns, all legitimate in the eyes of their respective countries. This was because every official and politician worth knowing in their home nations had their respective palms greased, or their loved ones threatened, thus ensuring that each of their businesses were never interfered with.

Carlos Mendez was the first to speak. He was a huge ugly person. His face looked as though it had seen better days. His nose bent to one side, was the result of a king hit at a nightclub in Bogota, his home-town. The guy who threw the punch didn't live long enough to see his handiwork. The Columbian addressed his two acquaintances gruffly. "I'm not at all happy with the Thai taking the attitude he has. We will need to take him down a peg or two. But we will hear him out. We all have worked through our differences over the years".

The smallish man, a Sicilian who went by the strange name of Rocky Alberto stood in front of Mendez, wheezed and mumbled in a sickly manner. No one seemed to know where he sprang from, but somehow he became a large dealer in cocaine and allied drugs. He had many useful cohorts in the industry and was an asset to the quartet of super criminals. He had the air of a loser, but was a pocket full of dynamite if anyone crossed swords with him. "Yes Carlos, I'm getting too old to change my established methods and the system has worked great for the past three decades or so. Why change a winning team?" He coughed, then wheezed again much to Mendez' discomfort. He was weasel of a being, made his fortune from Sicilian racketeering and mobster activities, but to look at him you'd think he couldn't say boo to a goose.

The other man, who had kept his silence during the last few minutes, stretched his arms above his head, yawned, scowled, and then added his thoughts to the conversation. "Maybe we might kick the old Thai out of the group. After all, he's been sort of dying for years now. By the way, nobody sees much of him these days and I don't think that he could fight back if he was put under pressure. His daughter Khanchana is his eyes and ears, but he presses the buttons. I say, listen, then we'll discern the way forward into the future. Poun has never caused us to lose any sleep so far, so let us give him a hearing." The man who had just spoken was known worldwide as the supremo of vice racketeering. An untouchable creature, a predator of the vilest kind and who, if it suited him, would dispose of his mother if it could earn him an easy buck. His name was Omar Ishmael, a Moroccan, home-based in Marrakech, among other hiding places.

Poun Thanong, the missing fourth member had, for decades, controlled the illicit trade in just about everything that flowed from the Golden Triangle in south-east Asia. He operated from his home, situated in the northern Thailand city of Chang Mai. This location gave him and his associates direct access to billions of dollars in opium, teak plantations, illegal trafficking in exotic wild life including many endangered species, as part of their portfolio of criminal activities.

The three had been standing on the patio, in front of Mendez's Monaco home, set in the area known as the Grande Cornishe. This is the highest part of the area. It was not only secluded but commanded a magnificent view of the coastline of this exclusive and expensive Principality. His neighbours were the elite of the sporting, film, and show-biz sets - not that he spent much time socializing in the area. The house was a convenient stopover point. It allowed him access to make furtive dealings in the comfort of a luxurious setting. It was not a holiday home. The rest of the players, who hung around the French, Italian and Spanish Riviera, did so for the fun things of life, but not

Mendez. He was a serious player, not one for fooling around, as he was interested in one matter only, money - and buckets of it. Woe betide those who got in the way of Carlos Mendez' ambitions.

A car suddenly appeared at the entrance to the house. It slid gracefully down the drive-way towards where the men were standing. The limousine came to a standstill right beside them. The back passenger side door opened and a very short woman with jet black hair, stepped onto the pavement. She was of Asian appearance, dressed in a black, expertly tailored suit, which pronounced her every curve and feature. She was a stunning looker, which none present could deny. Her hands were adorned in velvet gloves, which matched the hat that she was wearing. A turquoise coloring of the head and hands made her look distinctly Thai in appearance.

"Good afternoon, Miss Thanong", Mendez greeted her, then went to shake her hand, but she withdrew her hand before he could do so. The other two just nodded to her, not prepared to extend their hands in case of rebuttal as well. Mendez turned and motioned his guests into the mansion. The woman went first, followed by the men. She surveyed the inside of the main lounge room quickly, but did not comment. She refused to remove her jacket, nor be seated.

In the end no one sat down. The atmosphere was very tense. The men looked at her in unison, not sure what was about to happen next. The Moroccan broke the silence. "Miss we expected your father. It was he who called us here".

"My father is dead, he died a month ago. I am the one who called this meeting. I have an offer to each one of you. This, I expect you not to refuse." She brushed off an attempt by the three men to offer her their condolences. She then reached into her pocket. She removed three small envelopes. The envelopes were handed to each of the three men in turn.

"I am placing before you an ultimatum. It is this. I will assume all of your holdings. I will pay you each one hundred million American dollars in cash or in any form you desire. Before you reply, let me inform you of my master plan. Then, you may inquire of me any concerns that you may have regarding the offer." She then set out her vision to the men who were still trying to digest the news of the death of one of their associates of long standing. Poun was a person who shared mutual dealings with them for a very long time. The manner in which the news was conveyed to them was also a cause for concern.

The men were on the back foot, completely taken by surprise with the events of the past half hour. It was only through great experience that they allowed her to lead the discussion. Then they would, when the time was right, serve the ball straight back into her court with great vigor. She may not recover from the power of the serve. Mendez decided on a circuit breaker. He interjected to offer a round of drinks, and was pleasantly surprised when the woman agreed. His butler who was waiting patiently in the wings, obliged, and supplied whatever each requested. Then the host handed the floor back to the little woman.

Khanchana Thanong explained to the three men the grand plan she had in her mind. Firstly, she told them that she could foresee significant changes taking place in their respective organizations. To fit in with this as global operators they would need to move into the twenty-first century, and meet the current challenges. International terrorism had hurt their businesses. Law enforcement agencies in nearly all of the 'friendly' regimes had made significant inroads into their traditional commodity suppliers, whilst hunting for terrorist backers and the origins of the funds used for the different groups around the Globe. Some of their dealers had been swept up as the nets were thrown. Also the borders in most countries are now more tightly controlled. There was no room for too many players and she had the solution as far as they were concerned

Secondly, with India and China burgeoning onto the world stage, this was the area they should concentrate their efforts with the drugs and the insurance packages they were so competent in supplying. Her main efforts would be to solicit the millions of new rich and middle class Asians who were now embracing the habits only the West indulged in before this change in economic fortunes.

She went on, whilst they listened in stunned silence, not even interrupting with a query. All were preparing themselves for the matter of her offer, what a joke, to buy them out. Each man's devious mind was already planning the method that he could take this miserable little upstart out of this world. In fact, they were only half listening. Paying lip service, but thinking ahead. She had lost all the gloss she exuded when she first stepped from the car. Her demeanor was one of arrogance and superiority. Her overbearing attitude continued as she outlined her offer. They, the principals of their respective businesses, were to hand over their complete assets and sources of their commodities to her in toto. In return, she would give them the millions she outlined earlier. She would manage the entire empire with the aid of her five brothers from Chang Mai.

As far as she was concerned, the three could retire into oblivion. They really had no option, she re-iterated, as she was in a position to take over any area of their industries as she wished. This aggravated those present no end. Each would have strangled her on the spot, but Monaco was hallowed ground, in the sense that one indiscretion would blow their cover. The authorities knew of them and tolerated them, as they did with many other types of despots. Dictators and Mafia leaders played at the Grand Casino, alongside entertainers, Wimbledon winners, Olympians and Royalty, all under careful scrutiny of a variety of agencies.

There was a further reason for restraint on the part of the assembled group. The four had their bodyguards present. Stationed around the villa, well out of sight were more than a dozen highly trained killers. In the car which the young lady had arrived in, would no doubt, be an entourage of blood-thirsty individuals armed to the teeth and ready for any sign of trouble. The limousine was also bullet proofed. The three also knew that dealing with Asian martial arts would put them at a great disadvantage.

Each man had his yacht moored off the coast. The three boats were placed ten kilometres out to sea, and several kilometres apart from each other. The Moroccan had placed his boat directly out from Cannes, one of his favourite haunts. The Sicilian's was in line with the Palace at Monte Carlo, so he could attend the Grand Casino. Mendez left his luxurious indulgence off Nice, coming ashore in his chopper, as did, of course, the other two. All the boats were heavily guarded, with their usual crew of modern day pirates.

The Asian stood up abruptly, causing the others to do likewise. She spoke as a master addressing her servants. "I suggest you return to your water-craft, take your envelopes, and read the contents after you have considered you positions. I am moving to Paris. I will await your collective decisions. My brothers are within the vicinity, awaiting my directions, so please, for your own sakes, do not delay the replies. I do not expect you as a group, or individually, to immediately appreciate my forthrightness. But you will all see very soon that the conditions I have laid down will be the ones to prevail in the end. Thank you for hearing me out. Good-bye gentlemen." With that last statement, she turned, left the room and the property. None of the three followed her out. They did not even say farewell to her. They were preoccupied with their next moves.

Mendez yelled for his top operative, Nino Scarlati, to step into the room. Scarlati an Italian, Naples-based controller of the Columbian's Mediterranean interests, knew the area like the back of his hand, and was ruthless and decisive. Mendez ordered the helicopter for a quick flight to his yacht. The other two were in contact with their henchmen immediately, making plans for similar manoeuvres, then to return to their boats, as soon as was humanly possible.

"That bitch is up to no good. Check your craft and we'll call each other within the hour." They agreed, gathering their bodyguards, and whatever other support that they had concealed around the villa. An onlooker would have been amazed to see the number of figures with high-powered weaponry exiting the premises. Vehicles sped from the scene like a frenzy of bull-ants disturbed at their nest, going hither and thither down the road. Some were heading for Monaco, some for Nice, others heading in the direction of the vicinity of Cannes.

Mendez leapt from the limousine, sent the other members of the team to their hotels, to await further orders, and was in the chopper before Scarlati had collected the pilot. The pilot, who was asleep in the canteen at the airport, rubbed his eyes, asked why the hurry and received an earful of expletives from Mendez, who was in no mood for questions. He impressed upon the pilot that if he didn't step on it, he would get a thumping that he would never forget, if he survived it. The pilot made due haste and the aircraft touched down on the boat's landing pad within minutes.

Scarlati was out of the chopper in a flash, charging across the deck and down to the inner section of the three-storey craft, whilst Mendez, revolver in hand, wandered around the deck, checking for anything of a suspicious nature, not exactly knowing what he was looking for. Mendez shouted at Scarlati from the top of the stairway, "Well, what's holding you up?" Scarlati called his boss to come down to the lower decks, which he did post haste.

Mendez caught a strange stench to his nostrils, as he more or less tumbled down the stairs. Then he saw Scarlati bending over a body, lying at the bottom of the stairs. It was, he quickly noted, that of his Captain, Albass, who had kept all of his many craft afloat for many years. Then Scarlati pointed to the bunk rooms, of which each door was ajar. Mendez then kicked open the door of the nearest room. The three occupants were spread across each other dead as doormats. Their faces were twisted, as in agony. "What about the others?" He asked his junior, who replied that all twelve crew were dead.

Mendez was in a state of shock. In thirty years of throwing his weight around, in his gangster-related activities, it was he who called or fired the shots. Now a relatively unknown woman had spread havoc among his operational team, eliminating the finest of them. His very best men, except for the Italian Scarlati, who was his top man, were dead. This had far reaching implications for his future. How far had she got, whilst they were preoccupied with frivolous matters, taking things too lightly, rolling along on the wave of successful deals, but too stodgy in their old ways, to watch for the signs of ever present dangers.

Mendez, standing among the bodies of the deceased, cursed the woman, who had handed him this bitter pill. He stared at the remains of his servants, while he was fumbling with his cell phone. He called Ishmael, who sounded nearly incoherent. Yes, his crew was also devastated, all dead. His observations gave him the feeling that the crew was somehow taken by surprise and gassed. But why did none of these proven experts not even appear to fight back. Ishmael vowed to go after that woman and draw and quarter her before her own kin.

Mendez cut off the conversation with Ishmael to call Alberto, anticipating more of the same. And so it was. Alberto was cut to the quick, wheezing and cursing. His nine best operatives were gone, without showing any sign of any sort of resistance, as far as he could see. The Sicilian explained to Mendez that they must, however distasteful it was, dispose of all the dead before any of the coastguard boats return to the area. He agreed. After the call was terminated he instructed Scarlati to dump the bodies overboard when the boat was a little further out to sea. Scarlati was an expert in the disappearance of human beings. Mendez took the craft out several kilometres further, away from its original mooring place. His pilot and the Italian attended to the burials of the heavily-weighted corpses.

Mendez managed to extricate a bottle of whisky from one of the cupboards, foregoing the usual ice and water. He poured a large portion for himself and a similar amount for his two companions. His hands were shaking as he passed the drinks over, but his mind was seething with rage at the cards dealt him today. Plotting a course for his boys to take his boat away from the Riviera was on his agenda first. Then he would be free to plan his next manoeuvre, which would be on his own, and at his pace, which would be carried out with utmost urgency. He must check with his Columbian home base as soon as practicable. This could be done onshore, when he was free of the two who were at his side and who could be used an independent communication system. He could no longer trust a soul.

Many questions remained unanswered. How did the crews of the three yachts fall so easily? What type of gas or substance was used to kill the men? Who were the assailants? Did the Thai woman infiltrate the entire network of the three groups? Who sold out? He would personally eliminate any weak links. He would send Scarlati back to Italy. Then the chopper pilot could attend to the boat as well as the aircraft.

Then he remembered the letter in his pocket. He took it out. He opened the envelope with impatience, withdrew the sheet of paper from inside, and read it with incredulity.

There were only six words written on the sheet. It read in Spanish. "Three aces. Trumped by Rickety Kate."

FOR FEAR OF
LITTLE MEN

Nino Scarlati was a very desperate man. He left Monte Carlo in what one could only describe as a frightened and apprehensive demeanor. He had just disposed of the bodies of twelve of his close colleagues in a narcotics cartel. They were, it appears, executed aboard their employer's luxury yacht off the French Riviera, not far from Nice. Scarlati and Mendez discovered the bodies after returning to the yacht, following a meeting with the Golden Triangle's leading lady. She had thrown down the gauntlet to the three leaders of the drug trade in Columbia, Morocco and Sicily. She was moving in on the global vice supremos and flexing her muscles.

The discovery of the bodies also confirmed that her five brothers were in the area, ready to carry out her threats if the Cartel leaders didn't comply with her wishes. Similar murders of entire crews had occurred on the yachts of Alberto and Ishmael. The three Cartel leaders, laid the killings at the feet of the Thai woman and her family. But it was early days yet, and each needed to take stock of their respective home bases. This was made more difficult because they couldn't trust anybody until they cleared up the mess and clarified the situation.

Scarlati's boss, Mendez, the Columbian, had sent him back to Naples, his home town. He was instructed to lay low, and glean as much as possible about the Thai's movements. Mendez was to carefully check his own situation, and they would be in contact with each other when the time was right.

Mendez' custom in paying Scarlati was to deposit his salary, namely half a million American dollars, straight into his account. Scarlati was the eyes and ears of the Mendez operation in and around the Mediterranean area. He knew each individual spot like the back of his hand. He had contacts in all walks of life, both high and low. He was an indispensable part of the international scene, working for each of his boss's illicit enterprises. Mendez was in a quandary. Someone sold them out. That was the problem and the only one he trusted could be the one to undo him.

Nino Scarlati took the five-forty flight from Nice to Florence, then hired a car to take him to Rome. He left the car at a parking booth agreed upon by the rental company, once he had left the vicinity. He was covering his tracks in the same expert manner he'd always done. He had never come against any group as persistent as the Thai family that was harassing them now. He walked through the streets of Rome, hugging the old section, using the overwhelming surge of tourists as a shield, in case of trouble. After an hour of weaving and ducking, in and out of alleys, he finally felt safe, at least long enough to grab a bite to eat, and a long awaited mug of coffee

The next step was to find his way back to his home village in Naples, which was situated on the south side of the city, on a hill, overlooking the bay. He had several contingencies in place, in case some emergency would arise. Of course, he had anticipated problems from the law enforcement agencies, but not from opposing interests. The only ray of light was that his loving wife was in Lourdes with his mother, thankfully, for a couple of weeks, or so he thought. His only true belief was in the power of money, and lots of it His wife on the other hand was a devoted Catholic and an ardent traveller to holy sights and shrines of the faith. She was 'religious' to the extreme according to him, but as he was away so often, he didn't mind. It also kept his widowed mother off his back, as she shared the same passion as his wife

He was unaware that his wife, Maria, had returned home four days earlier. Her mother-in-law insisted that she would stay on, and felt Maria should go back a little earlier, to be there at home, in case Nino had returned from his travelling. Maria, her bags bursting with all types of artifacts and an impressive array of baubles, left the city of Lourdes, an inspired being. The stall keepers along the narrow streets insisted that she take with her Lourdes' Holy Water, Lourdes' Icons, and Lourdes' so many ideas - enough for all her friends. She had plenty for Christmas, Christenings, and a lot of other special occasions which had only sprung to her mind with a little prompting from the shop keeping fraternity, who were experts at transferring wealth from gullible pilgrims to themselves. She purchased a twenty-litre plastic container of 'holy water' from the Grotto which, unknown to her, was filled from a tap behind the shop.

Laden with 'holiness' and completely exhausted, Maria Scarlati boarded her outbound flight to return home. As she travelled, her thoughts, among other things reflected on her two children, studying in a Rome Exclusive Catholic girl's college. She hoped that someday, they, along with Nino would visit Lourdes with her together. She drifted off to sleep, until the aircraft was set to complete its landing procedures, then disembarking along with the multitude of packages that she had accumulated during her pilgrimage.

She was so preoccupied with the baggage and the parcels, that she took a taxi home, using the first driver who offered himself. Maria did not pay attention to the man, a Thai, as he placed her goods in the trunk, and deposited the water container beside her, on the back seat. She was so blasé that she hadn't even told the driver where to take her, but he was taking her in the right direction. He even called her Mme Scarlati. The taxi arrived at her home in due course, the courteous driver offering to bring the many parcels into the house, to save her lifting the very heavy ones. She agreed, and went to the front door, disarmed the alarm system, then opened the door. It still had not occurred to her that the driver, whom she had never laid eyes on before, knew her.

The driver inquired about where she had been. She told him. Then he said that he wished to see the Mona Lisa in the Louvre in Paris, but he would have to save for the trip first. She informed him that they had a large print of that very painting. It was in their downstairs room, and she offered to show it to him. He agreed to have a peek. Picking up the large package, which contained a plethora of rosary beads, she walked ahead, leading him down the staircase, into the spacious den below. The room was adorned with all the aplomb of the rich. It was a vast cavern of wonders, no doubt, obtained by her husband's wealth, from kick backs and illegal goings on. "There it is" she said, pointing to the large frame on the wall in front of them. They were the last words of Maria Scarlati.

The Thai, with meticulous ease and martial arts expertise, hit her before she even knew it. She fell to the floor, stone dead. He opened a wardrobe nearby, pushed the ski gear which was neatly arranged ready for the ensuing season, to one side. He then walked casually to the body, bent over, lifted it, and transferred it to the cupboard. After squeezing the late Mrs. Scarlati's body into the space, he pushed the door shut and turned the lock. He stepped towards the freezer and opened it. The upright deep freeze was stocked with frozen fish, bread, and among other things, packaged dinners, enough to feed an army. He noted the array of wine bottles along the wall. He placed the bag of rosary beads on a bookcase, then hastily stepped out of the room.

The taxi driver took all of the other evidence of Maria's early arrival with him. He closed the house and retreated to the car, leaving the property, without being noticed by a soul. He drove away with the intention of sifting through the baggage, for any saleable items. He would return to wait for her husband. His information was that Scarlati was already close by Rome's inner city. He did not expect the Italian home until late that evening, but he would be there and waiting to finish his assignment with due swiftness and his usual thoroughness.

The night was as still as the desert. The new moon hovered overhead, casting its light, which caused eerie shadows to linger around the lavish house. The Scarlatis had occupied this dwelling and enjoyed the tranquility of the neighbourhood for fifteen years. Nino reached Naples at ten fifteen, parked his Jaguar in a convenient spot three kilometres from his home, then commenced to walk to the house, by a pathway, known well to him personally. He would climb up a severe slope, then traverse some light scrub, and finish the final kilometre with stealth and utter watchfulness. As soon as he was on the path, and out of the light, he climbed a small tree, sat quietly, and catching his breath, waited for a few minutes.

It appeared that he was on his own in this particular section, but he would travel slowly. There was one more obstacle to his covertness. A small courtyard, which served the small housing precinct, lay directly ahead. This was a superlative ambush arena. He slowed then skirted the yard, hugging the walls, which fortunately were bathed in darkness, allowing him to slip through, completely unseen. He was sweating profusely, even as the night air hit his face with jets of coolness, the beads of perspiration poured from his chin

Moving ever slowly, with great caution, he crept along with alertness, looking from side to side, occasionally stopping to assess his position. Thank God, Maria and the two children were not here at this time. No sound, except his own heart-beat, which from his body, through to his brain, sounded as loud as a brass band in the still night air. He was now within sight of his home. He was near the spot that he buried Bruno, his faithful dog only a year ago.

He had made it to the perimeter of his property. So far, so good! The last thing that he needed at this point was a family pet to give him away. A two metre high fence was constructed around his place. The fence was made of thick concrete blocks with patterned holes, so one could peer through them at close up, but obscured the vision to any one else from a distance. The best of both worlds, he had once said, justifying his decision to make the walled enclosure his private fortress. Little did he expect to employ the fence in the way he would tonight. There was a long oblong, flat roofed garden shed at the rear of the block, it was from there he could check any intrusion tonight.

Bending to nearly a crouching position, he moved furtively towards the only side entrance of the block. The gate was a heavy metal one, with large hinges, that creaked a little, so he would need to be very careful when forcing it open. He had a key with him, which simplified matters. He lay on his side, staring into the darkness, looking for the slightest movement in or around the rear of the house. He waited. He sharpened his ears. A lone dog barked in the distance. No movement as yet. He was more frightened now than he had been for a very long time.

Probably the most disturbing factor for him was his adversaries. The Thai Landers, as he called them, were not only ruthless with guns and knives, but had an array of martial arts skills to call upon when in combat. No person, engaged in a battle at close range, could survive without the knowledge of the opponent's weaponry. He did not have the foggiest notion, of whom he was going to fight, but he did expect that it would be one or more of the Thais. He did know however, that he could not afford to allow the enemy to get close to him. He must be decisive at the outset of any engagement. He had fear of the little men.

The lighting around the house was poor. He believed that the less light the less chance of intruders at any time, so he had decided to forego security lighting around the home. Tonight this could be to his advantage. He waited a little longer. Time was not of the essence at this point. No movement as yet. He was treading water, going nowhere. He was scared stiff, but resolute. Then he noticed a glint in the moonlight.

It was over on the opposite side of the backyard. He watched with the eyes of a hawk. Then he saw the apparition in the gloom. The more he concentrated, the more outlines of the figure he could see.

His gaze was transfixed on the shadow, which now took shape, that of a short human. It seemed not to be looking his way, standing stock-still, just as it were waiting, as like a sentry, on watch at the battlements. He could wait. After all it was his home, and he would need to use his local knowledge to overcome, whoever it was out there, waiting for him. He did not move, but the other did. The sentry turned, and crept closer to the house into utter darkness. Scarlati's gaze followed him. The man walked to the far side of the house. Maybe he's checking the front area, Nino said to himself.

He made a bold movement. Quickly but silently opening the gate and squeezing between the garden shed and the fence, he tucked himself safely out of sight, but in a position to observe the whole yard from the spot he was crouching on. His planning brain began to function, as he summed up his position. The house was surrounded by an apron of concrete paving, two metres wide on each side and the rear, whilst the front had the triple driveway paved to the roadway. The yard was landscaped with various shrubs and potted-plants, none of which he knew the names, as that was his wife's forte. Then he remembered an important matter. Stored in the garden shed, were things other than gardening tools and sundries. His wife kept things such as the twenty-litre drum of olive oil. She was frightened that it could cause problems if it were to leak in the house, so into the shed it went.

A cat scurried across the yard, mounted the fence and disappeared into the night. It unnerved him a little. He kept his vigil and thought of the olive oil at the same time. He only had a small handgun and his flick blade on him. He decided to go for broke. He stood up slowly, surveyed his position, and then moved to the other end of the shed, to the only door it had. It was not locked. Opening the door he squeezed into the cluttered room. He reached to the spot were he was to find the oil. It had not been moved; for this he was thankful. He slowly lifted the drum, which appeared to be three quarters full and stepped toward the door.

He searched the night for danger. Nothing offered, so he exited from the shed. He set out for the nearest tree, only a few metres from the shed. He waited, tempted to look at his watch, but time did not really matter. With no movement around him, he made for the next shrub, then the one after that. He was now only five metres from the house, and three from the paved surrounds. He had taken a mallet from the shed as well as the oil. He took the cap off the olive oil container, stepping as near to the pavement he could get without exposing himself to any danger, he commenced to pour the oil onto the pathway. The olive oil spread rapidly over the concrete, until it covered most of it. It glistened in the moonlight He retreated to the bushes and picked up the mallet. He stood behind the shrub which gave him excellent protection, then tossed the can against the wall of the brick house.

Suddenly, he could discern footsteps coming from the front area of the house. A figure came into view, turning the corner, half enveloped in the darkness. The man encountered the olive oil, his feet flying from under him, sending him crashing into a large ceramic pot. Scarlati seized the moment, stepped speedily toward the prone figure, and brought the hammer down with all of his might. The man did not move a single hair. He was dead as a doornail. Scarlati dragged the body along the ground to the shed, opening the door just wide enough to pull the man inside. He stuffed the body into a corner. The man was definitely a Thai. He wore the trappings of a local taxi driver, but Scarlati knew there were few Asians in this part of town. He left the shed, stood at the back of the two-storey building and pondered what his next manoeuvre would be.

The Italian was now certain that this was not the end of the matter. It was possible that someone could be inside the house. This called for cast-iron resolutions on his part. He walked to a down-pipe in the middle of the back wall of the home. It was not a normal pipe but an imitation. He slowly levered the pipe apart revealing a folding ladder. He braced the ladder, then, after taking off his shoes commenced his ascent. Reaching the roof, he pulled himself onto it and as soon as he gained his balance, lifted a sky-light lid, which was hinged to the roof. He peered down into what was a spare bedroom, satisfied it was empty, swung through the sky-light, pulling it closed, then descended to the floor with as little sound as possible.

The room was as it always was, made up for the next guest. He found the house undisturbed, as he went from room to room. He decided to have a drink, so he walked to the basement room, to where his favorite drinks were kept in a refrigerator beside his lavish bar. This room, spacious as it was, was the focal point for most of his life at home. He could kick off his shoes, and booze away with his friends without the constraints of the main function areas, for his wife was a strict housekeeper, to the extent of paranoia. He couldn't help but marvel at the way his wife kept the house so neat. He poured himself a generous measure of whisky without ice or water, which he normally had, and sat on a sofa to reflect. He would need to remove the body before sunrise; it was already four in the morning.

Finishing the drink, placing the tumbler in the sink, at the end of the bar, he then moved to leave the room. His eyes fell on something, which was placed neatly on the table, adjacent the bar. It was a large, family Holy Bible, leather-bound. The Bible had a copper inlay with his name inscribed on it. He remembered that a year or so back, his wife had explained to his boss, that the family had lost their old leather one. Mendez told her that his own wife could access these things, so maybe this was it. Bless her, he thought as he lifted the cover. It was the last thing he would ever do.

The trigger, under the front cover, set off an almighty explosion. The force of the impact blew Scarlati to smithereens. The blast blew the cupboard, housing his late wife, to matchwood. The freezer regurgitated its contents. The liquor collection, held in racks that covered half the wall, flew to pieces. The prize collection disintegrated under the pressure of the explosion, spilling the wine, smashing all the glass, and spewing it in all directions. The bag, filled with rosary beads and various small icons flew everywhere. The Mona Lisa was shredded along with the curtains and blinds. The corpses of the late Mr. and Mrs. Scarlati joined the horrendous mess, all over the place, among the fish, the wine, the bread, the rosary beads and water pouring from ruptured taps added to the utter chaos. Poor Maria was floating amongst all the elements of her Christian faith

Carlos Mendez cancelled the transfer of the half a million dollars to Scarlati's account the very next day.

ABOUT THE
AUTHOR

Eddie Whitham was born in Wangaratta, Victoria, Australia in 1943. He was the second eldest of nine children of Jim and Esther Whitham. He left school at fifteen, and at the age of twenty-five moved from western Victoria, to Tamworth in NSW where he carried on a retail business along side his wife Barbara for more than thirty-five years. Since retirement, he and Barbara have travelled extensively throughout the world as well as Australia.

He made the effort to self educate himself and describes himself as a compassionate capitalist and world watcher. Travelling abroad extensively since the nineteen seventies, Eddie has gleaned amazing insight into other cultures and workings of most of the world's nations. He has been an advocate for refugees and migrants spanning more that thirty years and a lay preacher for twenty-five years. Being active in his own large world-wide family and the affairs of his city he is a well known and respected citizen. He took to writing twenty years ago, but only recently put the finishing touches to this collection.

To those who enjoy these stories, there are many more already set for publication. Despite his lack of schooling, his literal way of writing is refreshing.

ACKNOWLEDGEMENTS

My deepest appreciation to Doug Fenwick; my mentor and buddy, who put me on the right track when editing my raw material.

I am extremely grateful to Cathy Germon and Jan Eddison for assistance in the formatting rereading of my work.

My loving wife Barbara had to live through the stories time and time again. I am greatly indebted to her. She had to put up with my restlessness as I sank into an abyss trying to be creative in writing.

I would like to say 'thank you' to all of the others who read and contributed to the stories.